PAYBACK TIME

CAZ FINLAY

One More Chapter
a division of HarperCollins*Publishers* Ltd
1 London Bridge Street
London SE1 9GF
www.harpercollins.co.uk
HarperCollins*Publishers*
1st Floor, Watermarque Building, Ringsend Road
Dublin 4, Ireland

This paperback edition 2022
1
First published in Great Britain in ebook format
by HarperCollins*Publishers* 2022
Copyright © Caz Finlay 2022

A catalogue record of this book is available from the British Library
ISBN: 978-0-00-854526-0

This novel is entirely a work of fiction. The names, characters and
incidents portrayed in it are the work of the author's imagination. Any
resemblance to actual persons, living or dead, events or localities is
entirely coincidental.

Printed and bound in the UK using 100% Renewable Electricity
by CPI Group (UK) Ltd

To Eric and our boys, with all my love

Prologue

Former Chief Superintendent John Barrow lay back on his bunk with his hands behind his head.

'You all set for tomorrow?' he asked his pad-mate lying on the bunk above.

'Yeah. I can't fucking wait,' he replied with a contented sigh.

'And you remember everything we discussed?'

'Of course, John. We've gone over it half a dozen times. I'll make sure that things go according to plan. The wheels are already in motion. Don't worry.'

Barrow smiled to himself. He was facing life in prison with no chance of parole for another twenty-four years because of that bitch Grace Carter and her gang of thugs. The Carters were the scum of the earth as far as he was concerned, and he couldn't wait for the day when they were finally brought to their knees. They had ruled Liverpool for far too long and it was about time for a changing of the

1

guard. To his disgust, most of his colleagues and former friends had disowned him when he'd been arrested for murder and child sexual exploitation. People were hypocrites. Nobody had given a thought to the kind of women and girls he'd sought the services of when they were alive. That was how people like him had been able to prey on them so easily and for so long. But he still had enough contacts, and enough dirt on enough people, to be able to pull some strings – even from the confines of his cell in HMP Wymott.

The thing with prisoners like him was that they were all put on a wing together for their own protection. *Vulnerable prisoners.* So, when he bumped into a former associate of his, it wasn't a huge surprise. But it was a stroke of luck that this particular associate had a reason to hate the Carters just as much as he did. Well, one Carter in particular. The man who had stolen the love of his life – at least, that was what his pad-mate believed anyway. And John Barrow wasn't about to point out the sheer stupidity of doing anything for the love of a woman when it wasn't going to serve his own ends. He didn't care what his associates' motives were, he only cared that they shared a common goal – bringing down the Carters. If it hadn't been for their interfering in something that had fuck-all to do with them, he wouldn't be sitting in this tiny, stinking cell.

Since he was an ex-copper, most of the screws hated Barrow as much as the cons did, but there were some who recognised the authority and power he still held, and they treated him well. He was able to ensure that he and his old friend were padded up together, and with nothing but time on their hands, they had spent the last six months plotting the downfall of the Carter empire.

'Don't underestimate this new crew,' Barrow warned. 'They might be feral, but they are ruthless and not quite as stupid as they look.'

'I know the score,' came the reply. 'Stop fretting, John. I promise you that the Carters' days are numbered. I will bring them to their knees, and then I will take back what is rightfully mine.'

'I only wish I could be there to see the arrogant grins wiped off their faces when you do.'

'Hmm,' his cell mate mumbled into the darkness. 'Soon they will all know that *she* belonged to me first.'

Chapter One

Devlin King's fingers curled around the handle of the Beretta handgun as he stared out of the car window into the darkness. This shooter was the real deal. He'd used guns before plenty of times, but they were converted replicas or antiques and as such they weren't always reliable, as the missing tip of the thumb of his right hand could attest. But this one he held onto now was the dog's bollocks. He and his older brother, Jerrod, had a new benefactor, and while Devlin didn't trust him as much as Jerrod did, he had to admit he had come through for them in getting them four of the finest quality clean handguns Devlin had ever seen in his life in order to pull off this job. And given who they were going up against, they would need to prove that they had the balls and the resources to be contenders for the top spot.

Now the King brothers and two of their most experienced soldiers were sitting in an old Ford Estate on a dark country road somewhere in Scotland, waiting for a shipment of Connor Carter and Jake Conlon's cocaine to be delivered. The brothers had recently come by some new and interesting information about how the drugs were being transported, and it was too good an opportunity to miss out on. They were using a local car-hire firm to transport the goods from the border up to Glasgow, with minimal security. It was easy pickings as far as Devlin was concerned. The thing with Conlon and Carter was that they were a pair of arrogant pricks, and one day it was going to be their downfall. They believed they were untouchable. And while half of the city of Liverpool might shit their pants at the mere mention of their name, Devlin and his brother knew what they were really about. Too interested in looking pretty to get their hands dirty anymore. They sat in their fancy fucking cars and their flash designer suits, looking down at people like him, who knew what it was really like to graft your arse off to get what you want. Conlon and Carter had gone soft and now it was time for the Bridewell Blades to show everyone what they were capable of and step into the limelight for a change.

'Shouldn't he have been past by now?' Jerrod barked from the front seat of the car.

'It's only been ten minutes,' Devlin reminded him.

'We better not have missed them!' Jerrod growled.

'We haven't! Our lads saw the handover. He'll be here,' Devlin snapped. They had two of their men stationed four miles down the road where the drop-off was taking place, and they'd confirmed the drop had gone without incident.

'Here he is now. A white Renault Mégane, right?'

'That's them,' Jerrod snapped as he opened the car door and jumped out, quickly followed by the other three men. It was Jerrod who fired the first shot at the car, causing it to veer off the road and straight into a ditch.

The four men ran to the car. Devlin peered inside to see the driver slumped over the wheel with blood pouring from his head. He was either dead or unconscious. Devlin pointed the gun at the window beside his head. He may as well make sure, he thought to himself.

'Dev!' Jerrod shouted, full of excitement. 'We have hit the fucking jackpot here, kid! Come on. Give us a hand?'

Devlin lowered his gun and jogged to the back of the car where his brother and their two associates had forced open the boot to reveal four black holdalls full of cocaine. Devlin smiled at the sight as they lifted the bags from the car. This stuff had to be worth a fucking fortune, and if it was good-quality gear, they could cut it with something else and double their profits.

'Come on, before someone sees something and phones the bizzies,' Jerrod snapped again, breaking Devlin from his daze, as he was already thinking of the new motor he was going to buy himself. He took a holdall from his brother and the four ran back over the road to their own car, stashing the four black bags beneath the back seat before jumping inside. Adrenaline thundered around Devlin's body as the driver started the engine and sped off down the narrow country road.

'How fucking easy was that, lads?' Jerrod laughed

loudly and the rest of them joined in. The atmosphere in the car sizzled with excitement and electricity as they congratulated each other on a job well done.

'Big things are about to happen for us,' Jerrod went on excitedly. 'Those pretentious pricks aren't going to know what's hit them.'

'Too fucking right!' Devlin agreed with a vigorous nod of his head. They hadn't needed the shooters in the end, which only proved to him further that he and his brother didn't need anyone but themselves and their loyal soldiers.

Devlin leaned back against the seat and smiled to himself. Jerrod was right. Big things were about to happen for them. He could feel it in his bones.

Chapter Two

Two days later

Jake Conlon leaned back in his chair. The old leather creaked as it shifted under his weight. For a second, he was reminded of his father, Nathan Conlon, who had once owned this club and run Liverpool, and all from the comfort of this very same seat. Following his murder eight years earlier, Jake had taken over the reins at the age of just nineteen. Of course, he had been a complete idiot back then, and it had actually been his mum, Grace Carter, who had needed to step in and not only save his arse, but teach him how things were supposed to be run.

It was only then that Jake had learned who really ran the streets of Liverpool, and it was his own mum. She was everything his father wasn't. Smart. Calculated. Ruthless only when she needed to be, whereas his dad had been a vicious fucker just for the sake of it.

The Blue Rooms had been a seedy strip club back when his father owned the place, but now it was an exclusive Liverpool nightclub in the docklands, and it turned over enough of a profit to enable Jake and his business partner, Connor, to justify the lifestyle they both had, and also funnel a good portion of their illegitimate money through the books. Of course, they were also part-owners of Cartel Securities, the company that provided security for most of the Merseyside area.

Jake smiled to himself as he thought about how far he had come in those past eight years. How far all of them had come. He wasn't ashamed to admit who he was any longer. He owned his mistakes and his sexuality, which he had felt forced to hide for years. He was afraid of no one. Most of all, he was Grace Carter's son, and he was the new head of her empire.

'What you smiling about? Danny just been in?' Connor Carter said with a laugh as he strolled into the room.

'Fuck off, you knob,' Jake fired back good-naturedly. Connor was his stepbrother, business partner and best mate. They had been through a lot together in the past few years, including being arrested for murder, a paternity battle involving Jake's daughter, Isla, and most painfully, the murder of Connor's twin, Paul, who had been Jake's partner in every other sense.

Jake had been lost for a long time after Paul's death, wondering if he would ever feel happy again. But his family had pulled him out his pit of despair, and then he had met Danny Alexander. Danny was the Managing Director of

Cartel Securities, alongside his best mate, and Jake's uncle, Luke Sullivan. Danny had been a ladies' man, going through women at a rate of knots. He was so deep inside the closet that he hadn't even realised he was bisexual himself until one night after hours at the club, when one thing had led to another. It had taken Danny time to adjust and accept who he was, but now he and Jake were officially a couple and Jake had never been happier.

'Where is he anyway?' Connor said as he looked around the room. 'I thought him and Luke were meeting us here?'

'They were, but there was some trouble at one of the pubs over in the Wirral.'

'And they needed to deal with it?' Connor frowned. Pub scuffles were way below Danny and Luke's pay grade.

'Bizzies were crawling all over the place. One of the bouncers was stabbed,' Jake replied with a roll of his eyes. Danny and Luke used to have their own security firm, Sable Securities, and they had done well. But when rival firms kept trying to stage takeovers, they merged with Cartel Securities and became the new directors. They were well respected in their field and cultivated a fierce loyalty among their workforce, and part of the reason for that was that they looked after their employees well. They knew every one of their hundreds of staff by name and they always attended any incidents when one of them was seriously injured, which had been occurring more frequently of late.

'That's the second one this month.' Connor frowned as he sat on the sofa in the corner of the office.

'I know, mate.'

'You think it's random, or something more going on?' Connor asked as he helped himself to a can of Coke from the fridge beside him.

'Fuck knows. But Danny and Luke will sort it,' Jake replied. He and Connor had enough to deal with, without getting involved with the security firm too. They owned part of the company, but as far as Jake was concerned, it was very much Danny and Luke's domain now. Especially since his mum and stepdad, Michael, had gone to Spain for a few months to set up their new restaurant. They had finally handed over the reins to him and Connor, and while it had been a long time coming, Jake missed having both of them around. He knew they would be on a plane in a heartbeat if they ever needed them, but it wasn't the same as having them right on his doorstep.

'Yeah. We got enough on our plates with this fucking Scottish business,' Connor said with a scowl.

Jake nodded his agreement. He and Connor had controlled the supply routes to Scotland for years. It was one of their biggest earners. It had long been a target for wannabes to make their mark, or try to steal their product, but over the years they had fine-tuned their operation, and it rarely gave them much trouble. That was, until recently, when they'd changed their routine at the suggestion of one of their Scottish contacts, Derek McKeever, and as a result, they'd had almost half a million in gear stolen. Someone had fucked up and fucked them over, and once that someone was found, he would be spending the rest of his days in a deep, unmarked grave.

Jake checked his watch. 'What time we meeting them?'

'Half eleven,' Connor replied. 'We've got an hour yet.'

'I asked John to tag along, with Luke and Danny out of the picture. We can pick him up on the way.'

'Makes sense,' Connor replied with a nod. John Brennan had been Nathan Conlon's and, in later years, Grace Carter's right-hand man for as long as Jake could remember. John was loyal and trustworthy and he was built like a mountain. Jake and Connor worked with dozens of people every day, but there were few who were trusted enough to be allowed into their inner circle. John was one such man. Jake could handle himself when he needed to, but he preferred to let other people do the muscle work for him these days. It was something his mum and Michael had drummed into him and Connor over and over again, but after the two of them had done some time on remand for murder, they finally realised the sense in what their parents were saying.

Jake looked over at Connor as he took a swig of his Coke. He expected that it was probably easier for him to remain hands off than it was for his stepbrother. Connor loved a good scrap. They both worked out at a boxing gym five days a week, but it was Connor whom most people feared sparring with. He was strong and he was relentless. Along with his brother, Paul, he had once been one of the best and most expensive cleaners across the country. They were called 'cleaners' because they were paid well to clean up other people's problems, and that usually meant by making them disappear. Sometimes, Jake sensed Connor getting edgy when he hadn't been able to smash someone's face in for a while.

Connor ran a hand through his thick, dark hair. He was the image of his father Michael, but a little broader, because he was a keen weightlifter too. Like his father and uncle Sean before him, he had a reputation for violence that made most people who crossed him shit their pants.

'You think our issues with the gear going missing in Scotland have anything to do with these incidents with the clubs?' Connor asked with a frown. He didn't believe in coincidences, and in his experience, it paid to be suspicious of everything and everyone.

'Nah.' Jake shook his head. 'Someone had a tip-off about our new mode of transport, that's all. They chanced their arm and got lucky once, but it won't happen again. Not once we've put Degsy and his firm straight later and let them know they're going to be paying for our missing merchandise.'

'Hmm,' Connor mumbled, sucking on his top lip.

'You still worried about those Bridewell bell-ends?' Jake asked him.

The Bridewell Blades were a small, two-bit firm run by the feral King brothers. They had proposed going into business with Jake and Connor a few months earlier and had been laughed out of their office for their trouble. When there had been an attack at their security offices a few weeks later, during which Danny had been jumped and seriously injured, Connor and Jake had suspected that the King brothers might have been behind it. But they had hung them over the balcony of a tower block, and whilst they had both pissed their pants, neither of them had confessed, so they were either innocent of the crime or had balls of steel. Jake and Connor preferred to think it was the former.

'I dunno. They're just about fucking stupid enough to pull some shit, mate. That's all I'm saying. I've been hearing chatter about them and the shit they're into. Using kids no more than thirteen to fucking ferry their gear around. They got their own fucked-up version of Just Eat going on that estate, but it ain't Maccy's and KFC they're selling.'

'I know, Con. They're selling our gear, though. They may not get it directly from us, but that's where it comes from. You got a problem with what we do all of a sudden? Because it's a bit late to be growing a conscience now.'

Connor frowned at his stepbrother. Jake was a father too. But Isla was a girl and he supposed Jake didn't worry so much about her getting dragged into their world. Paul Junior was only eight months old, but Connor already worried that his son would follow in his footsteps, just like he and his twin brother had their own father's, as he had before them. One day the cycle had to break, didn't it?

Connor Carter respected his dad more than anyone else in the world. Despite what he did, he was a good man. He had done his best to steer his two sons away from the life he'd lived, but no matter what he'd done, it had never been enough. It was almost as though it was in their blood. Even when his twin had been murdered, Connor had never considered for a second walking away from his lifestyle. And if it was in his blood, then it was in Paul Junior's too.

'I just don't like the idea of young kids being involved, Jake. What grown-arse men and women do is their business,' he snapped as he took a long swig of his drink.

'Okay,' Jake said with a nod of his head, sensing his partner was ready to implode. Connor really did need a kick-off. He almost felt sorry for their Scottish contacts who had overseen the operation which had resulted in five hundred grand's worth of their product going astray, because Connor Carter was a man on the edge, and no doubt one of them would pay the price.

'It's not even just the kids doing their dealing, Jake. Apparently, they have these fucking initiation ceremonies involving girls, and the stuff they make them do…' Connor shook his head. 'I wouldn't believe it was true, mate, except there is something definitely missing with those King brothers.'

Jake screwed up his face in disgust. The King brothers were scum, and if he ever got the chance, or had any reason to, he would happily off the pair of them, because the world would be a better place without them in it. But it would simply create an opening for another crew to take their place. At least they knew the King brothers were a pair of inbred idiots. They were never going to have the nous, or the bollocks, to do anything that would touch him and Connor. Two hundred grand was nothing to them. They could lose it ten times over and not feel it, but it still had to be dealt with. Because you could not steal from Jake Conlon and Connor Carter without there being consequences. But they were so far above the likes of Jerrod and Devlin King that Jake didn't worry about them for a second longer than he had to.

'They'll be rotting in a ditch somewhere before we know it, Con, because everyone fucking hates them. Let other people worry about the Bridewell bell-ends. Like you said, we got enough on our plates without worrying about those fuck-nuggets too.'

Connor sighed, crushing his empty can and tossing it into the bin. 'Shall we get going? We can stop at KFC on the way. I'm fucking starving.'

'Jazz got you eating lentils and tofu for tea again?' Jake started to laugh. Connor and his wife, Jasmine, were on a health kick, but Connor missed his junk food, and whenever he had the opportunity he would sneak a cheeky takeaway in without his wife's knowledge.

'We had lentil dahl, actually.' Connor grinned at him.

'What the fuck is that?' Jake frowned as he stood up and shrugged on his suit jacket.

'It's nice. It's like a curry.'

'Whatever you say, mate. If it ain't got meat in it, I'm not interested.'

'Fucking philistine.'

'We're made to eat meat,' Jake protested.

'Actually, we're not. I've been reading up on it. Our teeth aren't made for meat.'

Jake shook his head, feigning exasperation. 'You getting veggie KFC then, are you?'

'What? Fuck, no!' Connor grinned at him and together they walked out of Jake's office.

Chapter Three

C onnor turned off the engine of his Range Rover
Overfinch and peered out into the dark car park in
the middle of the Lancashire countryside. He recognised the
silver Mercedes SUV as belonging to their associate, Derek
McKeever. Theirs were the only two cars in the car park and
they didn't expect anyone to disturb them here, which was
why it was the perfect meeting spot. He and Jake had done
business with Derek for years, and during that time, they'd
had very few issues with the man. Some of his employees
were complete divvies whom Connor had had cause to slap
on more than one occasion, but Derek himself was a good
businessman.

'They look like they brought any back-up?' John
Brennan asked from the back seat.

'Nope. You expecting trouble, big man?' Jake asked.

'Always,' John replied as he curled his fingers around
the small metal cosh in his coat pocket.

'Well, hopefully this won't take too long,' Connor said as he opened the car door. 'I got a hot date waiting at home for me.'

'Does your wife know you call her that?' John asked with a chuckle.

'Yeah, and she loves it.' Connor laughed too.

The three of them climbed out of the car and walked towards the silver Mercedes where Derek and two of his own employees were now waiting patiently.

'Derek,' Jake said as they reached the group.

Derek extended his hand in greeting. 'Jake. Connor,' he said with a nod as he shook their hands briefly. John lingered in the background, keeping an eye on Derek's two men behind him, as well as listening for any movement nearby.

'Tony. Go make sure we're not disturbed.' Derek indicated his head towards the car park entrance, and one of his men walked towards it to warn off any potential intruders. They had been disturbed before in this car park, by a horny young couple in an old Mondeo who were looking for somewhere with a little privacy themselves. Derek had killed their mood pretty quickly when he had told them to get lost in his own unique way.

'So, what the fuck happened, Degsy?' Jake asked as Tony walked away. Ordinarily, once their goods left Liverpool, it was up to the receivers of them to ensure they were kept safe and delivered to where they needed to be, but Derek had asked for this meeting personally.

'Somebody targeted the delivery, Jake. They knew where

and when it was coming into Glasgow, because the lads never even got it into their own vehicles before they were jumped.'

'You just persuaded us to start using this new car-hire company, though?' Connor frowned at him. 'You sure it's nothing to do with them? Because it seems kind of fucking coincidental to me.'

'No way.' Derek shook his head. 'That's my uncle's company. There is no way he would have me over like that, and we interrogated all of his men personally. I can assure you the problem is not from our end, boys. If it was, I'd have dealt with it myself. You know that.'

Jake frowned at his Scottish associate as his mind started to kick into overdrive. It was true that Derek rarely brought any problems to their door. He was a capable and ruthless businessman, which was why they had been working with him for so long. 'So, you're saying the problem is at our end?'

Derek sucked in a deep breath. It wasn't every day he accused men like Jake Conlon and Connor Carter of not having their house in order. 'Nobody knew about this new arrangement except for my right-hand man, my uncle and his two best drivers. I am one hundred per cent sure that the leak didn't come from any of us, and if I'm wrong,' he placed a hand over his heart, 'I will personally kill the fucker who has taken us all for mugs. But I'm not wrong, lads.'

'You think we have a snake working for us?' Connor scowled. It was true their organisation was much bigger than Derek's, but it was only a select number of trusted people who knew about the specifics of their bigger operations.

'I think it's worth exploring. Because nobody should have known about that exchange,' Derek replied.

'What the fuck?' Connor snarled as he clenched his fists by his sides and seriously considered taking his frustration out on Derek's face.

Sensing his partner's frustration, Jake spoke: 'We'll look into it.'

'I would appreciate that, lads,' Derek replied with a nod.

Jake glared at him. He'd had no cause not to trust Derek before today, but the accusation that someone close to them might have leaked information on that job stung.

'We'll still be expecting payment for the missing gear,' Connor snapped. 'Once it's in your city, it's your responsibility to make sure it gets where it needs to be.'

'Of course,' Derek replied with a nod, but the vein pulsed in his temple as he swallowed his anger at the unjustness of that. But as far and Jake and Connor were concerned, Derek should have taken every precaution to ensure that their drugs weren't stolen, and if they were stolen on his watch, then that was all on him, and they shouldn't be out of pocket because of it.

They were back on the M62 heading towards Liverpool when Connor asked the question they were all thinking about the answer to.

'So, who the fuck knew about that exchange?'

'Hardly anyone,' Jake replied with a shake of his head. 'Us three. Danny and Luke. And our driver, Ray.'

'Ray wouldn't,' John said, and both Jake and Connor nodded their agreement. Ray had been their father's driver before being theirs. He was professional and he was discreet, and he was paid a fuckload of money for his trouble. He had never given any reason to doubt him. He also lived alone and had no family to speak of, so it wasn't like he could be pressured in that way either. They all agreed he wasn't a suspect, and neither were Danny or Luke.

'Was there anything in the offices the night Danny was jumped?' John asked.

'You think we write this kind of shit down and leave it lying around, John?' Jake snarled.

'I'm just asking,' John snapped at him. 'It could have been a phone number or anything. You don't know how people get the information they do. Because if you're sure it's no one directly involved, it must be someone who has found out somehow.'

'Well, that's not fucking good either, is it?' Jake barked. 'We still have a fucking mole, and we're obviously leaving information around that any cretin can decipher.'

'I never said they were a cretin,' John interrupted him.

Jake snorted his response and John leaned forward in his seat. 'I have been in this game longer than you have been alive, lads, and the one thing I have learned time after time is that you should never underestimate anyone. Just because you think someone is a cretin, doesn't make it so.'

Jake clenched his jaw together, grinding his teeth in anger and frustration. There weren't many people who could get away with speaking to him and Connor like that, but fortunately for John, he happened to be one of them. And as much as he hated to admit it, John was probably right.

'I think we should pay those Bridewell bell-ends another visit,' Connor grumbled.

'You're just looking for someone to kick shite out of,' Jake answered him with a shake of his head.

'So?' Connor replied with a shrug. 'It would make me feel better, anyway. We need to ask Danny and Luke if there was anything in their office that night that someone might have seen.'

'And we still don't know who targeted Danny at Cartel Securities that night,' John reminded them. 'Maybe they went after the money? Or maybe they were after something else?'

'Hmm.' Jake ran a hand over his jaw. Whoever was behind the incident at Cartel Securities a few months earlier was still unclear, and although he'd written it off as someone trying to make some quick cash, he was starting to wonder if it was all part of a bigger and more worrying picture. 'So if we're thinking this is all connected and an inside job, we need to find out who knew Danny was going to the Cartel offices that night.'

'This is all getting far too fucking complicated for my

liking,' Connor said with a sigh. 'I remember when people were too fucking scared to take us on. Are we going soft?'

'I think you'll find it's always been the case that there is someone stupid enough and brave enough to take anyone on when there's money at stake,' John replied.

'You think they'd come back if we asked them?' Connor asked with a grin, referring to his dad and Grace and only half joking.

'Yes, they would. So don't bloody ask them. They deserve a bit of peace,' John replied before Jake could, causing Connor to laugh softly.

'I'll speak to Danny when he gets home and see if we can figure out who from our own firm knew where he was going that night,' Jake said. 'You got any other ideas, John?'

'Not yet,' John answered with a sigh. 'But leave it with me.'

'I can't believe we're being fucking bothered by this shit,' Connor grumbled in the front seat. 'Can't we pay other people to deal with this shit?'

John laughed in the back seat. 'No matter how big you are, you never stop being bothered by this shit.'

'For fuck's sake,' Jake groaned. 'Is this the kind of ball-ache my mum and Michael had to deal with all the time?'

'Every fucking day,' John replied.

Danny was home by the time Jake got back. He was freshly showered, his hair damp as he stood in the kitchen in only his shorts, having just made himself a bacon sandwich. Jake's eyes roamed over his muscular torso as he walked in and sat at the kitchen table.

'You want one?' Danny asked.

'Nah. Me and Connor had a KFC,' he replied.

'How did it go with Derek?'

'He thinks it was an inside job. But he thinks the problem is from our end,' Jake said with a sigh as he ran a hand through his thick dark hair.

'What the fuck?' Danny asked with a frown as he carried his sandwich to the table and sat down. 'You think he's right?'

'I dunno. Maybe. He reckons he's confident at his end, and let's face it, it's him who's out a few hundred grand, not us.'

'You trust him?' Danny asked as he took a bite of his food.

'I do, yeah. But nobody at our end knew.'

'Some of the lads did,' Danny reminded him.

'What?' Jake snapped. 'Which lads?'

'Some of the new bouncers. Jazz was in our office last week asking about the contract with that new car-hire firm. She wanted to know why we were paying them a shitload of money. I think she thought someone was pulling a fast one.' Danny winced, realising not only had he just landed Jazz in it, but he should probably have mentioned it at the time. It didn't help matters that Jake and Connor liked to keep their part of the business separate from the security firm, but they didn't seem to appreciate that it naturally crossed over, seeing as so many of their bouncers knew the dealers personally and some of them were also always up for a little extra courier work now and then.

'Fuck!' Jake said with a sigh and a shake of his head. 'So it is from our end, then?'

'Sorry, I should have mentioned it.'

Jake looked up at Danny's anxious face. He had no reason to be anxious though, Jake thought to himself, as he couldn't stay annoyed with Danny for longer than a few minutes.

'Don't worry about it,' he assured him. 'But how could Jazz have been so stupid as to announce that so openly? How many bouncers were there? I'm going to need to know exactly who was there, Dan.'

'Fuck! I'm not sure I remember. We'd just had a meeting. They were all milling in and out. At least five or six of them heard. Maybe more? I'll get you the names of everyone who was there, though,' Danny assured him.

'Yeah, and while you're at it, find out who in our own firm might have known that you were going to be going to Cartel Securities that night you got jumped.'

'You think that has something to do with this?' Danny asked with a frown.

'I don't think we can rule anything out right now. I know we deal with this kind of shit all the time, but there are things happening a little too frequently for my liking, and now that I know we might have a snake amongst our own, then I'm starting to wonder if it's much more than coincidence.'

Danny took a huge bite of his sandwich and mumbled his agreement.

'How was your night? What happened at the club?'

Danny swallowed his food. 'Seems like it was a bust-up between a stag do and some local lads, and one of our bouncers got caught up in the middle of it all.'

'Is he okay?'

'He'll be fine. He's going to be out of action for a few weeks, though.'

'If this leak is one of your bouncers, do you think these incidents in the clubs are linked somehow?'

'It's possible, I suppose, if you think we have someone on the inside working against us. On the surface they seem like isolated incidents, but it could be someone stirring up trouble. You know it doesn't take much to cause a kick-off when there's ale and coke involved.'

Jake nodded his agreement as Danny frowned. If it was one of his employees who'd had them over, he was going to string them up by their balls before Jake and Connor got their hands on them. He and Luke prided themselves on running a good business and vetted all of their employees personally. They had taken on a load of new staff in the past few months, though, and he made a mental note to look into all of them again.

'I'm sorry, Jake. If it is one of our lads...' he started to say, but Jake interrupted him.

'Then we'll find them and deal with them, Dan. There's nothing to apologise for. When we do what we do, there's always people who will want what we have.'

'I know that, but our lads are usually sound.'

'You have over three hundred people working for you. You can't keep an eye on them all, every minute of the day.'

'Me and Luke will do some digging. If there is a fucking snake among us, then we'll find him.'

'I know. And then if we can just stop Jazz from blurting out any more of our secrets, we'll be sound,' Jake said with a roll of his eyes.

'You can't be too hard on her. She's only been doing the job for a few weeks. She saw a huge account for a car-hire firm, and she queried it.'

'She should have done it in private,' Jake snapped. He loved Jazz, but she was so new to all this, it made him wonder if his mum and Michael had made the right decision in choosing her to be the new CEO of Cartel Securities.

'Maybe?' Danny shrugged. 'But maybe you and Connor should have told her about it, so she wouldn't have had to ask.'

Jake stared at him. Was Danny really trying to put some of the blame on him in this scenario? He wasn't used to people questioning his decisions, but the way Danny stuck up for the people he cared about was one of the many things Jake loved about him.

'So, it's mine and Connor's fault, is that it?' Jake asked, his eyes narrowed as he stared at Danny, who put the sandwich he was just about to take a bite out of back on his plate. If it had been Danny who'd fucked up, he would have apologised and taken it on the chin, not for a minute thinking of sticking up for himself. But he would argue the toss for other people without a second's thought.

'I never said that.' Danny glared back at him. 'But this is new for you all. Your mum and Michael knew everything that went on, everywhere, and you and Connor have been used to doing your own thing and not having to keep other people in the loop. But you can't do that now. Because you two are the ones in charge – well, you and Jazz.'

Jake looked at Danny and, much as he hated ever admitting being wrong, he couldn't deny that Danny had a point. He would speak to Connor tomorrow and then they could deal with the issue in whatever way Connor felt most comfortable with, given that it was his wife they were talking about. 'You know you're pretty smart for some hired muscle,' Jake said with a half-smile. It was a private joke between them, since Danny often referred to himself as Jake's hired muscle, despite him being so much more than that in many ways.

Danny's cheeks turned pink and he shook his head dismissively, making Jake laugh out loud. He really struggled with taking a compliment.

Jake stood up and walked around the table to him, placing his hand on the back of Danny's neck before leaning down and planting a kiss on the top of his head. 'I'm going to bed. Fancy joining me when you've finished that?' he offered.

Danny stuffed the remainder of his bacon butty into his mouth and pushed his chair back before following Jake out of the room. He didn't need asking twice.

Chapter Four

Connor walked into Maria's café on Liverpool's Dock Road and saw Jake sitting at their usual table. They had been meeting there every Friday morning for a fried breakfast for as long as he could remember.

'I ordered your usual,' Jake said with a smile as Connor sat down.

'Thanks, mate.'

Before either of them could say anything else, Maria bustled over to their table with two large mugs of steaming hot tea. 'Morning, boys,' she said with a smile. 'How are you both?'

'All good, thanks, love,' Connor replied. 'How are you doing?

'Can't complain,' she replied with a girlish giggle and a twinkle in her eye. She was at least sixty and had owned this café for thirty years. She was a Liverpool institution, and she had a thing for Connor Carter.

Jake chuckled in his seat as he watched her bat her eyelashes at his best mate. Maria was a fucking gem, and he and Connor always looked after her.

'You got any sugar for these?' Connor asked as he tapped a fingertip against his cheek, and she cackled loudly before she leaned down and gave him a quick peck.

'Mickey is just cooking your breakfast. Extra bacon,' she said before walking back to her counter.

'You thought any more about our meeting last night?' Connor asked as he poured a sachet of actual sugar into his tea.

'Yeah, and I think Derek was right. We could have a leak.'

'Did Danny know something?' Connor frowned while he stirred his tea.

'Not much, but he told me something that makes me think it is one of our own.'

'What's that?' Connor asked.

Jake purposely avoided the question, wondering at the best way to tell Connor what Jazz had done without sounding like he was accusing her. Connor adored his wife and he wouldn't take any possible criticism of her lightly. 'He's going to speak to Luke and they're going to look into a few people. Some of their newer recruits, as well as anyone who might have known Danny was going to the Cartel offices that night, along with anyone who was at a meeting a few weeks ago.'

'What meeting? And what did he tell you that made you think it's one of ours?'

Jake licked his lip as he wondered if he was about to get a smack in the mouth. He loved Connor Carter like a brother, but the man was a bad-tempered bastard at times, and Jake was about to accuse his wife of a major fuck-up.

'What?' Connor snapped.

'Some of the bouncers overheard a conversation about the new car-hire firm we're using in Scotland. Some of the payment has gone through the Cartel Securities books, like we planned.'

'Yeah?' Connor answered with a puzzled look on his face. 'We always do that.'

'I know, but Jazz didn't know that, did she?'

Connor's face darkened at the mention of his wife's name. 'What are you saying?'

'Jazz asked Danny and Luke about the payment in front of some of the bouncers last week.'

'She's not that fucking stupid, Jake,' Connor snarled.

'Are you calling Danny a liar, then?' Jake snarled back before he noted how Connor's knuckles were turning white on the table as he clenched his fists in anger. He realised he would do better to defuse the tension rather than ignite it further. 'Look, it was an oversight, probably. She was doing her job and checking on an anomaly in the books. We should have told her what we were doing, in her defence.'

Connor glared at him for a few seconds before he spoke again. 'For fuck's sake!' he hissed through clenched teeth. 'She knows better than that.'

'Yeah, but she's still finding her feet, mate. She probably didn't think. Besides, if she hadn't done that, we wouldn't have known we had a fucking snake working for us, would we? And now we do. Danny and Luke are getting us the names of the bouncers who were there that day, and they will find out which one of them is the leak, if you want? Or we can speak to them ourselves?'

Connor shook his head. 'We've got enough on our plate. It looks like this traitorous fuck works for Danny and Luke, so let them do their jobs and find out who it is. Then we can deal with whoever it is ourselves. But let me speak to Jazz, okay?'

Jake nodded, having no desire whatsoever to get involved in that conversation. 'Of course, mate.'

'I'll make sure it doesn't happen again,' Connor assured him.

'Good. And we should remember to keep her in the loop from now on.'

'Yeah,' Connor replied with a sigh as he ran his hands through his hair.

'Everything okay, mate?'

'When my dad and your mum told me about their plan to make Jazz CEO, I thought it was a good idea…'

'But now?' Jake probed him.

'I don't know, mate. I just don't like the idea of bringing her so deep into our world, you know? I kind of liked her being at home with Paul all the time. But I know that's not enough for her, and I want her to be happy more than anything. But now I get why my dad was always so worried about your mum.'

'Yeah, but I know she worried about him just as much,'

Jake offered. 'You can't be in our game and get to keep your family life out of it, mate. As much as we'd like to. You know that. She is your wife, and so she is involved whether you like it or not. Isn't it better that she's in the position she's in, so she knows exactly what's going on?' Jake was surprised he was arguing Jazz's case so passionately, but he acknowledged that he had perhaps been a little harsh in his judgement of her the previous night. And maybe Danny Alexander was rubbing off on him?

'I dunno. I'll talk to her this afternoon, though.'

'Good. Now you'd better stop looking like someone just shot your puppy, because Maria is on her way back over here with our brekkie, and she'll have you pressed up against her tits while she comforts you, if you're not careful,' Jake said with a grin.

Connor laughed and Jake was glad to have relieved the tension, for now at least. 'You all set for Danny's birthday tomorrow, then?' Connor asked as they each tucked into their fry-up.

'Yeah. Picking his watch up later,' Jake replied.

'I thought you already had it?'

'I did. But I got it engraved,' Jake replied with a flash of his eyebrows.

'What with?' Connor eyed him suspiciously.

'Come with me and find out.'

'Yeah, I might. I'll bring Paul with me. Jazz has some paperwork to catch up on.'

'Good,' Jake replied, although the mention of his nephew's name always reminded him of his namesake,

Connor's twin brother, and Jake swallowed the lump in his throat. It had taken him a long time to accept that Paul would have wanted him to be happy. Paul Carter had been even more fearsome and unhinged than his brother, but he was one of those people who grabbed life by the balls and lived by his own rules. He was the kind of person who would grab onto something that made him happy, regardless of what anyone else thought about him. Eventually, his death had taught Jake to do the same. Like Connor, he still missed Paul every day, but he no longer felt guilty for finding happiness with someone else, because he knew without a doubt that Paul would be cheering him on from the sidelines if he could.

Chapter Five

Connor pulled into the driveway of his house and parked up. He stayed in his car for a few minutes, looking up at his beautiful six-bedroomed house, with his gorgeous wife and son inside. It had been almost two years since he'd first met Jazz in a nightclub in Manchester. She was on a night out with her sister, and he'd been there with Paul. From the moment he had laid eyes on her, he'd been completely besotted. She'd been wearing a gold, shimmery dress, and unlike most of the other women in the club, she hadn't been showing off her tits and her arse, but that dress had been skintight and had clung to every single inch of her body. He smiled as he remembered having to rearrange himself in his trousers as he'd stood there watching her dance. She was mesmerising. All hips and arse and long, dark, curly hair.

He'd abandoned Paul and marched over to her. When he offered to buy her a drink she smiled at him, and he'd been done for. He'd fallen for her hook, line and sinker. She was nine years older than him but that hadn't mattered at all. She was the most beautiful and incredible woman he had ever met in his life. She had told him from the outset that she was married, but he hadn't cared. He had wanted her more than he'd ever wanted anyone or anything in his life. And she had wanted him too. She had been supposed to stay at her sister's, but Connor had taken her to a hotel instead and they had fucked until the sun came up.

She'd never done anything like that before and she'd told him they never could again, but Connor had been determined not to let her slip through his fingers. What they'd done hadn't been some one-night thing, and he knew that she had felt it too. So even when she'd told him that her husband was Sol Shepherd, the biggest gangster in Manchester and a man Connor's own father used to work for, he had been undeterred. He had pursued her relentlessly and she had been his willing prey.

He had been prepared to take Sol Shepherd out if it meant getting Jazz away from him, but somebody else beat him to it. Connor suspected it was his father, and that it had something to do with Paul being murdered, but his dad never spoke of it and they were painful wounds to open, so they never picked at that particular scab. Jazz had been pregnant with their son Paul at the time, and once Sol was dead, she had been free to move on with him, and they had never been happier.

Connor sighed and ran his hands through his hair. He was a lucky bastard, and he knew it, but he wasn't particularly looking forward to the conversation he was about to have. He could hardly believe Jazz had been stupid enough to discuss business in front of their employees like that. But then he had remembered her mentioning the car-hire firm to him some time last week and how she'd queried the invoice with Luke and Danny. He hadn't realised she'd done it out in the open like that.

He knew she'd been struggling with her new role. When Grace had suggested it to her, she had been tempted to turn it down, wondering if it was too big a job to take on. It had been Connor who had persuaded her otherwise, and now he wasn't sure if she hadn't been right all along. Perhaps it was too much for her, especially while their son was so young.

As he stepped out of the car, Connor's shoes crunched on the gravel path as he made his way into the house. The sound of Jazz singing along to the radio in the kitchen made him smile, despite everything. He walked in and stood in the doorway watching her as she danced along too, while she unloaded the dishwasher. The baby monitor was on the worktop, which meant that Paul was having his mid-morning nap in his cot, and so it was just him and her. He wished he could lift her onto the kitchen counter and bury himself inside her, instead of having to talk to her about being more discreet about their business dealings.

Jazz had been a dancer in her late teens and early twenties, and she still moved like one. She still had him completely hooked and he wondered what he had ever done to deserve the devotion of such an incredible woman.

She turned and caught him watching her, and it made her jump.

'Connor!' she shrieked, placing her hand on her chest. 'You scared the living daylights out of me.'

'Sorry, babe,' he said as he walked towards her. 'But you look pretty fucking hot dancing like that.' He grinned.

She smiled back at him. 'Well, you know I would dance for you any time you want me to,' she purred, and he wrapped his arms around her waist as he reached her. 'Paul is asleep.' She flashed her eyebrows at him and he sucked in a deep breath.

He loved that she wanted him just as much as he did her, and he would love nothing more than what she was suggesting. 'I need to talk to you first,' he said, looking down into her huge brown eyes.

'What is it?' she blinked at him.

'You remember that Scottish car-hire place you were asking Danny and Luke about the other week?'

'Yes. Why?'

'Were there other people around when you asked?'

'I don't know.' She frowned at him and then shook her head. 'Maybe?'

'Maybe, Jazz? For fuck's sake, babe.'

'What is it?' She tilted her head slightly as she searched his face.

'We had some gear go missing up there. Someone knew we were using that car-hire company to transport it. That was information that very few people should have been aware of.'

One of Jazz's hands flew to her mouth and he watched as her cheeks flushed pink and her eyes darkened in anger. He knew she was only angry at herself, though. She hated to make mistakes and he knew better than anyone the pressure she felt under to be the next Grace Carter. 'Oh my God, Connor, I'm so sorry. I just thought it was something to do with lease cars for the bouncers. If I had known…' She shook her head again and pulled back from him. 'I should have realised, though. I'm so sorry.'

'Jazz,' he said, reaching out and pulling her back into his arms. Seeing his wife hurt and annoyed with herself suddenly made what had happened seem insignificant. So what if they had lost a bit of money? Derek was going to pay it back anyway. 'It's okay, babe. At least we know now that someone in that room is working against us, and we would never have known that otherwise.'

'But I should have known. I can't believe I did something so stupid. It will never happen again, I swear.'

He placed his finger under her chin and tilted her head so she could look up at him. 'I know. But give yourself a break. You're new. You're learning. And me and Jake should have told you about the car-hire place and what they were doing. We will in future. And you just make sure that any conversations happen behind closed doors. Okay?'

'Okay.' She blinked at him and he placed his hand on her warm cheek, tracing her cheekbone with the pad of his thumb. 'What must Jake and Danny and Luke think of me?' She winced.

'Exactly the same as me. We all make mistakes, babe. It's

done. We're handling it. Now please don't worry about it anymore, because it fucking kills me when you doubt yourself.' He bent his head low and pressed his lips over hers, and she leaned into him. 'How long has he been asleep?' he growled as he broke their kiss.

'About ten minutes,' she breathed.

'So we got about half an hour, then?'

'Yes.' She bit her lip and looked up at him.

'Let's not waste any more time then, Mrs Carter.' He winked at her as he lifted her up onto the kitchen counter, making her squeal with laughter.

Chapter Six

J errod and Devlin King stood staring at the man in the
expensive suit. He was tall, lean, but muscular. With
ice-blue eyes that made Devlin shudder involuntarily
when he trained them on him. He also had a scar running
from the corner of his left eye to his lip, which made his
already menacing countenance even more so.

His accent was weird. The King brothers had never left
Liverpool, and rarely left their estate, so they didn't hear
many regional accents. This meant they had no idea where
their new associate was from – only that it wasn't Liverpool.
But they didn't care where he was from; all they cared about
was that he seemed to hate Jake Conlon and the Carters as
much as they did. What they did know was that Mr Savage
had money and he had some powerful people in his
pockets. He was able to make things happen, and quickly.
They had met him a few nights earlier when he'd turned up
at their local and presented them with an offer that seemed

too good to be true. Do one little job for him, and at the same time finally get rid of those two annoying pricks, Jake and Connor, and fuck up the whole of their empire while they were at it, leaving Liverpool for the Bridewell Blades crew. Jerrod and Devlin had laughed at him at first, and told him to fuck off. But he had taken down three of their best soldiers without even breaking a sweat, and then sat at their table anyway. That had certainly got their attention. And when he had told them about the people he had in his pockets and the strings he could pull because of it, they had paid even more attention. He'd left them to consider his proposal and gave them his number. The following day, when one of their crew had been stopped and found with two bags of brown, Jerrod had decided to call on their new, connected friend, Mr Savage, and give him a chance to prove his worth. A few phone calls later, their boy was back on the street.

'Can you take your hand out of your fucking pants when I'm talking to you?' Mr Savage snapped at Devlin.

'Prick,' Devlin muttered under his breath, earning him a nudge in the ribs from his older brother. Mr Savage might be a pretentious prick, but he had proven he had the money and the connections in Liverpool to help them take their firm to the next level, and Jerrod wanted in. He was fed up of people laughing at him. Fed up of people not taking him and Devlin seriously because they didn't dress fancy or have flash cars. It was time to step up and show that bunch of arrogant cunts just how smart he was. With Jake Conlon and Connor Carter out of the way, and Grace and Michael

Carter out of the country, there would be a void to fill, and Jerrod believed that he and Devlin were just the men to fill it. They had built their operation up from nothing, and they had a large and loyal crew and, as he saw it, they were primed and ready to slide seamlessly into that top spot as soon as it was vacated. They even had someone on the inside of the Carters' firm for them, and with some persuasion, he was sure plenty of their other ex-employees would turn once the dust had settled.

Mr Savage had a plan. And it was such a fucking good one that Jerrod was happy to execute it and take the credit. It was something he could never have come up with himself, not that he would admit that. But it was all so easy, especially when they had unwittingly done some of the legwork already. It seemed their expedition to Cartel Securities a few months earlier had netted them more than just a few grand; it was going to give them the whole fucking city. Everything was ready for them to pull the job off. All he and Devlin had to do was wait for the right time to make their move, and everything would fall into place.

'What did you just fucking say, son?' Mr Savage snarled as he advanced towards the youngest King brother.

Jerrod slapped his brother over the back of his head before their new associate had a chance to. 'I'll sort him out, Mr Savage. He gets a bit ahead of himself sometimes,' Jerrod said before glaring at Devlin.

Devlin glared back. He wasn't as convinced of Mr Savage's clout as Jerrod was. The incident with one of their firm had all been a little too convenient for his liking, but

Jerrod had dismissed him when he'd voiced such concerns. Devlin wasn't sure that Mr Savage's plan was as foolproof as he made it sound. But his older brother was so desperate to stick it to Conlon and Carter that he would do anything, including being someone else's fall guy.

'So, once this is done, you're just going to walk away from Liverpool and leave us to run things, are ya?' Devlin asked. He wasn't going to let this smarmy prick order him about in his own city.

The older man scowled at him, but after a few seconds he nodded. 'That's what I said. I have no interest in your city. I only want what's rightfully mine.'

'That stuck-up b—' Devlin was about to say 'bitch', but he wasn't completely stupid. He had seen how Mr Savage's whole personality had changed whenever *she* was mentioned. He went from being cool and collected to wide-eyed and feral in an instant. And although it was amusing to see, Devlin wasn't stupid enough to provoke the man so much by insulting the woman he was clearly obsessed with.

'Carter's wife?' Jerrod finished for him.

Mr Savage flinched, as though the words had cut him. 'Yes,' he eventually snarled. 'She is all I'm interested in. Everything else is yours.'

'Sound,' Jerrod replied with a grin, looking between his younger brother and their new business partner. 'When do we start?'

'No time like the present,' Mr Savage said as he checked his watch. 'The sooner we put the next stage of our plan into action, the sooner we can all get what we want, and I can get out of this fucking city.'

'We'll get one of our soldiers onto it right away,' Jerrod replied with a nod as he twisted the gold signet ring on his little finger. It had belonged to their mum and was one of the few things they had left of her. As the oldest, Jerrod had inherited it, and he never took it off.

'Good,' Mr Savage said before he smacked his lips together in satisfaction.

Devlin watched the two of them with a scowl on his face. Nothing this good ever came this easy. There had to be a catch somewhere. He just couldn't see what it was.

Chapter Seven

J ake looked around the table at the six faces of the people he trusted more than anyone else in the world. Since his mum and Michael had left for Spain two weeks earlier, it had just been the six of them running every aspect of their business, and things had been going okay – no more problematic than it usually was, anyway. He and Connor oversaw the dirtier side of things, while Danny Alexander and Luke Sullivan managed Cartel Securities, and Stacey managed the club and some of the restaurants now too, while their uncle Sean got back on his feet. He'd been shot in the chest a few months earlier and left for dead. The perpetrators had been dealt with, but Sean was lucky to have survived and he still wasn't back to full strength. And then there was Jazz, who was the respectable front of their whole organisation now, and despite her little mistake the week before, she was generally doing a good job of it.

'So, how does it feel being thirty, Danny?' Stacey asked with a grin.

'Exactly the same as it felt to be twenty-nine,' he replied with a frown.

'Hey. There's nothing wrong with being in your thirties,' Jasmine added as she downed a shot of tequila. 'And I could still outlast the lot of you.'

Connor slipped an arm around his wife's shoulders. 'I have no doubt about it, babe,' he said before kissing her forehead.

'So, let's see the bling Jake got you for your birthday, mate?' Luke said with a flash of his eyebrows.

Danny Alexander hated being the centre of attention and Jake watched as his cheeks flushed pink. Still, he held out his arm and showed off the Breitling watch to a chorus of appreciative noises.

'Wow. That must have cost more than your house, Dan,' Stacey said as she took hold of his wrist and inspected the timepiece. 'And what does it say on it?'

'What?' Danny stammered.

'We all know he got it engraved,' Luke answered with a grin.

'For fuck's sake, Jake,' Danny hissed as he unfastened it from his wrist and handed it to his younger sister. 'Is nothing sacred?'

'Not between us six, no.' Jake laughed in response as he watched Stacey's eyes brimming with tears as she read the inscription.

'Don't, Stace,' Danny said with a sigh.

Stacey looked up and smiled at him before she looked across at Jake. 'I didn't realise you were such a romantic,' she teased.

Jake shrugged in response. It had taken months for Danny to finally come out of the closet and open up about their relationship, and now that it was out there for everyone to know, he wasn't ashamed to admit that Danny made him happier than he had ever thought possible.

Connor had been with him when he'd picked up the watch and knew what the inscription read, so no doubt Jazz did too. But Luke stared at Stacey, waiting for her to let him in on the information, while Danny looked down at his pint.

Stacey swallowed the lump in her throat before she read it out loud: '*If I know what love is, it is because of you.*'

'Fuck!' Luke breathed.

'He's a soppy bastard really, aren't you, lad?' Connor laughed as he leaned over and ruffled Jake's hair.

'Fuck off!' Jake laughed too as he shook his head, while Danny kept his bent slightly until Luke, his best mate and the man who was like a brother to him, leaned over the table, placed his hands on Danny's cheeks and kissed him on the head. 'Happy birthday, mate.'

Danny looked up and gave a slight nod of his head. 'Thanks, mate,' he mumbled.

'It's beautiful, Dan,' Stacey said as she handed his watch back to him and he strapped it onto his wrist again.

'I know, yeah,' Danny replied with a smile before he turned and caught Jake's eye. 'Thanks,' he mouthed.

'So, who is going to split a garlic bread with me, then?' Stacey piped up.

'I suppose I might as well, seeing as it's me who has to kiss you at the end of the night,' Luke said with an exaggerated groan.

'Can you not talk about kissing my sister when I'm about to eat?' Danny rolled his eyes, and Stacey looked between him and Luke, not sure which of them she should pretend to be more annoyed at. She chose Luke and nudged him in the ribs, making him laugh.

Jake smiled as he looked around the table. Danny had been through a lot these past few months. Not only was he only just fully recovered from the attack at the Cartel Securities office; he had finally come out as gay, and had also cut ties with his rotten excuse for a mother. So, Jake had been determined that he would have the perfect birthday, and this birthday meal with their closest friends and family was the most fitting way to top it off.

As he was sitting, thinking about how great life was, Jake looked up and saw the figure approaching the table. Anger surged in his chest. 'Who the fuck let *her* in here?' he snarled as he stood up from the table.

Everyone else at the table turned too, to see Glenda Alexander walking towards them.

'Oh, God!' Stacey mumbled as she shifted in her seat, positioning her body so she was shielded by Luke.

'What the fuck are you doing in here?' Danny snapped as his mother reached him.

She held out a small parcel, that had been poorly

wrapped in faded balloon wrapping paper. 'Happy birthday, Danny boy,' she replied with a toothless smile and a glazed look in her eyes.

'Fuck off, Glenda!' he snarled at her, and her face crumpled in front of them, and if Jake didn't know her better, he would have thought she was genuinely upset by his reaction. Perhaps she was, but only because her personal cash machine had finally woken up and told her where to go.

'Danny?' she whimpered before she turned to Stacey, who hated her mother even more than her brother did, and had refused to talk to her since her return to Liverpool just a few months earlier. 'Stace?'

'What are you doing here, Glenda?' Luke snarled, his eyes narrowed as he glared at the woman who had given birth to his girlfriend and his best mate, but had done nothing else to deserve the title of mother.

'I miss my kids,' she snivelled as she turned to Jake now. 'Please, I just wanted to give my Danny his birthday present.'

Jake shook his head in annoyance as he signalled one of the bouncers to come over. How the hell had Glenda Alexander even got past them? Sofia's Kitchen was the most exclusive bar and restaurant in Liverpool's Albert Dock, and Glenda shouldn't have been anywhere near the place. Someone was going to have their arses handed to them before the night was through. Jake would happily remove her himself, but he knew that Danny's relationship with her was a complicated one, and he would rather not do anything further to ruin their night by manhandling Danny's mother.

Glenda continued to stand there, arm outstretched with her gift while the occupants of the table stared at her, except for Stacey, who refused to look at her and remained positioned behind Luke so she wouldn't have to. 'Get out, Mum. No one wants you here,' Danny said more calmly, trying to reason with her. But Glenda Alexander wasn't a woman who could be reasoned with, even when she wasn't as high as a kite, which she clearly was now, as she stood there in a face-off.

'Everything okay, Boss?' Nick, Sofia's head bouncer, asked as he jogged over.

Jake stepped closer to him and bent his head close to Nick's ear. 'No, it's fucking not, Nick. How the fuck did she get in here and anywhere near us?' he snarled.

Nick looked at the dishevelled figure, his Adam's apple bobbing in his throat as he swallowed hard. 'I don't know, Boss. I'll have a word with the lads on the door.'

'Have a word? I want to know who let her in here, because he will no longer be working in this cushy little number. And if any of your staff ever fuck up like this again, neither will you.'

Nick nodded and cleared his throat. 'I'll deal with whoever it was, Boss.'

'And escort this piece of shit out before she puts everyone in this restaurant off their food,' Jake snapped.

Nick turned and faced Glenda. 'Come on. Out,' he said as he walked towards her.

'And who the fuck are you?' Glenda screeched, as Danny groaned loudly and put his head in his hands.

'Come on now, love. Don't make a scene,' Nick said as he put his hand on her shoulder and attempted to guide her out.

'Get your fucking hands off me!' Glenda screeched again, causing every single person in the restaurant to look over at the commotion. Jake sucked in a deep breath in an attempt to calm his raging temper. He could quite happily throttle Glenda right now, but that wouldn't look good in front of a restaurant full of customers. This place was still his mum's pride and joy, and she would give him no end of earache if he caused that kind of scene in here – not to mention she had raised him to never lay his hands on a woman, even one as vile as Glenda.

'Get her the fuck out of here, Nick,' Luke snarled.

'I'm trying, Boss,' Nick replied with a look that conveyed he was conscious of all eyes on him too.

At the sound of Luke's voice again, Glenda's face contorted with venom until she was practically hissing as she wrenched herself from Nick's grip and stepped towards the table again. 'And you can shut the fuck up too!' She jabbed a finger in Luke's face, causing Stacey to stand up, no doubt prepared to throw her mother out herself now. 'Did you tell my children what you did?'

'I said get her out,' Luke said through clenched teeth as his hands balled into fists against the table top.

'Do they know you've been lying to them?'

Danny's head snapped up. 'What's she on about, Luke?'

'Nothing! She's a fucking nutcase,' he snapped back, his eyes dark with anger.

'What's going on?' Stacey added.

'Tell them. Go on!' Glenda snarled. 'Tell them how I came back for them but *you* paid me to stay away.' She started to cackle now as Nick stood beside her and shook his head, as though he had no idea how to handle this situation while everyone was looking on.

'What the fuck is she on about, Luke?' Danny shouted as Jake stood with his mouth open, watching the whole scene unfold like he was in some fucked-up soap opera.

'If you don't get her the fuck out of here right now, you will be out of a job,' Luke snarled at his head bouncer.

Nick nodded and put his hand on Glenda's shoulder again, but she bent her head and bit him hard. He winced in pain as he snatched his hand back. 'Bitch!' he hissed under his breath, holding onto his hand for a moment before he raised it again and looked as though he was about to knock her out, but before he could, Jasmine stood up, pushing her chair back.

'Go and get that seen to,' she said to Nick, who stopped in his tracks and blinked at her. 'Now!'

He nodded and walked away as Jasmine walked around the table to Glenda, who was practically foaming at the mouth now. 'You fancy a drink, Glenda? Something to calm you down, eh, love?' she said with a sweet, reassuring smile.

Glenda blinked at her in confusion, but it stopped her ranting, at least.

'Come on.' Jasmine put an arm around her shoulder. 'Leave this lot to their squabbling. I've got an incredible single malt in the back office. You look like you could do with something to warm you up?'

Glenda's face softened slightly and she nodded. 'All right, girl,' she sniffed, wiping her nose with the sleeve of her coat.

Jasmine looked at Connor and he winked at her before discreetly summoning one of the other bouncers who was hovering nearby, while Jasmine guided Glenda through the restaurant to the back office, where Jake's mum and Michael did indeed keep their finest whiskies, although Jake suspected Glenda wasn't going to get anywhere near them.

As the bouncer reached their table, he leaned down so Connor could speak quietly. 'Follow my wife, and do whatever the fuck she tells you to. And if a single hair on her head is harmed by that fruitcake you lot let in here, I will deal with every single one of you personally. You got that?'

'Yes, Boss,' the bouncer said, nodding before following the two women.

Jake smiled to himself as he sat back down at the table, confident that Jasmine would handle Glenda better than any of them could, and that the bouncers would be so terrified of getting on the wrong side of Connor, that she was perfectly safe. Not that Jasmine couldn't handle Glenda on her own. She was one of the toughest and shrewdest women Jake had ever met.

'So, what the fuck was she on about, Luke?' Danny

asked again as soon as Glenda was gone, and Jake groaned inwardly. Could they not just have one night out without any drama?

'Yeah?' Stacey added as the two of them glared at Luke, waiting for his response.

Luke sighed deeply, and the look on his face made Jake want to put his head in his hands, because he knew there was a bombshell coming, and suddenly he wasn't bothered about their night out anymore. If that was the only thing that was ruined after whatever Luke was about to confess, then it would be a good outcome. But Jake had a horrible feeling that all hell was about to break loose.

'Did she come back for us?' Stacey asked, her voice small and quiet, and nothing like the Stacey Jake had come to know and admire.

Luke looked between the two of them for a few seconds before he finally answered. 'Yeah,' he admitted.

Danny leaned forward in his chair and Jake felt the anger radiating from him. 'What? When?'

'Just after my mum died,' Luke replied.

'What the fuck, Luke? What happened? Why the fuck didn't you tell us?' Danny snarled as Stacey stared at her boyfriend with her mouth open in shock.

Luke shook his head. 'I found her going through my mum's things. She was looking for money. That was all she was after, Dan. You were just getting back on your feet after prison. I thought...'

He didn't get the chance to finish before Stacey

interrupted him. 'While I was in that horrible kids' home?' she said, blinking at him.

'Yeah.' He swallowed hard.

'She could have got me out of there, Luke,' she snapped. 'You knew they wouldn't let Danny take me out, but she could have.'

'She wouldn't have, though,' he replied.

'But you don't fucking know that!' Danny shouted at him.

The change in Luke's face was instantaneous as he leaned across the table, staring Danny in the eyes. 'She walked out on you both when you were only kids. She left you to live with your rotten prick of a stepfather. She never did anything for either of you, your whole fucking lives. And when she came back, she was after one thing. Money.'

'I don't give a shit,' Danny snarled. 'You had no fucking right to make that decision for us.'

'I did what I thought was best,' Luke snarled back.

'You did, eh? Well, guess what? You are not my fucking father, or hers, and you have no fucking right to do what is best for either of us. She was our mum, and she came back for us.'

'You really think that, Dan? She came back for you both? Did she ever do anything for you before?'

'She could have at least got Stacey out of that fucking hell-hole, you prick!'

Jake placed his hand on Danny's shoulder, knowing that he was about to say something he was going to regret, but

Danny shook him off and Jake sat back in his chair, glancing at Connor, who shrugged as if to tell him to leave them to it.

'You're talking about her like she is a normal person who actually cared about her kids,' Luke spat incredulously. 'But this is Glenda we're talking about here.'

'Yeah, well, we couldn't all have a fucking amazing ma like you, could we? But she was all we had, and you fucking sent her packing without even telling us?' Danny stood up, planting his hands on the table.

Luke stood too. 'You want to know how much it took for her to walk out on the pair of you? Two fucking grand. I waved it under her nose and she couldn't get out of there fast enough.'

'Fuck you!' Danny spat, as Stacey sat with her mouth hanging open in shock. 'I should kick your fucking head in.'

'I'd like to see you fucking try,' Luke challenged him, his eyes narrowed as the two of them stared each other down over the table.

Jake stood. He was not about to have these two going at it in the middle of the restaurant. He placed his hand on Danny's shoulder, gripping him firmly and not about to be brushed off for a second time. 'You need to calm down,' he said in his ear before turning to Luke. 'And you need to leave. Now.'

'What the fuck, Jake?' Luke frowned at him.

Jake took a deep breath. He knew Luke was hurting, and he understood why he'd done what he did. He would happily pay Glenda to stay out of Danny's life himself, if he thought the evil, greedy bitch would actually keep her word. But Danny was hurt too, and he was Jake's priority.

'Leave,' Jake repeated. 'I won't ask for a third time, Luke,' he warned him, and Connor stood too.

Luke looked between the three of them, his face contorted in anger and confusion, but he backed down. He looked down at Stacey and she looked away from him, blinking away tears as she did.

'You're all fucking nutcases,' Luke snarled before he walked out of the restaurant.

'Nutcases?' Connor turned to Jake and smiled, trying to lighten the mood and relieve some tension. 'If he wasn't your uncle...' He cocked his head.

Jake shook his head as he sat back down. He knew his stepbrother and best mate well enough to know that they were both thinking the same thing. This was a potential shitstorm of epic proportions, and they both needed Danny and Luke to sort out their differences, because the truth was, they needed Luke. He was amazing at his job. He was loyal and trustworthy and he had their backs, no matter what. He was one of them.

Jake glanced at Danny, who was sitting looking like his world had just ended, as he downed a shot of whisky that had been sitting on the table for the past half an hour. He didn't drink spirits much because he couldn't handle them. How had their night turned so sour in a matter of minutes? He wondered if Jasmine had dealt with Glenda yet, because if she was still in the building, he might go and wring her neck himself.

Chapter Eight

Jasmine Carter opened Grace Carter's office and stepped inside. With Grace and Michael gone, she occasionally used the place as a base for herself while she figured out where her own space could be. She had been the CEO of Cartel Securities for two weeks and was still finding her feet. Grace's shoes were big ones to fill. And if she had been hoping for some hands-on guidance from her mother-in-law and mentor, she was mistaken, as Grace and Michael had taken their youngest two children and moved to Spain for six months to set up their newest restaurant.

Jasmine didn't blame them for taking an extended break from Liverpool. They both deserved it after everything they'd been through and how hard they had worked running the Carter empire. It was about time they enjoyed the fruits of their labour, but she missed them like crazy and she knew that Connor and Jake did too. Not to mention

Luke, who had only recently discovered he had a sister. But Jasmine also knew that Grace had ulterior motives. She was the shrewdest woman Jasmine knew, and she was allowing her daughter-in-law the space and time to find her own way without the shadow of her predecessor always looming in the background. She knew that Grace was there on the end of a phone, or even a few hours' flight away, if they really needed her. But being out of Liverpool removed the temptation for people to constantly seek her advice and guidance, rather than figuring things out for themselves.

Grace and Michael adored their children and their grandchildren, and she knew how hard it must have been for them to take a step back and let them make their own mistakes, and she felt privileged to have been entrusted with their empire. She was going to make them, and Connor, proud.

'So, where is this good whisky you got, girl?' Glenda asked, rubbing her hands together.

'It's in here,' Jasmine replied with a smile, beckoning Glenda into the office. She had noticed the bouncer following at a discreet distance and gave him a nod to wait outside. She wouldn't be needing him just yet.

Glenda followed her into the room and Jazz indicated she should take a seat before she poured them each a glass of Scotch. She begrudged wasting such good-quality alcohol on Glenda, who would probably have been just as happy with a shot of paint-stripper, but she didn't have anything but the good whisky back there.

Glenda took a long sip of the whisky and smacked her

lips together in approval. 'Ooh, that is the good stuff,' she said as she leaned back in her chair, making Jasmine wonder if she was as half cut as she appeared.

'So, we need to talk about you coming into my family's restaurant and causing a scene, Glenda,' Jasmine said as she took a sip of the expensive single malt, which warmed her throat as she swallowed. There was a time when she had been forced to drink whatever she could get hands on too, just to numb the pain and get through the day back in her early twenties, when her life had been a far cry from what it was now. She had pulled herself up from the depths of the hell that she was sold into, and she had become something more. But she had never forgotten her roots. She never for one second forgot that she could have ended up just like Glenda Alexander, if she hadn't met Sol Shepherd. And as much as she hated her ex-husband for the violence and cruelty he showed her, she did owe him for taking her out of that life.

She had met and fallen for Connor while she was still married to Sol. He had beaten her black and blue when he suspected she had been having an affair, and then murdered Connor's twin Paul, believing him to be Connor, when he'd been leaving the gym one day. Then she had fallen pregnant with their son, and as Sol couldn't have children, she had known her days were numbered. She had been ready to kill Sol herself when Michael Carter had turned up like some knight in shining armour and done it himself as revenge for Sol killing his son.

Now she was married to the love of her life, and they

had an incredible little boy, whom they had named after his uncle, and she couldn't be happier. So, although she had some sympathy for Glenda Alexander, she couldn't fathom the woman wanting to cause her own children so much pain, and she wasn't about to allow her to cause any unrest in her family.

'It's my family too,' Glenda sniffed.

Jasmine arched an eyebrow at her. 'Really?'

'Yes. Now that Danny has finally admitted he's a fairy and he's with that Jake, well, I'm family too, aren't I?' She drained the last of her Scotch and smacked her lips again.

Jasmine felt the bile rise in her stomach and burn against the back of her throat. So, that was Glenda's new game, was it? She believed that because Jake and her son were a couple, somehow she was part of the Carter family too? And she had no doubt that Glenda was going to be a thorn in all of their sides. A permanent solution would have to be found for her, but right now, Jasmine would take a leaf from her predecessor's book.

Placing her glass onto the table, she walked around the desk, leaning her face close to Glenda's. 'Jake and Danny are a couple, yes. They'll probably even get married one day. Maybe have a few cute kids. But you will *never* be a part of this family, Glenda. I will make sure of it.'

Glenda frowned, her mouth open as though she was about to speak, but Jasmine didn't let her. 'Because you are poison. Everything you touch turns to shit. You cause nothing but pain and misery wherever you go. Just because you gave birth to Danny and Stacey doesn't give you any right to be in their lives. They have a new family now. A family who would do anything to protect them.'

'Who the fuck do you think you are?' Glenda spat, her face full of venom.

'Me?' Jasmine laughed in the older woman's face. 'I am Jasmine Carter. Remember my name, because if you ever come near any of my family again, I will fucking end you. And I'm not quite as forgiving as Grace was. I am giving you one warning, and you will not get a second.'

Glenda glared at her but Jasmine held her ground. 'Ben,' she shouted to the bouncer standing outside. She made a point of knowing the name of every single staff member employed by Cartel Securities and the Carter family.

Ben walked through the door a second later. 'You need me, Mrs Carter?'

'Kindly escort our guest out of the back and put her in a cab. I don't want her hanging around here any longer than she has to.'

'Of course,' he said with a nod as he approached Glenda, who looked like she was ready to launch herself at him as he reached her.

'There are no customers back here, Glenda,' Jasmine reminded her. 'He will not be so polite if you bite him too.' She winked at Ben, who nodded his understanding, then she gave him a pat on the shoulder before she walked out of the office and left him to deal with the problem.

Chapter Nine

Connor closed the door behind his grandparents, Patrick and Sue, who had been looking after baby Paul for the night, and went to find his wife, who was taking off her make-up in their bedroom. They had taken a cab home and then had a quick drink with Pat and Sue when they'd got in, so he hadn't had a chance to talk about what had happened at the restaurant earlier, or how she'd dealt with Glenda. But the old witch hadn't bothered them again, so whatever she had done had been effective.

'Hey,' she said with a smile as she saw him walking into the room.

'Hey,' he said with a sigh as he took off his suit jacket and sat on the bed beside her.

'That was some night.'

'I know. Poor Stacey,' Jasmine said with a shake of her head. 'She looked so upset.'

Connor nodded his agreement.

'And poor Danny and Luke too,' she added.

'Well, Luke kind of brought it on himself, though, didn't he?'

'Why do you say that?'

'He should never have lied to them, Jazz,' Connor replied as he started to unbutton his shirt.

'Well, sometimes lies are needed to protect people from the truth,' she suggested, and he frowned at her.

'No. Lies are never the way to go. Not when it concerns the people you love, anyway,' he snapped at her, and instantly regretted it when he saw the hurt on her face. But he had seen first-hand how lies could tear a family apart. However, the last thing he wanted was an argument with his wife right now, and especially not over Glenda Alexander. 'How did you get rid of her?' he asked as he brushed the hair back from her face.

'Ben threw her out. I just wanted to get her away from the customers. Sometimes a little niceness works better than aggression, you know?' She smiled sweetly at him, as if to prove her point.

Connor smiled back at her. 'You did good. Reminded me of someone else I know.'

'Oh. And who's that?'

'Hmm. I think you know who. But I really don't want to talk about my stepmum right now.' He chuckled before he pushed her back against the bed and rolled on top of her.

'Oh? What do you want to talk about?' she purred, and his dick twitched in his pants.

'Nothing. I just want to get these clothes off and have

you ride me like you stole me.' He flashed his eyebrows at her.

'Connor,' Jasmine shrieked as she pushed against his chest, feigning her protest even though she had every intention of doing exactly as he asked.

Chapter Ten

J ake shrugged off his suit jacket and threw it onto the bed, sighing inwardly as he watched Danny pacing up and down the room.

'I can't fucking believe Luke would do that to me. To Stacey. He had no right keeping that from us.'

Jake sat on the bed and let Danny vent, hoping that getting some of the rage and anger out of his system might help him to think more clearly about the whole situation. Because as much as he was on Danny's side, he could also see Luke's point of view. Glenda Alexander was a nasty piece of work, and Jake understood exactly why Luke had wanted her out of Danny and Stacey's lives. He wanted her out of Danny's life too. She was a vile excuse for a mother, and the only reason she was interested in her son was for his money. Jake could see the pound signs in her eyes every time she spoke to him. And Danny was too good a man to ever turn his mother away when she was crying poverty.

'You're very quiet on the whole subject,' Danny said once he had stopped ranting.

'You seemed like you needed to get it all off your chest,' Jake replied with a shrug as he started to unbutton his shirt.

'But you agree with me, don't you?'

'I can see why you're pissed off,' Jake replied.

'That's not what I asked you, though, Jake. I asked you if you agreed with me.'

'It's late. Can we go to bed and talk about this in the morning?' Jake asked with a sigh.

'No, we fucking can't,' Danny snapped, and Jake bristled at his tone. Nobody spoke to him like that – not even the man he shared his life with.

'I'm on your side, Dan. That's all that matters,' Jake snapped back.

'No, it's not. You think I'm in the wrong and not him, don't you?'

Jake stood up as he peeled his shirt off and tossed it into the laundry basket. 'It's not that fucking straightforward, though, is it?'

Danny walked over to him, his face full of anger and anguish. 'Seems pretty straightforward to me, Jake. You either agree with me, or you don't. Which is it?'

Jake glared at him. He didn't feel like an argument tonight. He was tired and all he wanted was a quick fuck and to go to sleep, but there seemed to be no way Danny was going to let this go. He sucked in the air through his teeth, trying to keep a lid on his temper because he knew how much Danny was hurting, and he hated to see him in pain.

'I agree with you, Dan. But I can see where Luke was coming from. I get why he wanted Glenda out of your life.'

'You do?'

'Yes. And if you weren't so fucking blinded by whatever hold your mother has over you, you'd see it too.'

'You think?' he sneered.

'Yes, I fucking do. What the hell do you think she came back for, all of those years ago? Exactly the same thing she came back for last year. Money!'

'That's not the fucking point!' Danny hissed. 'It was not Luke's fucking decision to make. It was mine and Stacey's. She could have got Stacey out of that awful fucking kids' home. But instead, Saint fucking Luke had to deal with it all on his own, didn't he? Our fucking white knight!' he spat.

'Look, Dan, all I know is that Luke has always had your back since you were kids. I don't agree with what he did, but at least you can try and see that he did it for the right reasons?' Jake suggested. 'You're going to throw away your relationship with the man who is like a brother to you, because of your rotten ma?'

'No, not because of her. Because I can't fucking trust him anymore,' Danny shouted.

Jake shook his head. 'Then you're giving your mother exactly what she wants.'

'What? I don't fucking believe this!'

Jake shrugged as he slipped off the rest of his clothes. 'Believe it or don't, I'm going to bed.'

'You're supposed to be on my fucking side, Jake. No matter what – remember?'

Jake spun on his heel and walked over to Danny, bringing his face close to his. 'And I am, Dan. Every fucking day. That is why I just threw my own fucking uncle out of our restaurant. Do you realise what this will do to our family? Our business? It's going to tear us apart.'

Danny opened his mouth to speak but Jake cut him off. 'But I stood there and I supported you in front of everyone, and I told Luke that he had to go, because I have your fucking back. I always fucking do, and don't you for one minute ever suggest that I don't.'

Danny blinked and Jake knew he had made his point, but he continued anyway. 'But in here, there's just me and you. In here, I can tell you that I think you're making a huge mistake, Dan. But I will support it every fucking step of the way, if this is really the road you want to go down.'

'It is.' Danny nodded. 'I can't trust him, Jake. He's lied to me for the past eight years.'

Jake sucked in a breath. He could see the hurt and betrayal in Danny's eyes and knew how much Luke's deceit had cut him deep. He recalled a similar feeling years earlier when he had been at loggerheads with Connor and Paul over secrets and lies, and at the time he had felt like his heart had been sliced wide open. It was his biggest regret in life that he had never made peace with Paul before he was murdered. Now, he and Connor were brothers again, and they had both made a vow that nothing would ever come between them again. All Jake could hope for was that, in time, Danny would realise that Luke belonged in his life. In all of their lives.

'Then he's a ghost,' Jake said softly. 'Now, for the love of God, come to bed. It's your fucking birthday, and if the inscription on that watch hasn't earned me a blow job tonight, then I'm clearly losing my touch.'

The hint of a smile pulled Danny's lips into a curve. 'You're really thinking about that right now?'

'I'm always thinking about that.' Jake arched an eyebrow. Danny narrowed his eyes at him and Jake smiled. 'You know I only ever think about that with you, Dan,' he said as he stepped closer.

Jake heard Danny's breath catch in his throat as he reached out and started to undo the buttons of his shirt.

'Fuck! I love you,' Danny hissed.

'I love you too. Now get your arse over here,' Jake said as he pulled Danny towards him and silenced him with a kiss.

Chapter Eleven

The following morning, when Luke saw Danny's car parked outside Stacey's flat, he groaned inwardly. He knew he had to face both of them eventually, and he was intending to go and see Danny after he'd spoken to Stacey anyway, but he had hoped to get the chance to speak to each of them alone. One stubborn Alexander was always easier to deal with than two. He closed his car door and walked over the road. The air had to be cleared – and fast.

It had killed him to walk out of the restaurant last night, especially as Stacey practically lived with him now. He couldn't even remember the last time she had stayed at her own place, preferring to stay at his house in Allerton instead. He had lain awake for hours waiting for her, but by three o'clock he'd finally admitted that she wasn't coming and had tried to get some sleep. But of course he hadn't been able to. Fucking Glenda Alexander. She was a fucking pain in his arse and she had been for as long as he could remember. Always showing up and screwing things up when Danny's and Stacey's lives were going well. He had always hated her for what she'd done to them. It was why he'd paid her to clear off out of their lives eight years earlier, but now she had fucked up his life too, and he could happily murder the old cow for it.

With a deep sigh, Luke pulled back his shoulders and rang the buzzer to Stacey's flat.

It was Danny who answered. 'Who is it?' he barked.

'It's me, Dan.'

'Fuck off. She doesn't want to speak to you,' he snarled before the line went dead.

Luke rang again. And again.

'I said fuck off,' Danny eventually answered.

'No. I'm going anywhere until I speak to you both. So either let me in or get the fuck down here and speak to me. You can't just keep on ignoring me.'

'If I come down there, I'll kick your fucking—'

'Danny! Just let him in.' Stacey's voice cut across him, and a few seconds later the door clicked to signal it was open. Luke pulled it open quickly, as though Danny might change his mind and it would somehow lock again. He jogged up the stairs to the second floor to find the door to Stacey's flat already open for him when he got there.

He walked inside to see Stacey and Danny sitting at her kitchen table, each of them with a mug of steaming hot tea in front of them. He winced as he wondered if he might be wearing it soon.

Danny avoided looking at him while Stacey glared at him. 'What do you want, Luke?'

'What do you think I want, Stace?' he replied with a frown. 'To talk to you. To explain what happened.'

It was at this point that Danny jumped up from his chair and Luke sighed. His best mate was a short-tempered bastard, but Luke could count on one hand the number of times he had been on the receiving end of it before. Danny was like his brother, and he couldn't stand the thought of both him and Stacey not talking to him. 'Explain what, Luke? How she came back for us and you fucking sent her away? And then you lied about it for the past eight years?' Danny shouted as he bounced up and down on his toes, his fists clenched by his sides.

Luke sucked in a breath. Danny gave Glenda far too much credit and he had no idea why. He, of all people, knew the type of woman she really was. 'Are you fucking serious, Dan? She didn't come back here for you, or for Stacey. She came back here to see what she could get from you. Just like she has now.'

Danny advanced towards him, practically foaming at the mouth. 'It doesn't matter why she did. You had no fucking right to keep that from us. You had no fucking right to send her packing without giving either of us the chance to speak to her. She is our fucking mother!' He snarled the words and Luke took a step back.

'You're right. I'm sorry,' he said, but Danny was already halfway through his rant and he had no intention of stopping.

'Just because you grew up in a fucking posh house with a ma that gave a shit about you, doesn't give you the right to decide what's best for us. You think you're better than us just because you lived in a nice house and never had to wash your fucking clothes in a sink with cold water and a bar of fucking soap!'

Luke frowned at him. That was completely uncalled for, and as much as he loved Danny, he was about five seconds away from knocking him on his arse.

'Danny,' Stacey said sternly as she stepped in between the two of them. 'Stop it. Please?'

Danny looked between Luke and his sister, and after a few seconds he clamped his lips together and stepped back.

'Can you give us a few minutes?' Stacey asked him, and he glared at her in response. 'Please?'

'Fine,' he snorted as he started to walk out of the door, but then he turned and pointed a finger at Luke. 'But you and me are done. You are no fucking mate of mine,' he snapped before he left the room.

His words hit Luke like a punch to the ribs, but he turned and focused on Stacey – the sane Alexander sibling. 'Stace?' he started, but she held up her hand and he stopped talking.

'I know, Luke…' she said softly and he felt the relief wash over him in a wave. But unfortunately for him, she hadn't finished speaking. 'I know that you're sorry, but it doesn't change what you did, or the fact that you lied about it. You left me to rot in that horrible kids' home.'

'I didn't know…'

'You didn't know how bad it was in there? *Really?*'

'I knew it wasn't great, Stace, but you only had a few months left. If I'd known how bad it was there, I'd have come and fucking taken you out of there myself.'

She laughed at that and he frowned at her.

'You think you can fix everything, don't you? And that's your problem. You don't stop to think that some people don't need fixing, Luke. You do not get to make decisions for other people because *you* think it's the best thing for them.'

'She was only after one thing, Stace. She would never have taken you out of that place, because there was nothing in it for her.'

'But you don't know that, Luke. Glenda might be an awful mother, but she is the only one we have.'

'I know, Stace.' He swallowed the lump in his throat.

'I hated every second I was in that kids' home. I know Glenda would've been bloody useless, but I could have lived with Danny.'

Luke's heart sank in his chest. He sat on the chair and put his head in his hands. As soon as Danny had been released from prison after serving four years for the manslaughter of their stepfather, he had applied for custody of Stacey, but the courts had refused him because he was an ex-con with a violent temper.

'I thought it was for the best, Stace. I knew you'd get out when you were sixteen, and I thought a few more months in there would be worth it to have her out of your lives. I wasn't thinking straight, I'm sorry.' He looked up at her with tears in his eyes as he thought back to that day Glenda had turned up at his mum's house looking for Danny, because she needed money. His own mum had just died. He was devastated, and he'd needed his best mate by his side, not distracted by his useless mother, so he'd been completely selfish and paid her to leave. And in his heart, he knew he'd done it just as much for his own benefit as he had for Danny and Stacey. But he hadn't realised what Stacey had been going through in that home, or the fact she was being groomed by her ex-boyfriend, Simon Jones, who was currently serving life for his part in the murder of a young woman and sex-trafficking crimes.

'It's not just the extra few months I spent in there, though, is it? If I had been living with Danny, I might never have run off to Manchester and got involved with Simon. My whole life might have turned out differently.' She sniffed as a tear rolled down her cheek, and Luke resisted the urge to wipe it away for her.

The thought that he could have prevented all of those awful things that happened to her at the hands of her ex-boyfriend cut him deep, and he would never forgive himself, so how could he expect her or Danny to forgive him either?

'I'm sorry, Stace,' he said again, because he didn't know what else there was to say.

'I know you are, Luke,' she sniffed as she wiped her cheek with the sleeve of her hoody. 'But it changes nothing.'

'So, what does this mean for us?' he asked as tears pricked at his own eyes. He knew the answer but until she said it, he could pretend that she could forgive him and they could work this out.

'I can't trust you, Luke. So this... us... it can't work.'

'Stacey?' he pleaded as he stood up and crossed the room to her.

'I can't be with you, Luke. Not after this. I can't look at you and not feel completely betrayed.' She looked up at him as the tears ran down her face. She was hurt and angry, but he knew that she wasn't just saying this to hurt him. It was the truth, and it was breaking his fucking heart.

'You can trust me, Stace.' He tried one last plea, even though he knew it was useless. 'Don't let one mistake fuck this up for us!' He slid her arms around his waist, expecting her to push him away, but she didn't. She pressed her cheek against his chest and he felt her tears soaking through the material of his shirt, and it broke him even more than if she'd shouted at him and told him to get out. He could deal with anger. It always faded eventually. But as he held onto her and realised it would probably be for the last time, he realised his world had just fallen apart.

A few moments later, Luke walked out of Stacey's flat. He didn't bother saying goodbye to Danny. He didn't have the energy for another argument with him. He had just fucked up the best thing in his whole life and there wasn't a single thing he could do about it. His heart hammered against his ribcage and he fought the urge to be sick as he crossed the road to his car. He wished Grace was here and not in Spain. She'd be able to talk some sense into everyone. She had a way of making people see things differently, and he could use a little of that right now. Not to mention some tea and sympathy. Without Stacey and Danny, he had no one. Jake might be his nephew, but Danny was his partner, and that would be where his loyalties lay.

As he replayed the events of the last twenty-four hours over and over in his head, Luke promised himself that if he ever saw Glenda Alexander again, he would fucking kill her.

Chapter Twelve

Jasmine Carter looked up from her desk at her temporary office in Sofia's Kitchen as she heard someone tapping lightly on the open door.

'Mind if I come in?' Luke asked softly.

'Of course. Close the door,' she said with a smile.

Luke did as she asked before taking a seat in the chair opposite her. Although he was dressed as impeccably as ever, she noted the dark circles under his eyes and the thick stubble on his usually clean-shaven face. It gave him a slightly dishevelled appearance and made her wonder if he'd slept at all the previous night.

'How are you doing?' she asked.

He ran a hand through his thick, dark hair and gave a deep sigh.

'That bad, huh?'

'And then some,' he said, leaning back in the chair.

Jasmine said nothing as she waited for him to speak. She

could see both sides of the argument, and she knew that Luke loved Stacey and Danny as much as if they were his own flesh and blood. He would never have hurt them deliberately. It was a pity that neither of the Alexander siblings could see that right now.

'What am I going to do, Jazz?' he asked eventually, looking at her like she held all of the answers.

'Have you spoken to Grace?' she asked.

'No!' Luke shook his head. 'And I'm not going to. Her and Michael are busy and she's probably fretting enough, worrying about us all back here without her. I'd rather we handled this without her or Michael knowing. The last thing I want to do is drag them into the middle of a family feud.'

Jasmine leaned back and looked at Luke. His shoulders slumped as he sat there looking at her, waiting for the magical answer to his problems. She wished she had one. But she wasn't Grace Carter, and she was painfully aware of it when things like this happened. Grace would find a way to get through to them all and make them see sense. There was no way she would stand for her own brother and her son's partner to be at loggerheads for long. Jasmine felt completely at a loss over what to do to resolve the situation, but Luke was waiting for an answer.

'I think all you can do is wait for the two of them to calm down and see some sense, Luke,' she eventually replied. 'I'm not sure there's anything else you can do. They are both as stubborn as each other. You know that better than anyone.'

'So, you don't think I completely fucked up, then? You see why I paid Glenda off and never told them?' he asked, desperate for someone to be in his corner.

'Of course I do. I even think that Danny and Stacey could understand why you did that, if they were honest with themselves. But I think it's the lying to them for all these years that they're struggling with more than anything.'

Luke hung his head and slammed his fists down on the armrests of the chair. 'Fuck!' he hissed.

'They'll come round, Luke. They love you too much to let this come between you all.'

Luke looked up at her again. 'You really think so?'

Jasmine swallowed. She certainly hoped so, and that would have to be enough for now. 'Yes.'

He nodded and the hint of a smile played on his lips.

'Did Jake or Danny have a chance to speak to you about what happened in Scotland?' she asked, keen to change the subject and get back to discussing something that she felt they could find solutions for.

'Yeah.' Luke sat straighter in his chair, his brow knitted in a frown. Despite his heartbreak, he was a professional and Jasmine enjoyed working with him. He was a good businessman and she saw why Grace valued him so highly, even before she had discovered he was her half-brother. 'Jake and Connor think it's an inside job. Maybe one of our bouncers heard something?'

'Yes,' Jasmine replied as heat crept over her cheeks. She was still kicking herself over discussing business so openly like that. She knew better than that and it annoyed her that she had dropped the ball just a few weeks into her role. 'When I asked you and Danny about that car-hire firm. I can't believe I was such an idiot,' she said with a soft sigh.

Luke narrowed his eyes at her. 'But if you hadn't, we might not have found out it was one of our own for a while. And who knows what damage they could have gone on to do?'

'That's exactly what Connor said.'

'Well, your husband is a smart guy. You should listen to him.'

Jasmine smiled at Luke. She really hoped he and Stacey could work through this, but mostly she hoped that he and Danny would be back on good terms again soon. They were a great partnership. Danny was short-tempered and could be a loose cannon without Luke's calming influence around him. Not that Luke wasn't just as vicious as his business partner, but he understood the nuances of business a little more than the rest of them, including Jake and Connor. He was just like his sister in that respect, and Jasmine wondered if he wouldn't have been a better fit to take over from Grace than she was. Not that she thought Jake or Connor would have accepted that as readily.

As if he was reading her mind, Luke spoke again. 'You've got this, Jazz. My sister knew what she was doing when she handed the reins to you.'

'Thanks, Luke.' She nodded and straightened her shoulders. He was right. Grace Carter knew what she was doing. She was Jasmine Carter and she could handle anything that the world threw at her. 'Do you know who was here that day and who might have overheard me?'

'Yeah. Between me and Danny we got a list together yesterday before the whole birthday drama unfolded. I'll start working through them today. It will give me something to do.'

'Yeah,' Jasmine agreed. It would be a good distraction for him and perhaps it was the best time to be doing something like this. Because anyone who crossed him today was likely to be on the receiving end of all of his anger and frustration from the past twenty-four hours, and a determined, angry Luke was a dangerous combination. 'Keep me posted, won't you?'

'Of course,' he replied as he pushed back his chair and stood up.

'If you need anything, you know where I am, Luke.'

He smiled at her. A genuine smile this time that reached his eyes. 'Yeah. Thanks, Jazz.'

As Luke walked out of the office, one of the waiters walked in carrying a huge bunch of white roses. Jasmine smiled widely. They were her favourite flowers, although it wasn't like Connor to send her them. He was romantic in lots of other ways but he didn't buy flowers because he said they were a pain in the arse when they shrivelled up and died.

'Are they for me?' she asked.

'Yep.' He placed the large bunch on her desk and handed her the card. 'Dropped off just now.'

'They're beautiful,' she said as she bent her head and

inhaled their fresh scent. She waited until she was alone before opening the card. She sat back in her chair and opened the small cream envelope. The handwriting was unfamiliar, but then lots of people bought online now, so that meant nothing. The note simply said:

Not so sweet as Jasmine. All my love. Xx

Jasmine frowned at the card. They must be from Connor, but that didn't sound like the kind of thing he'd say, even though something about that phrase was familiar to her, but she couldn't recall why. She tucked the card back into the envelope and placed it in the drawer inside her desk. She would thank Connor for the flowers later.

Chapter Thirteen

Danny stepped out of his BMW and glanced around the street. It was a quiet Sunday evening. The shops were closed and there was nobody around, which he was pleased about. He didn't want anyone seeing him associating with Glenda. But he had one final message to give her before she was out of his life for good.

He jogged over the road to her flat and rang the buzzer. A few moments later, she opened the door slightly and peered through the small crack.

'Danny,' she slurred, her face breaking into that semi-toothless smile, and he rolled his eyes. She was as high as a fucking kite, as usual. Perhaps that would make this easier?

'Can I come in?' he snapped as he glanced around the street again.

She didn't reply, but she opened the door wider and he stepped inside. The smell hit his nostrils as soon as he did, and he fought the urge not to puke onto the floor. He hated the rotten smell of her flat. It reminded him of their house when he was a little kid, and he would always spend hours in the bath trying to wash off the stench. Even now, after a visit to her flat, he felt the need to shower straight away and change his clothes, but no matter what he did, the foul smell would stay in his nose for hours. Jake called him a clean freak because he hated untidiness and he took at least two showers a day, but he couldn't help it.

Danny swallowed the bile in his throat and followed his mother up the stairs to her living room. She flopped down onto the sofa and picked up the lit cigarette that she had left in the ashtray on the arm of the chair. He shook his head in annoyance. She was going to burn the place down one of these days. But maybe that would be a good thing? A way to get her out of all of their lives for good?

'You come here to apologise?' Glenda said before sniffing loudly, as though he had offended her somehow.

'Me apologise to you? What the fuck for?' Danny said with a frown.

She stared at him as though he had two heads. 'For having that cheeky tart throw me out of your new fella's fancy restaurant, that's what,' she shrieked.

'I told you to stay away from me and Stacey,' Danny snarled. 'So no, I am not going to fucking apologise. I'm here to warn you for the last time, Glenda.' He spat her name as though it left a sour taste in his mouth. He couldn't bear to call her Mum anymore. She hadn't been a mother to him or Stacey for a very long time.

'You mind who you're talking to, Daniel,' she hissed as

she sat up straighter in her chair. 'I am still your mother.' She puffed out her chest and glared at him, and he shook his head in exasperation.

'Why the fuck did you do that?' he asked.

'Do what?' She frowned at him.

'Tell us about what happened between you and Luke?' He stared at her. Of all the things she had ever done, that had to be one of the cruellest. Luke had been the one constant in his and Stacey's lives for a long time. He was their only real family. Stacey was completely in love with him. Danny had never seen her so happy. So, why the fuck had Glenda walked in and tossed a grenade full of shit right into the middle of them? He hated that Luke had lied to them. He should never have done it. But, even full of anger at his best mate, Danny recognised that he had done it from a good place. It didn't make it hurt any less, and he still couldn't forgive him for it, but he understood it. What Glenda had done was born out of pure malice.

'You deserved to know what a lying snake your so-called best friend is,' she replied with a shrug. 'The way he walks around like some fucking holier-than-thou...' She mumbled the rest of her sentence before taking a swig of the cheap can of cider on the table in front of her.

God, the woman was fucking deluded. Was she talking about the same Luke he knew? One of the most humble men he had ever met. Even though he had plenty of reasons not to be. He was good-looking, rich, powerful, loyal. Danny missed him already. He could happily murder Glenda for what she'd done to him, but mostly for what she'd done to Stacey. How could any mother not be able to stand seeing her children happy? It was beyond him. It was unlikely he would ever have kids of his own. He had always been too worried about passing on his father's monstrous genes, but as he sat staring at the woman who gave birth to him, he realised with complete clarity that he was equally terrified of passing on his mother's too.

Danny's biological father was serving back-to-back life sentences for murder and sexual offences against kids, and Danny had never even met him, but he was terrified that there might be a part of his father inside him. He knew there was a load of research about mental health disorders and the like being genetic. He had read up on the subject as soon as he was old enough to start wondering about where he had come from, and he couldn't help but wonder whether a sickness like his father obviously had was hereditary too.

Jake had a daughter, Isla, whom Jake obviously adored, and Danny was coming to love too. She was a bright little kid, with her dad's blue eyes and his infectious laugh. Jake's ex-wife, Siobhan, shared custody, and despite their acrimonious split some years earlier after Jake had discovered he was gay, they had a great relationship and they co-parented well. Danny had been terrified to meet Siobhan, but she had welcomed him with open arms and had been nothing but lovely to him every time he'd seen her. That was what a real family was like. Looking out for each other and caring about the other person's feelings.

What a pity that he and Stacey had instead grown up with this poor excuse for a human being sitting in front of him.

'So?' Glenda piped up, snapping him from his thoughts.

'So, what?' he shook his head.

'My apology?'

Danny felt the anger surging in his chest like a river breaking a dam. All the years of pent-up anger and frustration, every punch he'd taken from his stepfather, every time someone had called him and Stacey names when they were kids, every single time this woman had let him down, came tumbling out of him. He crossed the room in two strides until he was standing before her, and she looked up at him through glassy eyes.

'I warned you to stay the fuck away from me,' he snarled. The hatred he felt for her coursed through his veins as though it was his very lifeblood. She was a poison and he had to cut her out of his life for good. He would never let her hurt him or Stacey ever again.

Chapter Fourteen

Jake was lying on the sofa watching TV when Danny came home, armed with two huge pizzas. 'You took your fucking time. I'm starving,' Jake said as he sat up straight.

'Sorry. Had to do something first,' Danny replied as he placed the pizzas on the coffee table before shrugging off his jacket.

'What did you need to do?' Jake asked with a frown as Danny hung up his coat. He never left anything out of place and his obsessive tidiness made Jake smile. He knew where it came from and it suited him fine. He liked an order to things himself. And he loved Danny's fresh-from-the-shower smell. As Danny sat beside him on the sofa, Jake caught the scent of his expensive shower gel and shampoo, and realised Danny hadn't answered his question.

'Where the fuck have you been that you needed to shower after, Dan?' he snapped. While one of Danny's

99

quirks was being a clean freak, one of Jake's was that he was possessive when it came to this man sat beside him.

He watched Danny's Adam's apple bob as he swallowed, and was beginning to dread what his answer was going to be.

'I went to see Glenda,' Danny finally admitted.

Jake sighed deeply before reaching for a slice of pizza. That explained the shower, then. Danny hated the smell of his mother's flat and was always paranoid about it after. 'Why the fuck did you go and see her, after what she did last night?' he asked.

'To tell her to leave me the fuck alone, Jake. She ruins every good thing in my life,' Danny snapped before stuffing half a slice of pepperoni pizza into his mouth.

'Not everything.' Jake flashed an eyebrow at him.

'Give her half a chance and she would turn you against me too,' Danny said with a sigh, and Jake wondered if there was something his boyfriend wasn't telling him.

'But we don't keep secrets from each other, do we?' Jake asked with a frown. 'So, there is nothing she could tell me about you that I don't already know, right?'

'Of course not. I'm just kidding,' Danny said dismissively.

Jake wasn't entirely convinced he had been joking and felt that something was off. He couldn't put his finger on it, but something had happened at Glenda's place. 'But you've told her before. What makes you think she'll listen now?'

'I dunno.' He shrugged. 'But I want her gone, Jake. I

want her out of my fucking life. I didn't know what else to do. She's fucking poison.'

'So what happened?'

'I told her how much I hated her.' Danny swallowed hard and Jake saw his eyes fill with tears. 'Like, really told her. I let it all out on her, Jake. The anger and the hate. Once I started I couldn't stop. I think this time she finally got it.'

Jake shook his head and sat back on the sofa. He wasn't convinced Glenda had taken any notice of Danny, because she never had before. He didn't know what they should do about her, though. He would pay someone to make her disappear if he thought Danny would be able to live with it, but he knew that he wouldn't. Despite his hard exterior and his short temper, Danny was a huge puppy-dog really.

'Why didn't you shower at home?' Jake asked while Danny helped himself to more food.

Danny turned to him. 'I had to drop some money at the office, so I showered there. I couldn't get the smell of that place off me. I'm gonna have to get the car valeted tomorrow as well. I can smell it everywhere,' he replied with a pained expression.

'I'll get one of the lads to sort it,' Jake said as he reached his arm out and pulled Danny into a headlock, kissing the top of his head and wishing he could figure out a solution to their Glenda problem. She was becoming a massive pain in everyone's arse and she needed dealing with, one way or another.

'You'll get pizza grease in my hair.' Danny laughed as he wriggled from Jake's grip.

'I'm gonna get pizza grease all over you in a minute.' Jake flashed an eyebrow at him.

'You're a sex pest.' Danny grinned at him as he flexed his shoulders and sat up straight.

'What's the scratch on your neck?' Jake asked with a frown as he noticed the red mark just below Danny's shirt collar.

'What?' Danny pulled at his collar and shook his head. 'Oh, Glenda did it.'

'She scratched you?'

'Yeah. She's mental, isn't she?' He shook his head and took another bite of his pizza.

'You might want to get it looked at, in case she's given you rabies or something.' Jake laughed, but Danny didn't seem to appreciate the joke. He turned away and concentrated on the TV instead, as though it was the most interesting thing in the world.

Chapter Fifteen

Devlin King scowled at Mr Savage as he popped the cork on the bottle of champagne. Jerrod held out his glass, waiting for it to be filled, with a stupid goofy grin on his face. Since when did he drink fucking champagne? His older brother acted differently when Savage was around, as though he was fucking royalty or something. Just because he was mates with an ex-copper who still had a bit of pull in Liverpool, Jerrod seemed to think that the sun shone out of his arse.

'You fancy some, kid?' Mr Savage said as he held the bottle in his outstretched hand.

'Nah.' Devlin shook his head and held up his pint of Stella. 'I'll stick to this, thanks.'

Jerrod turned to him, still with that idiotic grin on his face. 'But we're celebrating, Dev. Come on. Mr S bought the good stuff.'

'I don't fucking like it,' Devlin snapped.

'Suit yourself,' Mr Savage replied with a shrug of his shoulders as he turned back to Jerrod. 'I'm proud of you, kid. You stepped up and got the job done when the pressure was on.'

Jerrod beamed proudly and Devlin resisted the urge to stick his fingers down his throat. He had no idea why his older brother, who was usually far too smart to trust anyone, was fawning all over a prick like Savage. Just because he was promising the keys to the fucking kingdom, it didn't mean he could deliver. In fact, as far as Devlin could see, he and Jerrod were taking all the risks so far, while Savage sat back and watched them, like the puppet-master pulling at their strings. Well, Devlin wasn't quite as stupid as Savage thought he was. He was onto the pretentious prick.

'Thanks, Mr S,' Jerrod replied as he knocked back the glass of expensive bubbles. 'It was easy, really. In fact, we quite enjoyed ourselves, didn't we, Dev?'

'Hmm.' Devlin nodded as he sipped his pint. That much was true, but it didn't change the fact that they were the ones doing all the hard work while their supposed benefactor sat back and waited for things to pan out the way he hoped.

Mr Savage smiled at them both. 'You're good lads. That's why Mr Barrow suggested that I come to you both. He saw your potential. When the time is right, you are the perfect fit to take over the reins from Carter and Conlon.'

'You hear that, Dev? That bent copper saw our potential.' Jerrod laughed. 'I told you those pricks would be

kneeling at our feet one day, and that day is coming soon.'
He held out his glass to Mr Savage who topped it back up.

Devlin smiled at his older brother. It was hard not to get
a little swept up in Jerrod's excitement, and if Savage's plan
did pay off, then they would be sitting fucking pretty. But
that was a big if.

'You were both careful, yeah?' Mr Savage asked.

'Of course we were.' Jerrod nodded, his face suddenly
serious, as though to convince the older man he was the
ultimate professional. 'We did everything that copper said
to do, so we didn't leave any evidence behind.'

'Good.' Savage smiled before checking his watch. 'I
have another meeting I need to get to. So, I'll leave this
with you boys.' He placed the bottle of champagne onto
the table. 'And I'll catch up with you in the next few
days.'

'Okay, Mr S,' Jerrod replied. 'Do you need us to do
anything else?'

'Not for now.' Mr Savage shook his head. 'We'll wait and
see how things play out.'

'Sound,' Jerrod replied with a grin.

———————

Jerrod picked up the bottle of champagne and sat in the
booth opposite his brother as he watched Mr Savage walk
out of their local pub.

'This is nice, this, Dev. You should try some.'

'It's a fucking fags' drink,' Devlin spat. 'You ain't in Jake

Conlon's shoes yet, you know!' He laughed at his own joke but Jerrod didn't find it amusing.

'Fuck off, you little cunt. Why are you so fucking miserable, anyway? You heard Savage. Everything is going to plan.'

'Well, yeah. Coz we did everything ourselves, didn't we? It should have been one of our soldiers at that job, not us, but then all of a sudden it had to be us, because he didn't trust anyone else to do the job right.'

'Well, he had a fucking point, Dev. This had to be fucking spot-on. No mistakes. And me and you knew the score. We knew what had to happen. We couldn't have handed this over to one of our crew. It's too important. Once this all starts to go down, there will be fucking carnage. That prick Jake Conlon and the Carters are going to rip themselves apart once their golden boy is out of the picture, and me and you are going to be ready and waiting to take everything they've got when they do. This is the best chance we're ever going to have.'

Devlin sneered at him in response and Jerrod reached over and slapped his younger brother around the head. 'Have I ever fucking steered you wrong, lad?' he snarled. 'Didn't I take us from nothing to this?' He held out his arms and looked around the near-empty pub. It was their new base of operations now that they were moving up in the world.

'Yeah,' Devlin grudgingly agreed as he rubbed the back of his head.

'Yeah! And you heard what Savage said. We've got

potential. Him and Barrow could have gone to someone else with this opportunity. There's loads of people who'd be happy to take down that gang of arrogant cunts, but he came to us. So we do not want to blow it. Do we?'

'You just fucking act different around him, Jerrod,' Devlin sniffed. 'Like you think he's the fucking dog's bollocks or something.'

'He's a fucking legend, Dev. You heard what he used to do and who he used to work for back in Manchester.'

'Yeah, he was a big player once. Not anymore, though.' Devlin scowled at his brother.

'Well, maybe that's a good thing. Because if he did decide to make a grab for the top himself, no one in Liverpool would stand for it.'

'You really think this is going to work?' Devlin asked before he took a swig of his pint.

'I know it is, lad.' Jerrod grinned as, in the corner of his eye, he saw their cousin's boyfriend, Aaron, walking towards them. Jerrod frowned at him. He was late. He'd been hoping to introduce Aaron to Mr Savage. It was quite the feat to have their very own mole working on the inside. When their cousin, Chanel, had told him that she was seeing some bouncer she'd met in town and he'd got her up the duff, Jerrod had hoped he'd be one of those Cartel pricks, and he had been overjoyed to be proved right. Aaron was one of the newest members of Cartel Securities, and it had only taken the promise of some easy money to support his new growing family to persuade him to switch his loyalty from his new employer to them. He had already given them plenty of valuable information and had unwittingly provided them with the perfect means to execute Mr Savage's plan.

'Where have you been?' Jerrod frowned as Aaron slid into the booth beside him.

'Fucking working,' Aaron snapped. Jerrod and Devlin were his girlfriend's cousins. Had he known she had this kind of family when he first met her, he would have run a mile. But she had one of the hottest, tightest little bodies he'd ever seen and his cock had completely led him astray. Thankfully she seemed to have inherited the lion's share of looks in the entire family too, unlike this unfortunate pair sitting in front of him. He suspected that she had all the brains too, and now he'd gone and knocked her up, he was stuck with this lot for life. His own dad had never been around and he would be fucked if he would do that to any kid of his own.

But in the short time he'd known the King brothers, he'd grown to dislike them more and more. They were feral. He'd stupidly agreed to give them some information a few months earlier about one of his bosses, Danny Alexander, having a load of cash on him. He'd thought it was a way to make some quick, easy money, but these two fucktards had turned it into a massive fucking brawl that Jake Conlon and Connor Carter had got involved in. Now the pair of little scrotes had him over a barrel, threatening to tell his employers who'd done them over, unless he kept providing them with information they needed. He'd thought that giving them the information for the job in Scotland would have kept them satisfied for a while, but they were too greedy for their own good.

Aaron was good at fading into the background. He knew he had one of those faces that wasn't very memorable. Average. That was how anyone would describe him. He didn't stand out. He never had. He was always in the background or on the sidelines, and while he had hated that as a kid, now he had learned to use it to his advantage. So he took any opportunity to hang around the Cartel offices and try and pick up any snippets of information that might come in useful to him. When that stuck-up bitch Jasmine had started quizzing his bosses about a car-hire firm in Scotland, his ears had pricked up. He was a smart man. He knew Conlon and the Carters controlled most of the trade up north. Any jobs in Scotland meant big money.

To their credit, Jerrod and Devlin had put together a half-decent operation, and between them and their crew had managed to nick the entire shipment of Conlon and Carter's gear. He'd heard whispers around his colleagues that it was valued at half a million quid, but he knew the King brothers would cut it with any old shite and make it go even further. He'd netted himself fifty grand for that job. Once the dust was settled, he and Chanel were going to use it as a deposit to get themselves a decent little house somewhere, instead of her grotty little flat in Everton.

'You got anything for us, Az?' Jerrod asked as he swigged champagne from a wine glass.

Aaron bristled. Jerrod shortened everyone's name. He hated being called Az, but it was low on his list of annoyances regarding the King brothers, so he let it slide. 'No. And I'm not going to either. There's something going on with Luke and Danny that's got everyone on fucking pins, and not to mention they're looking into that Scotland job. If they find out it was me, I am a fucking dead man.'

'They won't find out it was you. Pin it on some other poor fucker instead.'

Aaron frowned. If only it was that easy. He would pin it on these two pricks if he thought they wouldn't take him down with them. 'Look, I need to lie low for a while. If they find out I'm related to you in any way, even if it's just through your cousin, they will fucking sack me on the spot, and maybe cut off my nuts for good measure. So, from now on, we don't know each other, all right?'

'Seems a bit extreme to me. What do you think, Dev?' Jerrod replied nonchalantly.

'I agree. Extreme.' Devlin smirked over the rim of his pint glass.

Aaron felt the anger bubbling in his chest. He cursed himself for ever getting involved with these idiots. But he had seen pound signs when he'd learned about all that cash Danny Alexander carried around, with no back-up. A quick snatch and grab was all it would have taken. He shook his head in annoyance. It was too late now, and until he could think of a way to get rid of these two permanently, he had to play along.

'Just until things die down a bit, that's all,' Aaron replied.

'Oh, things won't be dying down for your bosses any

time soon,' Jerrod said before he and Devlin started laughing.

'What's that supposed to mean?' Aaron asked with a frown.

'Watch and see, Az,' Jerrod chuckled.

'But their little world is about to come crashing down around their ears.'

'Just make sure my name stays out of anything,' Aaron hissed.

'Don't worry. In a few months' time, it will be me and Dev who run this city,' Jerrod replied with a wink.

Aaron stared at him. Jerrod King was fucking deluded if he thought that he and his brother had the brains or the balls to take down Jake and the Carters. But on the off-chance they did, God help them all.

Milo Savage walked towards his brand-new Audi and climbed into the car, thankful to be out of the grotty pub and away from the King brothers. His skin itched in his designer suit from just being in their company. Pair of scruffy fuckers.

He pulled at the collar of his shirt and shuddered in his seat as he started up the engine and drove out of the small car park, happy to be driving away from Liverpool. He didn't like the place. He hated Scousers and he always had done. Flicking through the numbers on the screen of his dashboard, he selected the one he was looking for and pressed call.

'Hello,' the voice answered.

'It's me,' Milo replied. 'Can you talk?'

'Yes. But make it quick. I got a new roommate today and he'll be back shortly.'

'Is he as charming as me?' Milo laughed softly, thinking of John Barrow still being stuck indoors while he was as free as a bird. It was quite poetic really. The former Chief Superintendent of Merseyside Police behind bars with so many of the criminals he had helped to put away. Who would have thought that he was more violent and depraved than the lot of them?

Barrow had a rough time of it when he'd first been sent down. Hated by both prisoners and screws alike – well, most of them anyway. He had a few prison officers who looked after him, for a princely sum. But Milo had been the only one who had seen the potential in him. They had worked together years before, and Milo knew that a man that powerful would still hold some pull, and with such intimate knowledge of the police system and the way they conducted their investigations, he was an ally worth cultivating, even if Milo did hate him.

'He's quiet and that is the only good thing I can say about him,' Barrow replied with a sigh. 'How is it all going?'

'Everything is going to plan. You were right about those idiots too. So fucking desperate to get to the top, they'll believe any old shite. In fact, they are the perfect amount of stupid and brutal for this job.' Milo laughed again.

'Good. So, it's done? And they followed my instructions?'

'Yes. And they added their own particular flair to proceedings.' Milo shuddered as he recalled the excitement on their faces when they told him in explicit detail about what they'd done.

'Not too much flair, I hope?' Barrow snapped.

'No. In fact, it's kind of perfect. I'd say they were geniuses, except they only did it for kicks. So, when do you expect things will start to happen?'

'Any time in the next few days, if the King brothers did the job right,' Barrow replied.

'Good. I am a patient man, JB, but there is only so much longer I can wait before I take back what's mine.'

Barrow didn't speak, but he made a noise that was somewhere between a groan and a growl that made the hairs on the back of Milo's neck stand on end. He knew what Barrow and the rest of them liked to do to women, but Milo didn't want *her* for that. He loved her. He would treat her right. Well, so long as she behaved herself, anyway.

'Will you send me pictures?' Barrow said with a cackle.

'Not a chance in fucking hell,' Milo snarled.

'Oh, come on. You know how lonely it gets in here.'

'Then get one of your mates to send you some. They're still at it, aren't they?'

'I have to go,' Barrow replied. 'Keep me posted.' He ended the call quickly and Milo wondered if his new pad-mate was aware that Barrow had a mobile phone. They weren't allowed in prison and if they were found in a cell search, you could lose some of your privileges, but they were easily accessible if you knew the right people, and so they were rife.

Milo frowned at the screen. He hoped Barrow was right that things would start happening soon, because all he could think about was getting her back. He imagined the look on her face when she saw him again after all these years. Shock? Relief that he was out of prison and her psychopathic ex-husband was finally dead? Now they could be together at last, the way they had always talked of.

Chapter Sixteen

Danny and Stacey stepped out of the lift and walked along the hallway to Jake's apartment, when they saw the two uniformed police officers standing at the door talking to Jake. Danny's stomach dropped through his knees and onto the floor and Stacey grabbed onto his arm.

'What the hell are they doing here?' Stacey whispered and Danny shook his head.

'No fucking idea. But it can't be good, can it?' he said with a frown. He'd invited Stacey round to have tea with him, Jake and Isla, to try and take her mind off the whole Luke situation. It had been four days since the incident at the restaurant and Danny had avoided his former best mate since he'd seen him at Stacey's flat. He knew that Luke had been working all day every day at Cartel Securities, which was why he'd stayed away from the place. He'd ignored Luke's calls and distracted himself by helping Stacey out at the club instead, but he knew that this couldn't go on much longer, given that he and Luke ran Cartel together. Something was going to have to give.

'Here he is now,' Jake said as Danny and Stacey approached the door.

'Mr Alexander?' the female police officer asked.

'Yeah. What's going on?' He looked between the officers and Jake, whose face was unreadable.

'It's about Glenda Alexander,' she replied. 'Can we come inside?'

Danny's heart started to hammer against his ribcage. The police turning up looking for him about his mother. This could only mean one thing, couldn't it?

'What is it?' Stacey asked, her voice trembling.

'This is my sister,' Danny said quietly.

'Then you should both step inside,' the female officer said softly.

Danny looked at Jake, who nodded at him reassuringly, before he stepped aside and let the two police officers inside his flat, with Stacey and Danny close behind.

Jake put Isla's favourite TV programme on for her and as soon as she was settled, he joined them all in the kitchen. Taking a seat beside Danny, he placed a hand on his shoulder while Stacey held her brother's hand tightly.

It was the male officer who spoke, taking Danny by surprise, as the woman had done all of the speaking up to now. She had one of those softly spoken voices that he assumed was supposed to put people at ease, but actually it just pissed him off. He told them his name was PC Rob Joseph, and his colleague was PC Rachel Quinn, but Danny had already forgotten their names. He wanted someone to cut to the chase and tell him what the fuck was going on.

'We found your mother dead at her flat this morning,' PC Joseph said.

'What?' Stacey gasped in shock while Danny hung his head low. 'What happened? Did she overdose? Or was it a heart attack or something?'

'We believe she was murdered,' he replied.

'Fuck!' Jake muttered under his breath as he squeezed Danny's shoulder.

Stacey's hand flew to her mouth and she let out a strangled yelp of shock and surprise, while Danny looked up and glared at the two intruders. 'What happened?'

PC Joseph swallowed. 'It was a violent attack. She sustained serious injuries.'

Danny felt the bile burning the back of his throat while Stacey turned her face against his shoulder and started to cry. Glenda might have been the world's worst mother, but she was the only one they had.

'Do you know who did it?' Jake asked, leaning forward in his chair.

'We're making enquiries,' PC Quinn replied. 'When was the last time either of you saw your mother?'

'What?' Jake snarled. 'Are they fucking suspects or something?'

'We're just trying to determine when the attack might have taken place,' she replied.

'You don't know that?' Danny blinked at her.

'She was in her flat for some time before she was found.

The owner of the nail salon below reported a strange smell,' PC Joseph added.

'Oh my God.' Stacey ran to the sink and started vomiting into it.

Jake got up and rubbed her back before handing her a clean towel. He looked back at Danny, who was sitting in a state of shock. He had seen his mother three days earlier. For a brief second, the thought that Danny was the last person to see her alive, and the strange mood he was in when he got home, crossed Jake's mind. But he admonished himself for even considering it.

'I saw her on Sunday night,' Danny replied.

'Okay.' PC Joseph took out his notebook. 'What time did you leave?'

'About half-past six,' Danny replied.

'Was anyone else there, while you were there, or after you left?'

'No.' Danny shook his head. 'Just me and her.'

'Did she say anything that seemed unusual? Speak about any visitors she was expecting?'

'No. Nothing.'

'And you haven't spoken to her since?' PC Joseph asked as he scribbled in his notebook.

'No.' Danny shook his head again.

'And what about you, Miss Alexander?' He turned to Stacey, who had stopped vomiting and was wiping her face with the towel.

'I haven't seen her since Saturday. We don't speak,' she sniffed.

'Oh?' PC Joseph replied as both he and his colleague visibly shifted in their seats. 'And why is that?'

Fucking pigs, Jake thought.

'Because she was the worst mother in the world,' Stacey replied.

'Stace!' Danny said with a sigh.

'Were you and your mother on speaking terms, Danny?' PC Joseph asked.

'No.' Danny shook his head.

'But you visited her on Sunday?'

'Yes.'

'Enough of this bullshit,' Jake interrupted. 'They've told you what you needed to know. Why are you interrogating them?'

'We're just trying to determine what happened to Ms Alexander,' PC Quinn replied in her soft voice.

'Well, they don't fucking know. They just told you they don't speak to her,' Jake snarled.

'Jake!' Danny snapped. 'It's fine.'

PC Joseph turned back to Danny. 'Sunday?' he reminded Danny of his question.

Danny explained briefly the events at his birthday dinner and how he had gone to his mother's address to ask her to leave him and Stacey alone. 'When I left, she was drunk, and on something, but she was fine. When do you think she was killed?'

'It's hard to say at this point,' the constable replied. 'Her body wasn't in good shape when she was found, but our best guess at this point is sometime Sunday night or Monday morning.'

Jake watched Danny's face drain of colour and he walked over and sat beside him. 'Do they need to identify the body?' Jake asked.

'No. Ms Alexander was well known to us, and given the circumstances, we have been able to identify her without the need to have her family do so. The tattoo on her ankle is quite distinctive.'

'The circumstances?' Jake frowned.

'Her face was unrecognisable,' PC Quinn replied quietly, and Jake squeezed Danny's hand. He had a complicated relationship with Glenda, but she was his mother. Even Jake was struggling to deal with the news, and he felt nothing but hatred for the woman.

'There's something else you should know,' PC Joseph said with a look on his face that made Jake groan inwardly. Whatever it was, he knew it was going to be fucking awful.

'What is it?' Stacey asked as she walked back to the table and took a seat.

If Jake had any lingering suspicions that Danny might have killed Glenda in a fit of rage, what the officers said next completely eradicated them.

'Your mother was also sexually assaulted before she was killed,' PC Quinn answered as Danny slumped forward with his head in his hands.

Jake shook his head and answered some more of the officers' questions while Stacey and Danny sat in silence.

Jake sat in bed with the TV on in the background while he watched Danny towel-drying his hair after his shower. It was the third one he'd taken that day, as though he could wash off what those police officers had told him. After the police had gone, Jake had left Danny and Stacey to process everything while he'd taken Isla to McDonalds for her tea. It had given Stacey and Danny a chance to talk, while also getting Isla out of the tense atmosphere. She was supposed to be sleeping over, but Jake had taken her home to her mum, explaining the situation and not wanting his daughter overhearing anything she shouldn't, or asking why Danny and Stacey were so upset.

Jake's ex-wife, Siobhan, had moved back to Liverpool from Lytham two months earlier, and it made the co-parenting of their daughter so much easier. Once he'd told her what had happened, she had agreed that it would be better for Isla not to be there, and Jake had dropped her off and promised to take her to the park after school the following day.

Stacey was sleeping in Isla's bed now after Danny had refused to let her go home to her empty flat alone. When his hair was almost dry, Danny pulled on a pair of clean boxers and climbed into bed.

'How you doing?' Jake asked as he wrapped an arm around his shoulder.

'I don't fucking know, Jake,' he said with a shake of his

head. 'Who would do that to her? Who would…' He couldn't bring himself to finish the sentence.

'I have no fucking clue, mate. Some people are just sick fucks.'

'You think she owed someone money or something?'

'If she did, we will know about it within the next twenty-four hours, I promise you,' Jake replied. Between him and Connor and the rest of their workforce, they knew every dealer in the North-West. If Glenda owed anyone drug money, then it wouldn't be difficult for them to find out about it.

'What if it happened just after I left? What if I'd hung around a bit longer? Maybe given her some money. She might have gone to the pub or something instead. What if she tried to tell me but I was too angry to listen?'

Jake cursed Glenda Alexander. Even in death she had Danny full of guilt. 'There was nothing you could have done, Dan.'

'I could have got her out of those flats. We know it's dodgy round there. I could have found her somewhere safer to live, couldn't I? It's not like I don't have the money.'

'Danny!' Jake snapped. 'You gave her more than she ever deserved. She would have bled you dry if you'd let her, mate. Can you honestly tell me, if you'd put her up in some fancy pad, she wouldn't have flogged the furniture, or sub-let the place the first chance she got?'

Danny sighed deeply and shook his head. 'I know,' he whispered. 'I just feel so fucking guilty.'

Jake wrapped his arm tighter around Danny's neck,

pulling him closer to him. 'I know you do, but you have nothing to feel guilty about. You were a better son to her than she ever deserved.'

'Hmm,' Danny mumbled but Jake knew he wasn't convinced.

'I'll speak to our police contacts tomorrow and see what information they can get me about the investigation. Okay? It's about time DI Webster started earning that bung he gets from us every month.'

'Okay.'

'And we will find who did this ourselves, if that's what you want?'

Danny shook his head. 'No. Let the police sort it, Jake. I don't want anything to do with it. I don't even want to think about it.'

'Whatever you want,' Jake whispered. But he didn't trust the police and he never would. Half of them didn't know their arse from their own elbow and he had no confidence in them finding out who killed Glenda, at least not before he could. And he knew that Danny wouldn't be able to move on until they did.

Chapter Seventeen

Luke Sullivan stuffed his hands into his pockets while he waited for the door to be answered. He had been to this house dozens of times before, but he was no longer sure how welcome he was, given everything that had gone on lately. But when Jake had called him earlier that morning to tell him about Glenda, he had been desperate to talk to Danny and Stacey. They still weren't talking to him, though, and he needed to talk to someone about what had happened, if only to make sure that Danny and Stacey were okay. He'd thought about phoning Grace, but he didn't want her panicking and flying home. She and Michael had handed over the reins of the business and they deserved to enjoy their new slower pace of life. Sooner or later, they were all going to have to find a way to deal with their problems on their own.

The door opened a few seconds later, and Connor's face appeared.

'Luke?' He looked at him in surprise as he peered out into the driveway. 'How did you get in here?'

'Someone left the gates open,' Luke replied with a shrug. The house was set in its own grounds with huge steel gates that had to be opened with a security fob, or from inside the house.

'Oh, yeah. We were a bit distracted last night, with everything,' Connor replied as he ran a hand through his hair. 'Come in, mate.' He opened the door wider and allowed Luke inside. 'You heard about Glenda, then?' Connor asked as Luke followed him down the hallway to the kitchen.

'Yeah. I can't fucking believe it, mate.'

'You hear what they did to her?' Connor said, his face screwed up in disgust.

'Jake told me,' Luke answered as he winced instinctively. The visiting police officers had given Danny and Stacey the sanitised version of events, from what Jake had told him. Jake had learned the true extent of Glenda's injuries from one of his police contacts. Glenda had been beaten and raped with the leg of a coffee table. Her face was unrecognisable, and thankfully Danny and Stacey had been spared the ordeal of having to identify their mother's battered body.

'Fucking mental, mate. I know we do some fucked-up shit, but who would do that to someone who couldn't even defend herself?'

Luke swallowed hard. 'No idea.'

They were stopped in their tracks by Jasmine walking

out of the kitchen with baby Paul in her arms. 'Luke?' she said with a strange look on her face that Luke could only describe as sympathy mixed with surprise.

Connor looked down at his son and laughed. He was covered in porridge. It was in his hair, his ears, and all over his clothes. 'What happened? Did someone let off a porridge bomb?' he chuckled.

'Oh, Con. I swear I turned my back on him for thirty seconds. He is definitely *your* son.' She flashed her eyebrows in amusement.

'What? I haven't tried to wash my hair with porridge for years now.' He laughed as he took Paul from his wife's arms.

Jasmine gave him a playful nudge on the arm. 'He's a handful, just like you. I'm going to be grey by the time I'm forty, I can already tell.'

'You're an angel, aren't you, son?' Connor said as he lifted his son into the air, making him giggle and squeal in delight. 'Now, if he takes after his uncle Paul, then you'll have to worry, Jazz. He was a little fucker when he was a kid.' Connor laughed loudly and Luke laughed too, thankful for some normality in his otherwise fucked-up life. Connor and Jasmine had the kind of relationship he'd hoped he and Stacey would have one day. They were such a good team. They could face anything together and it only seemed to make them stronger.

'I'll go get him washed and changed. Put the kettle on for this poor sod, will you, babe?' Connor said as he winked at Luke.

'Of course.' Jasmine linked her arm through Luke's. 'Come on through. But don't sit anywhere until you've made sure it's not covered in porridge first,' she said, chuckling, as they walked into the kitchen while Connor took Paul upstairs.

Jasmine put the kettle on while Luke sat on a stool at the breakfast bar, checking he wasn't about to sit in a lump of gloop first. When she had made two mugs of tea, she placed them down on the worktop and sat opposite him.

'How are you doing?' she asked, her voice full of concern.

Luke sucked in a deep breath. 'I just want to talk to them, Jazz. Especially after what's happened to Glenda. I don't think I've ever gone a day in my life without talking to Danny. Even when he was inside, he used to phone me every day. And Stace.' He shook his head as the emotion threatened to overwhelm him. 'I thought me and her had something, you know?'

Jasmine placed her warm hand over his and squeezed gently. 'You do, soft lad, and you will again. They just need time. And now they're dealing with Glenda's murder too. It must be hard for them to wrap their heads around. She might have been an evil witch but she was their mum. I can imagine them being all over the place.' She shook her head and wiped a tear from her eye.

'You okay, Jazz?' Luke asked, getting the sense that she was speaking from experience. He knew she hadn't had the best of childhoods herself, although she didn't really speak of it. She had one older sister, Rose, and the two of them had been in the care system since their early teens.

'My own mum wasn't the best. I mean, she wasn't on Glenda's level, but she was pretty useless, you know? By the time she died, me and Rose hadn't seen her for months. Fed up of all her broken promises and her turning our lives upside down every few months, we cut off contact with her. She had stopped being any kind of mum years before, and when she died, although I was sad, I was mostly relieved. And then I felt so guilty about that for a very long time.'

Luke nodded. Although he couldn't fully understand what Jasmine had gone through, given that his own mum had been an amazing one, he could appreciate the conflicting feelings their mother's death must have brought up for her and her sister, similar to what Danny and Stacey must be feeling now. It made him want to talk to them even more. Danny would be stoic and keep everything in, the way he always dealt with everything. He would be Stacey's rock, but she would be worrying about Danny and how he wasn't dealing with his emotions. They both needed him right now, even if they refused to admit it.

'You have any idea who might do that to her?' Jasmine asked as she took a sip of her tea.

Luke shook his head. 'Plenty of people who would like to see her dead, but none who would do that.' He shuddered as he recalled again what Jake had told him earlier that morning.

'A coffee-table leg?' Jasmine shuddered too. 'I can't even imagine.'

'It's fucking twisted.' Luke grimaced before taking a swig of his tea. 'I'm really worried about Danny, though.'

'I know.' Jasmine nodded her agreement. 'We all are. But Jake will look after him. We all will.'

Jasmine's heart broke for Luke as he sat in front of her staring into his mug of tea. She knew he must have felt like he had lost everything in a matter of a week. Not only Danny and Stacey, but the rest of the family too. Jake had understandably sided with Danny, and as close and Jake and Connor were, it must have felt like Connor had sided with him, and, by the same logic, Jasmine too. If Grace was there, she would pull them all into line. Jasmine only wished that she had the same clout.

'We're still your family, Luke,' she assured him. 'We are always here for you. And some day soon, Danny and Stacey will come to their senses.'

'Thanks, Jazz,' he replied with a faint smile as he looked up at her.

'I wish I could fall asleep that easily.' Connor's loud voice boomed across the kitchen, making Jasmine and Luke look up.

'He's asleep?' Jasmine smiled.

'Yep. As soon as I put his clean clothes on, he went out like a light.' Connor grinned as he joined them at the breakfast bar, sitting next to Jasmine and kissing her cheek.

'He always falls asleep after a bath,' Jasmine said with a

smile. 'Grace used to say that he sleeps so well because he knows he is loved.'

Luke smiled at her and Connor wrapped his arm around her shoulders. 'It's true,' he whispered.

'I should leave you two in peace.' Luke cleared his throat, feeling like he was intruding on their alone time now.

'Don't be daft.' Connor sat up and looked at him. 'Tell me how things are going at Cartel while Danny is pretending you don't exist.'

Luke rolled his eyes. 'It's a fucking pain in the arse, but we're on top of things. Nothing to worry about.'

'Yeah? Well, I can't imagine it's easy trying to run a business with someone who refuses to speak to you. I tried it once.'

'When you and Jake fell out?' Luke asked.

'Hmm. But we never speak of it,' Connor whispered before grinning and stealing Jasmine's mug of tea and taking a swig.

'You were such a bad boy, Connor Carter.' Jasmine nudged him in the ribs.

'I know,' he said, nodding in agreement. 'I was an idiot. But I'm a reformed character now. The love of a good woman and all that.' He chuckled softly before finishing the rest of the tea.

'Hmm,' Luke mumbled and Jasmine shot Connor a look.

'She'll come round, mate. She fucking adores you,' Connor said.

Luke shook his head. He wished he could believe that

was true. 'I've got the names of all of the bouncers who were in the office after our meeting and might have heard about the contract with the car-hire firm in Scotland. I'm working through the list, but so far I haven't come up with anything suspicious. You still okay for me to deal with them myself?'

Jasmine shifted in her seat as she recalled how she'd messed up talking about that in front of their employees. 'I'm so sorry about that.'

Luke was about to tell her that she had no need to apologise again, when Connor spoke instead. 'I've told you to stop apologising, Jazz. It was a mistake. And one that will end up working out in our favour, once we find out which sneaky cunt fucked us over.'

'Yeah,' Luke agreed. 'We wouldn't have known otherwise.'

'Well, thank you both for being so gracious about it.'

'If you could handle it, mate, it would take a load off. I don't expect Danny is going to be much use these next few days, and that means Jake is going to be distracted too,' Connor said, answering Luke's question.

'Of course. I'll crack on today. To be honest, as much as it pisses me off that one of our own has stabbed us in the back, it's been good to have something to keep my mind occupied,' Luke replied with a sigh. Whilst the task of interrogating some of his employees without Danny by his side was a depressing one, it was still a much-needed distraction.

'Maybe ask John to go with you?' Connor offered. 'No fun doing that shit on your own.'

'Yeah. I think I will,' Luke agreed. He liked working with John Brennan. He had been Grace's right-hand man for years, and after a brief hiatus when he'd shacked up with a copper for a few months, he was back to doing what he did best. He was level-headed and professional, as well as being one of the meanest-looking fuckers Luke had ever met. If Danny couldn't be at Luke's side when they were interrogating half of their employees, then John was a good second choice.

'But let me know when you do find out who it is. I want to deal with the cunt myself,' Connor snarled.

'Of course, mate.' Luke nodded and then he checked his watch. 'If I'm going to rope the big man into this, I'd better catch him before he heads off to the gym. Thanks for the tea and sympathy.'

'Any time, Luke.' Jasmine smiled at him.

Connor walked Luke to the door. 'Things will be back to normal soon, mate. I know it doesn't feel like that now, but they will.'

'Yeah.' Luke nodded as he shoved his hands in his pockets. 'Let me know how Danny and Stacey are, will you?'

'Of course, mate. I'll speak to you soon.'

Luke smiled and walked out of the door. He took his phone out of his pocket and dialled John Brennan's number. 'Hiya, big man,' he said when John answered the call. 'Fancy coming to help me sniff out some wrong 'uns?'

'You still looking into the Scotland job?'

'Yep,' Luke replied as he reached his car and unlocked the door.

'Then yes. Where and when you do need me?'

'I'll pick you up in fifteen, mate?'

'Sound. I'll see you then.'

Luke ended the call and climbed into his car. He had a list of names and had spoken to half of them already. Most of them had worked for him and Danny for years. He considered himself to have a good bullshit detector and he believed that none of the men he had spoken to so far had betrayed them. He opened up his phone and looked at the list of names that his and Danny's secretary had written down for him. Thirty-three men listed in alphabetical order from Lenny Allen to Aaron Williams. He still had seventeen people to speak to, but hopefully, with John helping him out, they would weed out the snake sooner rather than later. Because that was when the real fun could begin, and Luke was in the mood to cause someone some damage.

Chapter Eighteen

Luke rolled his eyes at John Brennan as they stood outside the door of the flat in Everton, waiting for it to be answered. Dogs barked as they heard a woman screech at them, 'Shut the fuck up!'

'This is the last name on your list, right?' John asked.

'Yep,' Luke replied with a nod. It was almost midnight and he and John had worked their way through most of the list with limited success. Four of the men on it were on a lads' holiday together in Spain, and while Luke had contemplated giving Michael Carter a call and asking him to pay them a quick visit, he'd decided against it. They would be back in three days and Luke supposed it could wait. Besides, it was time to stop relying on Michael and Grace now. He and the rest of the family were more than capable of handling stuff on their own.

John banged on the door again. 'You know much about

this one?' he asked as the woman's voice shouted, 'Hang the fuck on!'

'Aaron. Started working for us a few months back. Met him a few times. Nothing stands out.'

'Hmm,' John said quietly as the door finally opened.

'Who the fuck are you and what do you want?' a pint-sized blonde with her hair in rollers snarled as she answered the door, wearing just knickers and a white vest that barely covered her modesty and showed her nipples. John averted his eyes while Luke tried to keep staring at her face. When he did look down for a brief second, he noticed the roundness of her stomach.

'We're looking for Aaron,' Luke replied.

'Huh,' she snorted. 'If you find the prick, tell him I am too.'

'We were told he was living here with you,' Luke replied.

'He is. Well, he's supposed to be.' She looked down at her stomach. 'Maybe the kid scared him off. Some men have the balls to make babies but not to stick around and take responsibility for them,' she sneered.

Luke saw John roll his eyes and wondered if they were both thinking the same thing – Aaron was probably more terrified of this little firecracker than he was of any baby. 'How long since you saw him last?' Luke asked.

'Why?' She narrowed her eyes at him. 'Who are you?'

'I'm his employer.'

'He's on holiday this week,' she snapped.

'Yeah. So when did you see him?' Luke asked again. She was stalling, but she was a tiny pregnant woman, and he drew the line at manhandling her out of the way and forcing his way into her flat. Aaron Williams had suddenly become his number-one suspect and he would find him soon enough.

'This morning,' she said with a sniff, crossing her arms over her chest. 'But then he didn't come home.'

'But he will, though? It's only midnight. He might be out with his mates or something?'

For some reason, that made her laugh and Luke frowned at her. 'He doesn't have any mates,' she spat.

'Where did he use to live before he met you?' Luke snapped, growing tired of her. Something about her was off. She was kind of pretty until she opened her mouth, and then she just seemed kind of... feral?

'How the fuck would I know?' she snarled. 'Now, it's late and I'm fucking tired. So can you piss off and let me go back to bed?'

John sighed deeply, shaking his head in exasperation.

Luke shared his frustration and he sucked in a deep breath. 'Tell Aaron that Luke needs a word with him about his shifts at the weekend.'

'If I see him,' she replied with a shrug before she closed the door, leaving Luke and John staring at each other in bewilderment.

'Fuck, she was rough,' John said with a chuckle as they started to make their way back to the car. 'No wonder he didn't come home.'

'You buy that? That he wasn't there?' Luke frowned at him.

'Nah.' John shook his head. 'He was in there. Someone must have been keeping the dogs from barking.'

'Hmm,' Luke agreed.

'I think we just found our snake,' John said with a flash of his eyebrows.

'I think you might be right.'

'What do you want to do? Wait until he comes out?'

Luke shuddered. He was exhausted and he could think of nothing worse than sitting in a cold car all night on the off-chance Aaron might make an appearance. 'No. That could take all fucking night. Maybe all week. Let's get some kip. We'll call back tomorrow. Let him sweat a little, wondering if he's been found out. We'll catch up with the little fucker eventually.'

'Sounds like a plan,' John agreed, and the two of them climbed into Luke's car.

Chapter Nineteen

J ake sat up in bed. Something woke him with a start
but as he blinked in the dark room, he couldn't figure
out what it was. It wasn't until he heard it again that
his heart sank in his chest, as he wondered who it was they
had come for.

'Police! Open the door!' The shouting and hammering
on the door were almost deafening and Jake scowled in
annoyance. What the fuck were the filth trying to pin on one
of them now?

Jake jumped out of bed as Danny sat up, rubbing his
eyes and frowning in sleepy confusion. Jake knew from
experience that the battering ram would be out soon if he
didn't open the door voluntarily. The bizzies hated him and
his family, and they were always overly heavy-handed.
They'd break down the door and tear the place apart, given
the slightest opportunity.

He pulled on his tracksuit bottoms and jogged out of the

room with Danny close behind him. 'I'm fucking coming, you shower of pricks!' he shouted as he approached the hallway.

When he opened the door a moment later, he came face to face with four officers. Two plain-clothes and two uniforms – and no battering ram in sight. 'What the fuck is this about?' he snarled.

One of the plain-clothes held up his warrant card, but he looked directly past Jake and at Danny standing behind him. 'Daniel Alexander?'

'Yeah?' Danny snapped as he stepped forward.

'I am arresting you on suspicion of the sexual assault and murder of Glenda Alexander.'

'What?' Danny stammered as the detective continued reading him his rights. He looked at Jake, his eyes wide, full of fear and confusion. Jake stared back. He didn't have any answers for him.

'Are your fucking mental? He didn't fucking assault or murder anyone,' Jake shouted as one of the constables put the cuffs on Danny.

'Jake? What the fuck? I didn't do anything to her,' Danny said as he continued staring at him, waiting for Jake to make this go away. But he couldn't. Not right now, anyway.

'Don't worry. This is bullshit, Dan. I'll call Faye now and she'll have you out in a few hours.' Faye Donovan had been their family lawyer for years. She was a Rottweiler and a miracle worker. If anyone could get these trumped-up charges against Danny dealt with, it was her.

Danny nodded as one of the officers started to lead him out of the door.

'Can you at least let him put some fucking shoes on, you cunts?' Jake shouted.

The officer holding onto Danny looked down at his bare feet. 'Hurry up,' he said with a dramatic sigh.

Jake grabbed his boyfriend's trainers from the hallway and put them on the floor, allowing Danny to slip his feet inside. He grabbed his hooded sweatshirt from the coatrack too and handed it to one of the plain-clothes officers. 'He might need that as well once you pricks take those cuffs off him,' he spat.

The officer rolled her eyes, but she took the sweatshirt from him and tucked it under her arm.

'I'll have you out of there in a few hours, Dan,' Jake promised. Then all Jake could do was watch as the man he loved was escorted down the hallway. It took all of his willpower not to run right after them and forcibly carry Danny back into the apartment. The old him probably would have done that, but he knew better these days. That would achieve nothing other than getting himself locked up as well.

Once Danny and the police officers had disappeared from sight, Jake closed the apartment door and walked back to the bedroom to get his mobile phone. As soon as it was in his hand, he dialled Faye Donovan's number. It was 1 a.m., but it wouldn't be the first time she'd been woken by one of his family in the middle of the night. She had come through for them countless times before and he only hoped she could do it again, because the thought of Danny going to prison for what had happened to Glenda made him sick to his stomach.

He had never been more terrified in his life. If Danny went inside, there was every chance he might not come back out again. Danny could handle jail time, no problem. He'd done it before. But the kind of jail time you did when you were accused of raping your own mother was a whole different ball game.

Chapter Twenty

Jake kicked at the kerb, scuffing his expensive Prada trainers as he waited for Faye Donovan to finally come out of St Anne's Street police station. He had called her and she'd spoken to him briefly outside the station, but he didn't have much to tell her. And his contacts in the police knew very little at this stage, so he was left to wait and wonder what the hell was going on, whilst also hoping that Faye was able to work some magic and get Danny out of there.

Jake's heart sank as Faye walked out of the station alone. He had hoped that she would come out of there with Danny and tell him this was all a huge misunderstanding. A vein pulsed in his neck as he clenched his jaw and waited for her to cross the road to him.

'So, where is he?' he snarled as soon as Faye reached him.

She stared right at him, her face serious but completely

unreadable. 'They've charged him, Jake,' she said with a frown.

'What the fuck?' he snapped, running his hands through his hair as he began to pace up and down the street. 'Already?'

'Shall we talk in the car?' Faye asked, glancing around the street. It was almost eight o'clock in the morning and the road was starting to get busy with commuters.

'No. Just tell me what we're dealing with, Faye, and when you can get him out of there.'

'Okay,' Faye replied with a sigh. 'He's been charged with murder and sexual assault by penetration, so there is no chance of bail. He's being remanded into Liverpool Prison this morning.'

'He's going to Walton nick?' Jake looked across the road at the station, desperately trying to think of a way to get Danny out of there.

'We'll push for a quick trial,' she started to say, but Jake interrupted her.

'A quick trial? No fucking trial, Faye. He didn't do it.'

'But the trial is where we prove that, or at least cast enough doubt on his guilt to make a jury believe that.'

Jake stared at her, completely dumbfounded that she was taking this lying down. Danny was about to be carted off to Walton Prison and she was talking to him about trials and juries instead of how to get Danny out of there today. 'Do you realise what happens to people in prison who've been accused of raping their own mother, Faye?' he snarled at her, with nowhere else to direct his rage at that moment.

'Yes,' she replied with a sigh. 'He'll be protected, though. They have special wings.'

'You're suggesting putting him on a nonce wing, then?' Jake snapped.

'All I'm saying is that there are protections in place. And surely you have people in there who will look out for him?'

'That's not the fucking point, Faye,' he shouted. 'We pay you a small fucking fortune to deal with shit like this, and the first time I really need you, you let me down completely.'

Faye sucked in a breath. Jake was worried and anxious and she dealt with that a lot, so she resisted the urge to tell him that she had helped his mother out of far worse scrapes than this, including when Jake himself was arrested for murder along with Connor, and never once had Grace Carter spoken to her the way that he just had. But he was not his mother. So, she let it go.

'This isn't the place to discuss this, Jake. Please, let's go to your car.'

'Fine!' Jake snapped as he turned on his heel and walked the few streets to where he had parked. The car beeped to life as he approached it with the key fob in his pocket, and both he and Faye climbed inside.

Jake took a deep breath and looked at Faye. 'So, what can you tell me?' he asked, slightly calmer now.

'Glenda was brutally beaten with the leg of a coffee table. She was then raped with the same weapon, Jake.'

'Fuck!' Jake swallowed the bile that burned in his throat. He had already been given some details of Glenda's assault and murder, but it still didn't make it any easier to hear, especially now that Danny was being accused of it.

'It was a length of wood. Four by six inches. Her internal injuries were horrific.'

Jake held up his hand to stop Faye from talking for a minute. He didn't need to know any further detail about Glenda's attack.

'Their case against him is pretty tight, Jake. They have his DNA evidence. It was under Glenda's fingernails…'

'She scratched him, that's why,' Jake interrupted her.

'I know. He told me that. But they also have evidence on the implement that was used to rape the victim.'

'What?' He frowned at her. 'What kind of evidence?'

'His fingerprints are all over it, and there are traces of his blood on it too,' Faye replied softly, and Jake felt a momentary rush of relief. His blood and fingerprints were explainable, but in cases of rape… well, there was another type of evidence that wasn't quite so easy to explain away. He hated himself for doubting Danny for even a second.

Jake listened as Faye talked him through the rest of the details of the case. When she was done he ran a hand over his face as his anger was replaced with despair and his shoulders dropped in defeat.

'His fingerprints and his DNA? Even though it could be explained, that's enough to charge with him murder?'

'They also have motive,' Faye added. 'Their case suggests that the level of violence used is consistent with someone who held a lot of anger towards Glenda. They are aware of the incident in the restaurant the previous evening.

Danny himself admitted that he had an argument with her before she died.'

'But he wouldn't admit that if he'd done it, would he?' Jake snapped.

'The point is, Danny and Glenda's relationship was a volatile one. And he had means, motive and opportunity. Not to mention his previous form.'

'What?' Jake scowled at her.

'You know that he served four years for killing his stepfather when he was seventeen?'

'Yeah. But that was completely different. He was protecting his sister. He got done for manslaughter, not murder!'

'I'm just presenting you with the facts, Jake. Just like the police will do to a jury, and I'm telling you that their case is pretty solid.'

'Well, do what you can to undermine it then, Faye.' He stared at her.

Faye shook her head. If only it was that easy. 'Go home and get some rest, Jake. Let me get on with what I need to do at my end, and I promise you I will get him out of there as soon as possible.'

He looked up and blinked at her. 'Rest? How do I rest when he's in there, Faye?'

'Then don't rest,' she replied with a sigh. 'Do your thing and find out who did this, if you don't believe that Danny did.'

'Do you think he did it?' Jake frowned.

'It doesn't matter what I think,' she replied with a shake

of her head. 'I'll do whatever I can, regardless.'

'It matters to me.'

'I don't know, Jake. They have evidence. They have motive. And I don't know Danny, so I don't know what he is capable of. He pleaded his innocence in there, and convincingly so, but perhaps he is a good liar?' she said with a shrug.

'He's a shite liar,' Jake replied.

'Well, you know him better than I do. And like I said, no matter what, I will do everything I can to get him out of there.'

'My mum fucking adores him,' Jake said with a lump in his throat. 'Does that make you any more likely to believe he didn't do that? He's not capable of it, Faye. He's a fucking pussy cat.'

'Well, your mum has always been a good judge of character,' she said as she placed a cool hand on Jake's arm. 'Now please try and get some rest, because you are no good to him if you're not on the top of your game.'

Jake nodded. 'Yeah.'

'I'll be in touch later today. Okay?'

Chapter Twenty-One

Luke Sullivan's blood thundered in his ears as he walked down the corridor of The Blue Rooms. He'd received a phone call an hour earlier from a distraught Jake, telling him that Danny had been arrested and telling him to meet him at the club. It had been difficult to get much sense from Jake, so he had called Connor as soon as he'd hung up the phone, and he had told Luke the full story. When Luke had heard the words, he had almost stopped breathing. It was unthinkable. There was no way in hell Danny had done what they were accusing him of. He had thought about phoning Stacey, but she still wasn't speaking to him and he wondered if his calling would only make her feel worse.

So he had showered and dressed before jumping into his car and driving to The Blue Rooms as quickly as possible. The door to Jake's office was open when he reached it. Jake, Connor and John Brennan were already inside. Given that

John had worked for the Carters for years, it was no surprise to see him in there too. Jake sat behind his desk while Connor perched on the edge of it and John sat on the sofa in the corner, almost filling the entire two-seater with his huge frame. Luke sat on the chair opposite Jake and swallowed hard. He hadn't seen Jake since the whole incident involving Glenda. At that time, Luke had threatened to kill her himself, and he couldn't help but wonder if he was under any kind of suspicion here.

'Thanks for getting here so quickly, mate,' Jake said with a deep sigh that made Connor reach back and place his hand over Jake's.

'We're going to get him out of there, Jake,' he said reassuringly.

'Yeah,' Luke agreed, although he still didn't have the full details.

'Now that we're all here, tell us what we need to know,' Connor added as he stood up and pulled over another chair for himself.

Jake cleared his throat. 'So, Glenda was murdered. They've pinpointed the time to somewhere between 6 p.m. and midnight on Sunday. She was beaten to death. From what Faye said, it sounded like she really suffered. So she was either murdered by someone who really hated her, or someone who at least wanted it to appear like it had been done by someone who hated her.'

'Someone like Danny?' Connor interrupted with an arch of one eyebrow.

Luke shifted in his seat. Or someone like him? 'But they had to have evidence to charge him?'

'Oh, they've got plenty. He's been there God knows how many times. His fingerprints are all over her flat. He even visited her that day, so they have his car on traffic cameras around the time of the murder. Because she wasn't found for a few days, they can't pinpoint an exact time of death.'

'That's all circumstantial though, surely?' Luke frowned as he wondered what it was Jake wasn't telling him.

'They also have his DNA under her fingernails and his prints and blood on the weapon. It was...' Jake cleared his throat. In the world he lived in, he had seen plenty of things that should have given him nightmares but didn't, and stuff like this didn't usually bother him. But this was about his Danny, and what they were claiming he had done to his own mother.

'Was what?' Luke asked as he sat forward in his seat.

Jake shook his head and took a breath before he carried on speaking. 'Glenda wasn't just murdered. She was sexually assaulted too with the same thing that she was killed with. It was a piece of wood. They say it was the leg of a coffee table or something. Danny's fingerprints and traces of his blood were on it.' He closed his eyes and sucked in a deep breath.

Luke felt the bile burning the back of his throat. 'What the fuck?' he frowned.

'Exactly,' Jake replied.

'So, you think he was framed?' John asked from the corner of the room.

'Well, I don't think he raped his own fucking mum, John,' Jake snapped.

John nodded, aware of the insensitive nature of his question in the incredibly tense atmosphere of the small room.

Luke's mind raced with questions. 'But maybe it was something he'd touched before when he'd been at Glenda's flat? That would explain his fingerprints, wouldn't it?'

'But not his blood. Faye says the prints are in a handprint pattern that fits with holding it like a weapon, not just touching it at some point. Besides, it didn't match any piece of furniture in Glenda's flat so the police are saying that the killer brought it with them.'

'So someone has definitely set him up then,' Luke said.

'Yeah,' Jake said with a nod. 'Now, I know he hated her…'

'He would never do anything like that,' Luke finished for him.

Jake stared at him, his jaw clenched. 'I know. So, who the fuck did?'

'If you think he's been framed…' John said as he stood up.

'He has been,' Jake snarled before John could finish his sentence.

'I know,' John replied softly before he went on. 'Well, it has to be someone with a big enough grudge against him, or you, to go to those lengths. Because framing someone for the rape and murder of their own ma is pretty fucking extreme.'

'And pretty fucking clever,' Connor added.

'So, who the hell have we pissed off lately?' Jake asked as he ran a hand over the dark stubble on his jaw.

'Who haven't we pissed off?' Connor said with a sigh.

'No one that much, Con. This is fucking next-level shit,' Jake said.

'And how did they get a table leg with his blood and fingerprints on it?' Luke asked as he racked his brain for answers that just wouldn't come.

'I don't know.' Jake put his head in his hands.

'Those Bridewell bell-ends have been a pain in our arses lately,' Connor said as he shoved his hands into his pockets.

Jake looked up at him and shook his head. 'That shower of fuck-nuggets? You really think they have the brains to pull something like this off?'

Connor sucked on his top lip for a few seconds before he answered. 'Nah. Not even on a good day.'

Luke ran his hands through his hair. His best mate was in Walton Prison and there wasn't a single thing he could do about it.

'You think it's worth speaking to Leigh, John?' Jake asked.

The look on John's face when her name was mentioned was unmissable. He and DI Leigh Moss had been in a relationship for a few months, until she had found out about John's part in the kidnapping of her ex-boyfriend and called it off, breaking the big man's heart in the process.

'I think it couldn't hurt. But if you're asking me to do it, well, I'm not sure that would go down very well. You'd be better speaking to her yourself. I've still got her number, if you need it?'

Jake shook his head. 'It's better done face to face. I'll speak to her today. See what she knows about the whole thing.'

'Don't be expecting her to be pleased to see you,' John said with a shake of his head. 'Things between us ended pretty badly.'

'I know. But I will try fucking anything right now,' Jake said with a sigh.

Luke sat up in his chair. 'If the police think they've got their man, then they won't be doing any more investigating, will they? I'll have a sniff around and see what I can find out about who else might have been visiting Glenda.'

'I'll help you out,' John said with a nod, no doubt pleased to have something practical to do. Every man in this room understood what happened to people in prison who had been accused of the kind of thing Danny had.

Jake glanced at his watch. 'I've got a meeting with Faye in an hour. You think we can get a hold of our governor friend before then, so he can sort me out some Visiting Orders? I want to get in and see Danny as soon as,' he asked Connor.

'Yeah. I'll get onto him now. We'll make sure he's looked after.'

'When you speak to him, tell him...' Luke started to say but didn't know how to finish that sentence. He and Danny had never fallen out in the entire time they had known each other, and he didn't know what to say under these circumstances.

'I will, mate,' Jake replied, understanding exactly what he meant even if Luke couldn't find the words to say it.

Chapter Twenty-Two

L eigh Moss rolled her eyes and groaned out loud as she saw the familiar figure of Jake Conlon leaning against her red BMW in the car park of her gym. She had heard about Danny Alexander's arrest and wondered how long it would be before one of the Carters tried to rope her into something.

'What the hell do you want?' she snapped as she approached him.

Leigh had met Jake on a handful of occasions. She had always found him to be arrogant and cocky, exactly like his father Nathan had been. Always dressed in the finest tailored suits and expensive shoes, driving his flash cars. He looked just like his father too; in fact, she wondered if he was even better looking than Nathan. He had Nathan's piercing blue eyes and his square jaw, but he had Grace's dark hair and full lips. She supposed she understood why people usually fell at his feet. But she was not one of those people.

'I need your help, Leigh,' he said as he stared into her eyes, and she was taken aback by the desperation and humility in his tone. She took a second to compose herself. She was done with the Carters and every single person who had anything to do with them.

'I can't help you. Now please move,' she said as she smoothed back her damp hair.

'Please, Leigh? He didn't do what they said he did.'

She shook her head. 'That investigation has nothing to do with me, or my team. I owe your family nothing, Jake. I have no interest in any of this.'

Jake frowned at her. 'I never liked you,' he said with a frown, and Leigh shook her head. There was the Jake she knew. Charming! 'Well, you did put me away for a murder I didn't commit,' he went on, tilting his head as he continued to stare at her.

She laughed out loud. 'You and I both know it was you and Connor who killed Billy Johnson, so don't insult my intelligence, Jake.'

He shrugged and she tried to move past him but he stood rooted to the spot. 'Move!' she hissed at him.

'I don't like you, Leigh, but my mum always did. And the reason she liked you was because she always said you had integrity.'

Leigh frowned at him. 'Integrity? Even though I'm standing here talking to the biggest gangster in Liverpool, and have been to your mother's house for dinner?' She didn't add her relationship with John Brennan, mostly because it still hurt too much to think about.

'Yeah. Well, the kind of integrity she values, anyway. And that is someone who is willing to do what is right, even when everyone around them tells them it's wrong.'

Leigh shook her head. 'Your mum knows nothing about the kind of woman I am,' she snapped.

'Nobody will miss Glenda Alexander, Leigh. Not a single person will mourn her passing. But somebody raped her with a splintered leg from a coffee table, Leigh. Then they beat her to death. Her injuries were so severe, she had to be identified by a tattoo on her ankle.'

'I know what happened to her, Jake,' Leigh spat. The brutality involved in Glenda's murder was so shocking that the whole force were talking about it. And given that she headed up Merseyside Police's specialist rape and sexual offences team, Leigh had been consulted on the initial investigation. She had met Danny only once before, and she didn't know the type of man he was, but it was hard to believe anyone could be capable of doing that to their own mother.

'So, help me, Leigh. Whoever did that to her is out there – because I am telling you, it wasn't Danny.'

'The evidence against him is overwhelming, Jake,' she said with a frown, annoyed at herself for even getting drawn into a conversation about this, but he knew exactly how to press her buttons.

'I know that. But it's all circumstantial. He visited her that day, but then he came home to me. She was killed after he'd been there.'

'He had motive, Jake.'

'I fucking know that. He had more reason than anyone I know to want her dead, but I think I'd have noticed if he'd murdered someone.'

She arched an eyebrow at him.

'What? You think he would have just casually walked into our apartment and watched *Top Gear* with me after he'd bludgeoned his own mother to death? He didn't do it, Leigh.'

Leigh sucked in a deep breath. 'Then he'll have a chance to prove that when he goes to trial. There is nothing I can do to help you, Jake. Now, please, step out of my way.'

Jake stared at her for a few more seconds before he finally moved, walking away to his own car without a backward glance.

By the time Leigh got to the station an hour later, she couldn't stop going over the conversation with Jake in her head. Because the truth was, there was something not right about the whole investigation into Glenda Alexander's murder, and now it was niggling her like an itch that she couldn't quite scratch. Danny Alexander was not a stupid man. Before he got into bed with the Carters, he and his partner, Luke Sullivan, had built up a multi-million-pound business. Whilst she didn't know whether or not he was capable of doing what he'd been accused of, she did wonder why he would leave a murder weapon covered in his DNA and fingerprints at the crime scene. Even if he had acted in a fit of rage and blind panic afterwards, he'd had days to cover up what he'd done before Glenda's body was discovered.

The other strange element to this case was that the murder weapon was a leg from a wooden table of some sort. A short one, like a coffee or a side table, yet it matched no piece of furniture in Glenda's flat. So, the killer either brought it with them or Glenda had a single coffee table leg hanging around which the killer picked up at random. Neither of those solutions made any sense to Leigh. If the killer brought the weapon, then they chose it purposely, and why would anyone choose to kill someone with a table leg? Why not opt for something more effective? And if the killer didn't bring it, why the hell would Glenda have a random table leg in her flat?

Leigh turned on her computer and pulled up the file that the DI in the Major Incidents Team had sent her. The photographs of Glenda's injuries were horrific but there was one she was particularly interested in. A photograph of Glenda's temple. Her face was barely recognisable, but there, just above her eye, was a mark that looked distinctly like the partial imprint of a ring. As far as Leigh was aware, no such ring had been found at Danny's house, or Jake's apartment, and she was sure she hadn't seen him wearing any jewellery on the one occasion she had met him before. Of course, alone, it meant nothing. But, along with that niggling feeling that just wouldn't go away, it was enough to make Leigh wonder if Danny Alexander was responsible for the crimes he'd been locked up for.

Chapter Twenty-Three

Jerrod and Devlin King began relaying the events of the past few days to Aaron, whose face became paler with each passing second. 'Stop.' Aaron held his hand up. 'I don't want to know any more.'

'Why the fuck not?' Devlin scowled at him.

'The less I know, the less my employers can torture out of me.' He shuddered. 'Do you have any idea who you're fucking with?' he asked with a shake of his head.

'Yes! And we did what fucking needed to be done. Don't you be getting all fucking twitchy now, shit-house,' Jerrod snarled. 'You're in this as deep as we are. We told you we've got backing for this. And when shit goes down, you're going to want to be on the right side of the war, aren't you?'

Aaron closed his eyes. That was certainly true, but he wasn't sure the right side was with this pair of clowns. Surely it was no coincidence that Luke Sullivan and John Brennan had come looking for him at Chanel's flat. He had almost shat a brick when he'd seen them standing outside, sure that they had found out what he'd done. But Chanel had played a blinder and convinced them he wasn't there, and fortunately, the arrest of Connor Carter would have them all distracted for now, which gave him some much-needed breathing room while he figured out his next move.

Jerrod glared at Aaron and was about to give him a mouthful of abuse when his phone started ringing on the table in front of him. He recognised the number as Mr Savage's, and he answered it with a smile on his face, waiting for the praise that his new mentor was about to heap on him.

'Hey, Mr S,' he said as he leaned back in his seat with his hand down his pants.

'What the fuck did you two muppets do?' he snarled. 'You had one fucking job!'

'And we did it. We told you. We did everything you told us to,' Jerrod said with a frown.

'No. You fucked up! Big time!'

'What? I don't understand. We heard someone was arrested today.'

'Yes! But not the right fucking someone. You fucking idiots!'

'What?' Jerrod asked again, his mouth opening and closing like a goldfish's. They had done everything Mr Savage had told them to, and a little extra for good measure. But they had been careful, and they had done what they were supposed to.

'I thought you were supposed to be connected in

Liverpool? So, how you do not know what the fuck is going on is beyond me,' said Savage with a sigh.

'What's gone on?' Jerrod frowned, looking at Aaron as though he might have the answer.

'Ask that fuckwit you've got on the inside. That little present he gave you. It wasn't what you thought it was. So instead of taking out the top dog, you've only taken out one of his fucking henchmen. Now do me a favour, lie low and keep your traps shut until I can figure out how we can move forward with the plan,' Mr Savage hissed. 'I'll be in touch in a few days.'

Jerrod listened as the line went dead and then he placed the phone on the table as he scratched his balls in bewilderment.

'What is it?' Devlin asked with a frown.

Jerrod looked at the stupid fucker sitting across the table from him. If Aaron had ruined their deal with Mr Savage, then he and Devlin would make sure he paid the price. 'You fucked up, knobhead!' he hissed. 'You said Connor Carter was arrested today.'

'Wasn't he?' Aaron swallowed hard. He hadn't heard the specifics of what had gone down but he knew that one of the top men had been arrested in the early hours of the morning.

'No he fucking wasn't, fuckface! So who was?'

'I don't know,' Aaron shook his head as Jerrod and Devlin glared at him. What the hell had he been thinking, ever getting involved with these two lunatics?

Milo Savage clenched his jaw so tightly that he thought he might give himself lockjaw. He knew as soon as he'd met those two fucking idiots from Liverpool that they couldn't be trusted to pull off a job. If they hadn't been personally chosen by Barrow, he would have run a mile. But Barrow had been right about one thing: they were the perfect fucking mix of stupid and cruel. At least if the shit really did hit the fan, then the two of them would make ideal scapegoats. There was nothing to tie Milo or Barrow to anything at all. They would both get what they wanted – to take down the Carters – and the fuckwit King brothers could either take Liverpool, until someone with more brains took it right back from them, or they could take the fall. Milo didn't care one way or the other, as long as he got her back by the end of it all.

He dialled Barrow's number and waited for him to answer. He couldn't always reach him on the phone in his cell, as he had it switched off most of the time, but he was relieved when Barrow answered after a few rings.

'I heard,' Barrow said before Milo could even speak.

Milo licked his lower lip, annoyed at himself as well as the King brothers. Of course Barrow knew. He still had a few contacts in Merseyside Police, and the continued friendship of a small, but powerful group of individuals. The kind that only money could buy.

'Yep. Pair of fucking idiots told me they had something they didn't.'

'It could still work in our favour,' Barrow said quietly. 'Take out one, and you can take them all. They're too reliant on each other, and I hear that Mr Alexander is the current plaything of Jake Conlon. He's not exactly stable, is he? So strike now, while they are all in chaos wondering if one of their own is truly capable of such a heinous crime.'

'Yeah,' Milo said with a sigh. It wasn't supposed to have been this hard. Connor Carter was supposed to be going away for life for murder, *not* Danny Alexander.

'And if you don't want to get your hands dirty, send those feral little bastards to do it instead.'

'Yeah,' Milo answered, although he wasn't sure he'd trust the King brothers to pull off a pair of fucking gloves without supervision, never mind a job against the Carters.

'They don't have to do it well,' Barrow said with a chuckle. 'They just need to provide some distractions.'

'I'll think about our next move,' Milo answered, unsure of whether he had the patience or the stomach to plan anything with Jerrod and Devlin King. He ended the call to Barrow and threw his phone onto the sofa beside him. He closed his eyes and pictured her face. He would have her back soon. The memory of her hands on his body was enough to make him hard, and he unzipped his trousers and began to relieve some of the tension that had been building all day.

Chapter Twenty-Four

Connor pulled up outside The Blue Rooms, leaving the engine running as he waited for Jake to come out. It had been less than twenty-four hours since Danny had been arrested for murder, but Connor felt like he hadn't come up for breath all day. He'd been making phone calls to every useful contact they had, trying to pull as many strings as possible to make sure that Danny's time inside was as comfortable as it could be. Danny was as hard as nails and he'd done a hefty sentence before, but being accused of sexually assaulting your own mother – well, that was not the kind of thing that other prisoners thought highly of. There was a hierarchy inside, and the likes of Danny Alexander would ordinarily be at the top, but what he was supposed to have done would knock him down to the very bottom. Connor knew as well as anyone that they had to work fast to get him out of there.

Connor flexed his neck, cracking the muscles to ease

some of the tension in his body. He needed to let off some steam soon or he might explode, and the best way to do that was to get his hands a little dirty. As he stared at the door, he wondered how Jake was coping with everything. When Paul had been murdered a few years earlier, Jake had gone to pieces, losing himself in drugs and whisky to get through the day. He was clean now, though, and didn't do drugs anymore and only drank shorts on special occasions. Connor hoped Jake didn't choose that route again, because he needed him sharp and on the ball.

Connor felt the emotion stick in his throat as he thought about how much he missed his dad and Grace. They would be all over this Danny situation. He realised how much he and Jake had relied on them to sort out their messes, and how being at the top with no one to answer to wasn't all it was cracked up to be. Connor preferred to be in the thick of the action and he missed those days, even if he did understand why he had to take a more strategic approach. But it wasn't in his nature to sit behind a desk all day. Jake had taken to that side of the business much better than he had, but he supposed that was why they made such a good team.

The fire-exit door opened and Jake walked out and into the car park, snapping Connor from his thoughts. He looked sharp and sober, which made Connor heave a sigh of relief. Jake climbed into the car. 'You speak to McCarthy?' he asked.

'Yeah,' Connor replied. George McCarthy was the number-two governor at Walton Prison. 'He said he'll sort you a VO out as soon as he can, but you know what he's like – we'll need to keep on at him to make sure he delivers.'

'Yeah,' Jake replied with a frown.

'Where to?' Connor asked, hoping that whichever avenue Jake wanted to explore next involved beating someone to a pulp.

'I thought we could speak to some of the dealers around Huyton who would have sold to Glenda. She was on that much gear, she'd have been getting it every other day at least. You think?'

'Sounds like a plan,' Connor said with a smile. His evening was starting to look brighter already. 'Did you speak to Leigh?' he asked as he drove out of the car park and onto the main road.

'Yeah. She was fucking useless,' Jake snarled.

'Maybe we should ask John to have a word?' Connor suggested.

'Yeah,' Jake replied absent-mindedly as he stared out of the window.

'We'll get him out of there, mate.'

Jake turned in his seat and stared at Connor. 'What if we don't, though? What if...?'

'We will,' Connor interrupted him. 'Someone killed Glenda and we are going to find out who. Have you spoken to Luke and John?'

'Yeah. They've been out all day. Nothing yet.' Jake shook his head.

'Well, let's hope we find something out then, eh?'

Connor said, although he didn't hold out much hope of finding Glenda's killer easily. She hadn't been murdered over drugs. It had been far too brutal a killing. No, her death had been personal. But perhaps one of her suppliers had seen something that might be useful information to them.

Two hours later, Jake looked at his best mate and business partner as he had one of the local dealers pinned to an armchair. Jake didn't even know what his name was, but it didn't matter because he was going to die anyway. This was the third person they'd visited that evening, and although they'd had limited success with the first two, they had learned that this lanky string of piss was Glenda's main supplier.

However, upon seeing Jake and Connor coming through his front door a few minutes earlier, he had shat a brick and tried to run. Connor had caught him and snapped both of his ankles, causing him to howl and cry in pain, and then he'd thrown him onto the faded armchair in the living room. That was when the daft fucker had sealed his fate, because he had then blatantly lied to them both about not knowing Glenda.

Jake glared at him as he approached. 'You sure about that?' he snarled as Connor gripped the trembling man's jaw hard, ignoring the snot and tears that were running down his face.

'Yeah,' he wailed, trying to nod but unable to, as Connor held his head in place.

'But every single dealer on this estate knew Glenda Alexander.' Jake frowned at him. 'And we just got reliably informed that you were her main supplier.'

The man's eyes widened in fear as Jake drew closer. 'I didn't do n-nothing to her,' he stammered.

'So you did know her?' Jake narrowed his eyes at him as he noted the wet stain spreading over the crotch of his grey tracksuit bottoms.

'I think so,' he mumbled as his eyes darted around the room as though he was looking for someone to rescue him.

Connor shook his head roughly, like a bulldog shaking a chew toy. 'You think?' he snarled.

'Okay. I knew her,' he cried out in pain. 'But I didn't touch her.'

Jake smiled at him. 'Okay. I believe you. We're all friends here,' he lied as he winked at Connor, who he could sense was chomping at the bit to rip this man's head clean off his shoulders. He was like a caged animal who hadn't been let out for far too long. 'You know who did?' Jake asked, his voice calm and softer now.

'No. I haven't seen her for weeks.'

'Why not? She owe you money?'

The look on the other man's face was enough to confirm this to be true.

'You sure you didn't go looking for some money and lose your temper with her?' Jake asked.

'No,' he started to cry again. 'I swear. I don't know anything about what happened to her.'

Jake looked at Connor. 'You believe him?' he asked.

Connor shrugged. 'You want me to cut off his balls and see if that jogs his memory?'

'What? No!' he shrieked like a weasel drowning in boiling water. 'I don't know. I'm not lying now. I don't know anything.' His sobs grew louder and louder until Jake ran out of patience. He looked at the pathetic trembling mess on the armchair and didn't even have the energy or the will to test him any further. He didn't believe he knew anything, and asking him more questions was only wasting precious time. Time during which Danny was rotting in some filthy prison cell.

'He's all yours, Con,' Jake said as he took a seat on the sofa. Then he sat back and watched while Connor Carter took out all of his frustration and anger on him. Jake didn't flinch as Connor spent the next few minutes beating the other man to death with his bare hands. He ignored the sound of breaking bone and the screams and pleas for mercy as Connor gouged out his eyes. When he sliced out his tongue, his cries changed to strangled gargles of pain, but Jake continued to watch. It was the stupid cunt's own fault for lying to them. Whatever was going on lately, people were starting to take the piss, and neither he nor Connor could have anyone thinking they were soft touches. Maybe this was exactly what was needed to remind everyone just who they were and what they were capable of.

Chapter Twenty-Five

Jake rolled over and stretched his arm out. For a brief second, he forgot that Danny wasn't there and he groaned loudly when he recalled the truth and the events of the last twenty-four hours. Sitting up in bed, he rubbed his eyes and checked the time on the clock on his bedside table. It was a little after 7 a.m. He hadn't gone to bed until after three, and he'd slept fitfully for those few hours. He was exhausted, but there was no way he could go back to sleep now. There was too much to be done. He needed to check in with Faye and see if she had any new information that might help Danny's case. He needed to speak to Luke and John and make sure they were following any leads that they could. But most of all, he had to see Danny today. It was killing him not knowing how he was, and not being able to talk to him. He should have been passed a mobile phone by now, but Jake had yet to hear from him.

He picked up his mobile phone and checked it. No missed calls or texts. Frowning, he opened up his contact list and dialled the number of the number-two governor of Walton Prison. It took a few rings before George picked up.

'Hey,' he answered.

'You got my VO sorted yet, George?' Jake snarled.

'I'm working on it. He was only brought in yesterday, Jake. I'm not a fucking miracle worker.'

'Well, you'd better work some miracles today, George, because if I don't see him by the end of the day, I will be letting your employers know whose payroll you're really on. And all of those holidays to the Caribbean with your missus are gonna come to an abrupt end, aren't they? And it will be her waiting for a VO to see you.'

'I'm doing what I can, Jake,' George hissed. 'You know I answer to Cain.'

Jake shook his head in annoyance. Lincoln Cain was the number-one governor of HMP Liverpool, and much to Jake and his family's annoyance, he was apparently incorruptible. George, on the other hand, was as bent as a nine-bob note.

'Well, do whatever you have to in order to get me in there today, or I might just give your boss a call instead,' Jake snapped and ended the call, throwing his phone onto the bed in exasperation.

He felt completely useless. All of the resources at his disposal, and he couldn't do a thing about Danny being stuck in that godforsaken shit-hole. He knew how bad it was because he'd been in there himself, but at least he'd been there with Connor. And the two of them had been charged with the murder of one of the Johnson brothers, a family that most of the prison despised. Danny was in there on his own, and for the kind of thing that wasn't forgiven or excusable, no matter who you were. And once people found out who his real dad was too, Jake worried for Danny's safety more than he had ever worried about anything else in his life. If a bunch of inmates decided that Danny needed to pay for what he was supposed to have done to his mum, and for what his dad had done to those little kids, then there wasn't a single thing Jake could do about it, and that thought terrified him.

As his mind started working into overdrive, Jake's phone rang on the bed beside him. It was an unknown number and he answered it quickly.

'Hello?'

'It's me,' Danny replied quietly.

'Danny? Thank fuck,' he breathed as the relief washed over him in a wave. 'I thought you'd have phoned me last night. Are you okay, mate?'

'Yeah.' Danny cleared his throat. 'I wasn't let out of my pad until this morning. Ste Mac was waiting outside for me. He gave me the phone.'

'Make sure you stash it,' Jake warned him.

'I've been in prison before, Jake,' Danny reminded him.

'I know. I'm just…' He swallowed the emotion that stuck in his throat. The last thing Danny needed was to know how worried he was. 'Me and Faye are working on getting you out of there, okay?'

'Yeah. Faye is coming in to see me this morning.'

'Good. I'm hoping I can get in there myself later.'

'You gonna scale the walls or something?' Danny laughed.

Jake laughed too. It was so good to hear Danny's voice. 'Well, I would, but I heard the rooms aren't all that much and the food is shit.'

'Food's not that bad.'

'George McCarthy is going to sort me a VO as soon as. You have any problems at all, you speak to him. Okay?'

'Fuck off, Jake. I'm not running to the governor. If there are any problems, I'll sort it.'

Jake sucked in a breath. He didn't want to argue with him, but he had known this would be Danny's reaction. He was too proud to ask for help from anyone, especially someone like George.

'Well, just remember that he works for us, okay? That means he works for you too.'

'Got it,' Danny replied. 'I've got to go. The screws are hanging around.'

'Okay. I'll see you later.'

'Yeah. Bye.'

'Bye, mate. I love you,' Jake said.

Danny was silent on the other end of the phone for a few seconds. 'You too,' he finally replied before he ended the call. Jake leaned back against his pillows and closed his eyes. He had to get Danny out of there, and soon.

Chapter Twenty-Six

Jake walked into Donovan, Haigh and Macaulay Solicitors in Castle Street and headed up to Faye's office on the top floor. Her door was open and she was busy putting files into her briefcase when he arrived.

'Morning, Faye,' he said with a faint smile as he strolled inside. He knew he'd been a bit of a dick to her the day before, but he guessed she was used to that in her line of work.

'Morning, Jake. Thanks for coming so early, but I'm going in to see Danny at half-past ten.'

'Yeah. He said you had a visit this morning.'

She blew a strand of hair from her face. 'Have a seat.' She indicated the chair opposite her desk. 'You want a coffee or anything?'

'No. I'm good, thanks.' Jake shook his head and waited for her to sit down so she could bring him up to speed on Danny's case.

Faye sat down and crossed her long legs. Her tight-fitting pencil skirt rode up her thighs just enough to give a glimpse of the top of her stockings, and Jake averted his gaze. The female form did nothing for him.

'I've been going through the file and as far as I can see, the prosecution's case relies heavily on the murder weapon, and Danny's prints and DNA and being on it, as well as beneath Glenda's fingernails.'

'What about the CCTV?' Jake asked with a frown.

'The police can't pinpoint exact time of death, only a six-hour window. Danny freely admitted that he visited his mother on Sunday evening, so I'm confident we can put enough doubt in the jury's mind about that being circumstantial.'

'You keep focusing on a trial, Faye. I want him out of there now. I don't think he'll last until a trial.'

Faye nodded at him, her eyes full of concern. 'I have to focus on the trial, because that's my job, Jake.'

'What do we have to do to get him out, though? How did you get me and Connor out so quickly?'

'We found the real perpetrator,' she said with a flash of her eyebrows. Both she and Jake knew that he and Connor were the perpetrators. 'Bradley Johnson confessed to the murder of his brother, Billy, and he was charged, meaning you and Connor were released.'

'So, we need someone else to confess to Glenda's murder?'

Faye pressed her lips together as she appeared deep in thought. 'It's not quite that straightforward in this case.'

'Why not?' Jake frowned.

'Because of the DNA evidence, and also the other person would need motive and opportunity. It would need to be convincing.'

'I don't know what you mean.' Jake shook his head. Perhaps he was overly tired, but he felt like Faye was talking in riddles, which wasn't like her. She was usually completely straight.

'What I mean is, you can't just go and force someone to confess to Glenda's murder. Or pay them to take the fall. It doesn't work like that.'

'For fuck's sake, Faye. I wasn't suggesting that. I'm talking about finding the person who actually killed Glenda and getting them to confess, not just some random off the fucking street.'

'Okay.' She held her hands up in defence.

'So, the DNA evidence?' Jake went on, rolling his neck to relieve the tension in his shoulders. 'What do we do about that?'

'Danny's prints in Glenda's flat can be explained easily enough. Even the DNA beneath her fingernails – it's pretty damning, but it can be explained by the scratch on Danny's neck. The prosecution will argue that she scratched him in the attack.'

'But she didn't,' Jake snapped.

'Well, that's what we'll argue.' She nodded her agreement. 'But this coffee-table leg. How did Danny's blood and prints get on it? That is the crucial piece of evidence. Altogether, it's pretty convincing, but that is the prosecution's trump card. So, when I speak to Danny this morning, I'm going to be exploring how this piece of furniture ended up in Glenda's flat with his blood on it.'

'Okay. Maybe he cut himself one time he was there?' Jake suggested.

'Perhaps. But the table leg was not from any piece of furniture in Glenda's flat. And no killer would take the table and leave the one piece of incriminating evidence. It makes no sense.'

'Unless you were trying to frame someone else for the crime? Which is what we know is happening,' Jake said with a frown.

'Yes. Or, as the prosecution allege, the killer brought it with them. Now, they have searched your place, Danny's house and his office, and can't find a piece of furniture that matches the murder weapon.'

'Well, it wouldn't. Because Danny didn't do it.'

'So, how did his blood and prints get on it?' She arched her eyebrows at him.

Jake leaned back in his seat. 'Fuck knows. But hopefully Danny will know.'

'I hope so too,' Faye said with a nod as she checked her watch. 'I'd better be leaving soon.'

'You do believe he didn't do it, don't you, Faye?' he asked her.

'I told you, Jake, it doesn't matter what I believe.'

'It matters to me. How can you defend someone when you know they did it?'

'It's my job. I've done it plenty of times before.' She narrowed her eyes at him.

'I know that. But this is different. What they're saying he did...' Jake put his head in his hands.

'If you want the truth, I don't know yet,' Faye admitted. 'Maybe I'll have a better idea after I see him today. But I promise you, I will fight for him as hard as I fought for you and Connor. Okay?'

'Okay.' He nodded. 'Thanks, Faye.'

'Any time.' She smiled.

Chapter Twenty-Seven

D anny Alexander walked down the landing and kept his head bent low. He heard the whispers as he passed and he sucked in a deep breath, trying to close himself off from the constant noise and stares. He knew what they all thought of him, and he fucking hated it. He wanted to lash out at every single one of them, but they were all in on it, and he couldn't take on the whole fucking wing, although if it went on any longer, he just might try.

But not right now. He had a legal visit, and he couldn't miss it. Because Faye Donovan was a shit-hot lawyer and she was quite possibly the only way he was ever getting out of this hell-hole.

Thirty minutes later, Danny was sitting in one of the small legal visit rooms with Faye opposite him. She had a brown folder on the desk in front of them, and in it were all the details of his case, including photographs of his mother's injuries. Danny had no desire whatsoever to see them.

'How are you doing, Danny?' Faye asked with a smile.

'Okay.' He nodded. 'But can you get me out of here?'

'I'm doing my best, I promise,' she assured him. 'But there are a few things I need to go over. That okay?'

'Of course.'

'Can you remind me again what happened the last time you saw your mother? Leave nothing out. Even if it seems insignificant.'

Danny licked his lips and swallowed. 'Okay.' Then he gave Faye a detailed account of his visit to his mother, up until the few moments before he left.

'And what happened when she scratched you? Remind me again?' She had heard his explanation twice already, but she wanted to hear it again.

'I was about to leave. I walked over to her and I was standing over her. I was really fucking angry with her. Maybe she thought I was going to hit her or something, I don't know, but she jumped up and made a grab for my throat. I jumped back and she scratched me. Then I told her I never wanted to see her again, and I left.' He wiped away a tear from his cheek as he finished.

'Okay,' Faye said quietly as she took some notes.

'I wonder if he was watching me?' He added a few seconds later.

'Who?' Faye frowned at him.

'Whoever really killed her.'

Faye didn't reply. She considered herself a very good reader of people, but she still had no idea at all whether Danny Alexander was guilty or innocent.

'Traces of your blood were found on the coffee-table leg. If someone else took it to your mother's flat and killed her with it, do you have any idea how your blood or your fingerprints got on it?'

Danny shook his head. 'No.'

Faye took a photograph out of the folder and placed it on the small table. It was the picture of the table leg. 'Have you ever seen that before, Danny?'

'No.' He shook his head. 'I already told you and the police all this, Faye.'

'I know that,' she said quietly, trying to keep him calm. 'But this isn't about proving you did it, Danny. This is about us proving your innocence. This is the key piece of evidence. The murder weapon with your fingerprints and your blood on it. And I sure as hell don't know how it got there, so I need you to help me out here.'

Danny swallowed and nodded. 'Could someone have got my blood and wiped it on it somehow?'

Faye shook her head. 'The blood pattern is consistent with droplets, and not a wipe. Unless someone had a vial of your blood, it would be very difficult to replicate that pattern. And replicating your fingerprint would be even harder. Anyone got a vial of blood or a set of your prints that you know of?' She arched an eyebrow at him.

'No.'

'Have you assaulted anyone else with a table leg recently?' she asked.

'No.'

'So, how did your blood and your fingerprints get on this, Danny?'

'I don't know, Faye.' He shook his head. 'I wish I did.'

As Danny walked back to his cell, he heard them whispering again as he passed. His meeting with Faye hadn't exactly gone well and he was no closer to getting out than he had been earlier that morning.

'Nonce,' he heard one of them mumble, and the anger that he had been trying to deal with for the past day and a half came spilling out. He turned on his heel, glaring at the short stocky man with a ginger beard and tattoos on his neck, who was standing grinning at him.

'What the fuck did you just say?' Danny snarled.

'Nonce!' he replied, pressing his face close to Danny's. It was all the provocation Danny needed. Pulling his arm back, he swung it forwards, connecting with the ginger man's jaw and sending him sprawling backwards. That was when he felt someone on his back, a powerful forearm around his throat, cutting off his oxygen supply, while he punched Danny on the side of his face with his free hand.

Danny struggled to breathe. Reaching behind him, he pulled at the man on his back while all around him the other prisoners cheered on the fight. The distraction gave his tattooed attacker time to recover and he came back at him, punching Danny in the face and causing him to stagger backwards. But his tumble dislodged the second attacker slightly, giving Danny the opportunity to reach up and pull the other man over his head and throw him onto the floor. Danny stamped on his head and watched in satisfaction as his nose burst open like a ripe peach. He looked up at the man with the ginger beard and licked the blood from the cut on his lip as he glared at him

'You want some of this?' Danny growled and the look of fear that flashed across the other man's face made him smile. He advanced on him, punching him repeatedly in the face and body, and letting out all of his pent-up rage and aggression, until he was pulled off by Ste Mac, one of Jake and Connor's most trusted men.

Ste was a big lad himself, and he wrapped his arms around Danny. 'Come on, lad. The screws are coming and you don't want to end up in the block because of this pair of cunts. Now, let's move.'

Ste's voice snapped him from his rage and he stepped back, shrugging the other man off him. He looked down at the two bleeding men on the floor, before scanning the faces of the prisoners standing around him. 'Anyone else fancy a go?' he challenged them, and they all shook their heads and began to disperse.

'Come on, mate.' Ste pulled on his arm and they walked back along the landing to Danny's cell.

Jake held the phone to his ear as he crossed the road. George McCarthy answered on the second ring.

'Yeah?'

'I just had my visit with Danny,' Jake snarled.

'Did it go well?'

'No, it fucking didn't, you prick!'

'W-what?' George stammered. 'Hang on a minute.'

Jake listened as George told someone, probably his wife, that he was taking the call in the other room. A few seconds later, he spoke again. 'Why? What happened? Did you have any problems getting in?'

'I got in fine. But you mind telling me why Danny has a fucking black eye and a split lip?'

George sucked in a breath on the other end of the line. 'It's a prison, Jake. People have fights every day.'

'I pay you to look after our boys in there, and *he* is our boy. He is my number-one fucking priority, so that makes him yours too. You got that?'

'I can't watch him twenty-four hours a day,' George said.

'Then you'd better think of a fucking way to, George, because if he gets so much as another scratch while he's on your watch, your kids will become fucking orphans, mate.'

'I could put him on the VP wing?' George suggested.

'No. He's not going on no nonce wing, because he's not a nonce,' Jake snapped, knowing that Danny would hate that to happen, and Jake didn't want to make his time inside any more difficult than it already was. 'And no putting him in seg either. You just make sure he's fucking looked after. Okay?'

'Okay. I'll see what I can do.'

'You'd better do more than that!' Jake warned before he ended the call and crossed the road. With a final glance back at the old Victorian prison, he got into his car and drove to his club.

Chapter Twenty-Eight

Danny slipped the orange vest over his head and walked through the visit hall. One of the perks of being Jake Conlon's significant other was that he was given additional visits. He'd been in this shit-hole for six days now but had already seen Jake twice, and he wondered who else was here to see him.

He approached one of the guards, who pointed him in the direction of the table his visitor was at. Danny looked across the room and his heart sank in his chest as he noticed the familiar face sitting waiting for him. He wasn't sure he could do this right now. But, the alternative was leaving the visit hall and going back to his miserable cell, so he sucked in a breath and made his way over.

'I didn't expect to see you here,' he said as he sat on the plastic chair.

Luke shrugged. 'I persuaded Jake to give me his Visiting Order. He said he'll call you later.'

Danny nodded, thinking of the mobile phone stashed in his pad.

'How are you?' Luke asked, his eyes searching Danny's face and lingering on his recent black eye.

Danny brushed his fingertips over the bruise on his face. After the incident on the wing a few days earlier, things had been much calmer, but he still heard the whispers about him everywhere he went. He hated this place and every day he woke up in there, he couldn't help but wonder if it would be his last. There was no escaping the fact he had a massive target on his back, not only because of what he was supposed to have done, but also because of who he was. Being Jake Conlon's partner might have its perks, but it had plenty of drawbacks too. The Carter family had pissed off so many people during their reign that they had more enemies than Genghis Khan. Danny's last jail time had been a picnic compared to this. 'I'm okay,' he lied.

'You need anything?'

'Why? You brought me a cake with a file in it?' he snapped.

'I'd swap places with you if I could, mate,' Luke said with a deep sigh. Danny looked at him and knew that Luke was speaking the truth, because Danny would do the same for him. Despite everything that had happened between them, they were brothers, even if not by blood, and they always would be.

'I didn't do it, Luke,' Danny replied. 'I swear I didn't touch her.'

Luke frowned at him and shook his head lightly. 'I know that, Danny.'

'You do?' Danny felt a wave of relief washing over him.

'Of course I fucking do, Dan. I've known you for ever.'

Danny swallowed. 'I know. I just thought... I was a bit of a prick to you, the last time we spoke.'

'Well, I deserved it, after what I did. Besides, you think any fight we could ever have would make me think you were the kind of person who would do that?'

Danny ran his hands through his hair. 'I don't know what to think anymore, Luke. I don't know who I can trust. I see people looking at me,' he shook his head, 'wondering if I did it. Whispering about me when my back is turned and wondering if I really am just like my dad.'

'You are nothing like him. You were set up, Dan. And Jake is doing everything he can to get you out of here. We all are.'

'I know,' Danny replied. 'But can you all do it faster, because this place is driving me crazy.' He laughed to soften the impact of his words, but he already knew that Luke saw right through him anyway. 'But enough about my worries. Have you had any luck finding out if the Scotland hit was an inside job?'

Luke winced. In all of the drama of the last few days, finding Aaron Williams had fallen way down on his list of priorities. He'd paid another visit to his flat, only to be met by his angry girlfriend again, claiming she hadn't seen him. Luke and John had been focusing their attention on scouring every crack den in Merseyside, trying to find out if anyone might have wanted Glenda Alexander dead.

'I'm sorry I didn't help out with that, by the way,' Danny added, feeling guilty for leaving it for Luke to deal with.

'Don't worry about it. John helped me out.'

'And? You find anything out?'

'Maybe.' Luke ran a hand over the stubble on his jaw. 'Aaron Williams? You remember him?'

'Vaguely,' Danny said as he tried to recall Aaron's face, but to no avail. He definitely knew the name, though, and would know him if he saw him. 'Works at the Dog on Friday nights?'

'Yeah, that's him. Well, he's been dodging us. Didn't turn up for work last night either. So, something feels off. You know?'

'Yeah,' Danny nodded. 'What's his backstory?'

'No red flags, mate. Not related to anyone he shouldn't be. Nothing untoward, according to the last people he worked for. He's just knocked some girl up, though. She's a few months, I reckon. Maybe he suddenly needed the money?'

'Maybe,' Danny agreed. 'I wish I could help you out.'

'Me too. But you'll be out of here before you know it,' Luke said with a confidence he didn't feel.

Danny smiled at his best mate, wishing he could believe him.

Chapter Twenty-Nine

It was late afternoon by the time Luke arrived at The Blue Rooms. The place was closed, but it was Jake and Connor's main base of operations, so it was where he seemed to spend most of his time lately too. Stacey was the club manager, but Jake had given her a few days off because she had been so upset by what had happened to Danny. She kept bursting into tears, and it only reminded Jake even more that Danny wasn't there. Luke was relieved she wasn't around either, not because he didn't want to see her, but he hated to see her upset and not be able to comfort her.

So, he was taken completely by surprise a few moments later when he saw her walking down the corridor towards him. He stopped in his tracks, which also happened to be outside her office.

'How are you doing, Stace?' he asked as she reached him.

She shrugged. 'Okay, I suppose. Jake told me to take

some time off, but it was even worse being at home on my own. I miss him, Luke.'

'I know. We all do.'

'Do you think he'll get out?' She looked up at him with her big brown eyes and he had to force himself not to wrap his arms around her.

'Of course he will,' he said with a false confidence. Because while Luke believed with absolute conviction that Danny did not do what they had accused him of, he also knew that the evidence against him was pretty damning. And until he saw his best mate walk out of that prison, he couldn't be sure of anything.

'Are Jake and Connor in?' he asked, desperate to change the subject before she saw right through him.

'No. But they said they'd be back shortly. You can wait in here if you want?' She indicated her head towards her office and he nodded his agreement. He walked inside and Stacey closed the door behind him. He could smell her perfume. He saw her favourite cashmere cardigan hanging over her chair, and the memory of her wearing nothing but that in his house a few weeks earlier flashed through his mind. Suddenly, a few minutes alone with her in a confined space didn't seem like such a good idea after all.

'Actually, I could do with a coffee. Want one?' Luke asked as he turned back to the door.

'Luke,' Stacey called just as his fingers gripped the door handle.

He drew in a deep breath and turned to face her. 'I miss

you,' she said so quietly that he wondered if he'd misheard her. Because surely she wasn't doing this to him right now?

'I miss you too, Stace. But you already know that,' he replied.

She leaned against her desk and stared at him. 'I wish I could get past what you did,' she said with a shake of her head.

Luke sighed. He wished she could too, because life without her and his best mate was fucking miserable. He crossed the small office in two strides until he was standing directly in front of her. She looked up at him, her eyes wide as she chewed on her lip, and all of the blood in his body rushed straight to his groin.

'What can I do to make you forgive me, Stace?' he asked.

'I don't know. I wish that I did,' she sniffed.

He frowned at her as he wondered if she had any idea of the effect she had on him, because what was the point of telling him that she missed him? The answer became suddenly clearer as she slid her warm hands inside his suit jacket and pressed her body against his. 'I miss the way you make me laugh. I miss the way you play with my hair. And I miss waking up in bed with you every morning.'

'Fuck, Stace. What are you trying to do to me?' he growled as he looked down at her beautiful face. He loved her so much, it made his heart physically hurt.

'What's happened to Danny, and even to Glenda, has made me realise that life is far too short to let happiness slip through my fingers, Luke. I am so lonely without you.'

He brushed her hair back from her face. This was exactly

what he wanted to hear, but this was her grief talking. 'You're upset because of Danny – we all are.'

'I know, but I was lonely before Danny was arrested,' she said, shaking her head again. 'Being without you makes me miserable, Luke. I hate that you kept Glenda from coming back to me. I hate that you took that choice away from me… But I love you and I hate not being with you, Luke.' She pressed her body closer to his as her hands roamed over his back, and she began to pepper soft kisses along his throat.

'Your boss will be back soon,' he groaned.

'Then you'd better be quick,' she purred against his skin, and that was all the encouragement he needed.

———

Twenty minutes later, Luke opened the door of Stacey's office and glanced up and down the hallway while Stacey tried to peer over his shoulder.

'He will go fucking mental if he catches you two fucking on the job,' Connor said with a wink as he walked past. 'Especially as he's not getting any action.'

'Fuck! Where did you come from?' Luke said, his heart pounding in his chest as he stepped into the corridor.

'We got back about five minutes ago. I came to find you because you said you'd be here. Stacey's office door was closed. I heard some strange noises coming from inside there, so I went to the bar to get me and Jake a drink,' he held up two mugs of tea, 'and to keep Jake from finding you, because he is like a bear with a fucking sore head today.'

'Thanks, mate. I appreciate it.' Luke flashed his eyebrows at him before turning to give Stacey a brief kiss on the cheek. 'Will you come round later? We need to talk about...' He didn't finish his sentence because he didn't know what that had just been in her office. Were they back together? Was Stacey just seeking some comfort, or scratching an itch?

'Yes, okay,' she said with a faint smile.

'I'll be home late.'

'I still have a key. I'll wait for you.'

'I'll see you later, then,' he said with a smile before turning back to Connor.

'Anything other than the obvious crawled up his arse today, then?' Luke asked as they walked towards Jake's office together.

'Nah. He's just frustrated, mate. Faye has got that private detective of hers looking into some leads too. Me and Jake have been literally twisting people's arms up their backs for info, but it feels like we keep getting nowhere. You and John come up with anything?'

'No.' Luke shook his head and frowned. 'I think John might consider going to speak to Leigh, though. He's working himself up to it.'

'Well, it can't hurt, can it?' Connor said with a sigh and a shake of his head. 'Well, unless she kicks him in the nuts for his trouble, and I wouldn't put it past her.'

'Break-ups are a bitch!' Luke said with a frown.

'I'm glad you and Stacey have sorted your shit out, though. You were miserable apart.'

'Thanks, mate. So am I.'

Connor didn't ask how his visit with Danny went, because Jake was about to ask him that very same question in less than half a minute, but he hoped that had gone well too. They had enough trouble from outside the family to deal with, without having in-fighting going on too.

———

Jake was on the phone when Luke and Connor walked into his office a moment later. Upon seeing them, he ended his call and threw his phone onto his desk.

'Where the fuck have you two been?' Jake snarled.

Connor sucked in a breath and reminded himself that Jake was struggling right now and he didn't mean to be a complete arsehole. 'I've been making a brew, and Luke only just got back,' he replied as he placed the mugs on Jake's desk.

'Your visit ended two fucking hours ago.' Jake glared at Luke.

'I know. But I had to deal with something on the way back,' Luke replied.

'Deal with what?' Jake snarled.

'None of your fucking business is what, mate,' Luke said, trying to keep a lid on his temper. Jake might technically be his boss, but he wasn't his keeper.

'How was he, anyway?' Jake asked as he sat down.

'He was okay, considering,' Luke replied, knowing as well as Jake did that Danny wouldn't let on if he wasn't.

'How was his face?'

'His black eye is fading slightly. He had no other injuries that I could see and he swore he's not had any more trouble since.'

'Fuck. We need to get him out of there,' Jake growled as he slammed his fist onto his desk.

'We're doing our best, Jake,' Connor interrupted him.

'Are we?' Jake shouted. 'Because you're pissing about making fucking cups of tea, while he's doing fuck knows what.' He nodded towards Luke.

Connor planted his hands on the desk and leaned towards his best mate. Nobody spoke to him like that, no matter who they were and what they were dealing with. 'Well, if all I'm doing is pissing about, I'll go home, because I have better things to do with my time,' he snarled.

'Better things than trying to get Danny out of prison?' Jake stood up, planting his hands on the desk too and leaning his face close to Connor's.

Luke stood up from his seat and rolled his eyes. 'Can you two stop with the pissing contest? We don't have time for this!'

Connor turned to him with a frown on his face. 'But you just had time to fuck your girlfriend in her office, though, right?'

'What?' Jake spat.

'Oh, come on!' Luke scowled at the pair of them. 'Like you haven't fucked plenty of people in here before.'

'It's my fucking club,' Jake snarled.

Luke shook his head before glaring at Connor. 'Thanks, mate,' he hissed.

'Fuck the pair of you!' Connor shouted before he stormed out of the office.

Luke watched him leave and then he looked at Jake, who stood glaring at him with a look of murderous intent on his face. He was angry about Danny and his inability to do anything about the whole situation, but someone was going to feel his wrath soon, and Luke would be fucked if he'd let it be him.

'I'm going to see if John's found anything yet,' he said with a sigh before he walked out of Jake's office too.

Jake sank back down into his chair and put his head in his hands. He felt like his whole world was crashing down around his ears, and it seemed like there wasn't a single fucking thing he could do about it.

Chapter Thirty

Jasmine's heels clicked on the tiled floor as she walked along the corridor of The Blue Rooms to Jake's office. She had asked to meet him there, along with Luke. Connor walked beside her, like a sullen teenager who was being taken to the headmaster's office. He'd come home the day before like a bear with a sore head and had been a grumpy sod ever since. He'd told her about his fight with Jake, and after waiting for them to calm down and hoping they would sort things out themselves, she decided she'd had enough of their fighting. It was about time they all learned to play nicely again.

Jake was sitting behind his desk when Jasmine and Connor walked into his office. He sat with his elbows on the desk and his hands steepled beneath his chin. A position of power. Jasmine sat down opposite him and smiled, and he narrowed his eyes in response. Connor sat down beside her with a sigh and a few seconds later, Luke walked into the office too and pulled up a chair.

'So, what's this about, Jazz?' Jake asked.

Connor glared at his best mate, ready to pounce if he showed even an ounce of disrespect to his wife.

'I asked you all to meet so we could put an end to the petty squabbling and get back to doing what we do best,' she replied calmly.

'Petty squabbling?' Jake snapped, but Jasmine held up her hand, and to Connor and Luke's amazement, he stopped talking.

'What is the single most important thing we should be focusing on right now?' she asked him.

'Getting Danny out of prison,' he replied with a scowl.

Jasmine turned to Luke. 'Luke?'

'Getting Danny out of prison,' he agreed.

'Connor?' she asked as she looked at her husband.

'Same,' he said with a roll of his eyes.

She sat up straighter in her chair and glared at each of them in turn. 'Exactly. Danny is currently sitting in a prison cell, wishing he could be here with us right now. The police don't care about the fact that he's innocent. As far as they're concerned, they've got their man. You three are it. He needs you all now more than he ever has.'

'We know, Jazz,' Jake said with a frown.

'You know, do you? So, tell me why the hell you three are at each other's throats instead of working together to find out who set him up, so we can get him out of there?'

she asked. She didn't shout, in fact her voice was the same level as normal, but there was something about the tone of it that made the hairs on the backs of the boys' necks stand on end.

'We have enough enemies to contend with outside of these walls, without arguing amongst ourselves. The reason we are at the top of the fucking tree is because we have each other's backs. No matter what. So, grow the fuck up, boys, suck it up, and get back to work!' With that last remark, she stood up, straightening her dress as she did.

'Fucking hell, babe.' Connor grinned at her.

She leaned down and gave him a kiss on the cheek. 'I'll see you later. I'm going to find Stacey,' she said with a last look at them all, before she disappeared out of the room.

'Fuck me, Con!' Jake said with a shake of his head and a wry smile. 'Did she just channel my ma then or something? Because I feel like I just got told off!'

'Tell me about it,' Luke agreed with a laugh.

'What can I say?' Connor replied with a shrug and an unmistakeable look of pride on his face. 'My wife just made you two shit your pants.'

'I wouldn't go that far,' Jake said as he pushed his chair back and stood up. 'But you heard the lady.'

'Fancy a fry-up first? I'm starving, and we only had fucking buckwheat pancakes for breakfast,' Connor suggested.

'What the fuck are buckwheat pancakes?' Luke asked with a frown.

'Fuck knows, mate,' Connor replied. 'Jazz makes them. They're nice enough, but I think she forgets I'm a growing lad.'

'She still got you on that health kick?' Jake asked as he walked around the desk and grabbed his coat.

'Yep. And I swear, one day it's going to fucking kill me.' Connor winked at them both and they walked out of Jake's office together, arguing good-naturedly over who was going to drive.

———————

Jasmine and Stacey watched the three men leave as they walked past Stacey's office.

'You worked a miracle there, Jazz,' Stacey said with a sigh. 'Jake and Luke have been right moody sods since yesterday, with the three of them bickering.'

'They just needed reminding how stupid they were being,' Jasmine said with a smile. 'Now that they're back on track, we need to get our heads together too, and think about anyone else who might have had a grudge against your mum.'

Stacey shook her head. 'I've racked my brains, Jazz. I can't think of anyone. I mean, I'm sure lots of people didn't particularly like her. But what they did to her...' Stacey swallowed the ball of emotion in her throat. 'I can't think of anyone who would want to do that to someone.'

Jasmine nodded. She knew that Jake had spoken to

Leigh Moss and had got nowhere. Jazz had helped Leigh out once before. Maybe it was time for Leigh to return the favour?

Chapter Thirty-One

Jasmine pulled up outside the three-bedroomed house in Crosby and was pleased to see Leigh Moss's distinctive red BMW parked outside. Turning off her engine, she climbed out of her car and walked up the short gravel path. She didn't expect a warm welcome, but she was prepared to camp out on Leigh's doorstep if she had to.

As Jasmine waited for Leigh to open the door, she thought about the last time they had seen each other. They had been in Grazia's restaurant, along with Grace and Stacey, celebrating the fact that Leigh's team had solved the case of the Liverpool Ripper. It was a case that had shocked the city and had baffled the police. Leigh and her team had solved it with the help of all of the women who had sat around that table. Despite their obvious differences, the four women had a lot in common, and it could have been the start of a friendship, but when Leigh's relationship with

John Brennan had turned sour, she had turned her back on them all and refocused on her career.

'Hi, Leigh,' Jasmine said a few moments later when Leigh's face appeared at the crack in the door.

Leigh rolled her eyes. 'I already told Jake I can't help you.'

Jasmine tilted her head as she looked at the older woman, noting the dark rings under her eyes and the smell of stale alcohol coming from her. 'Like I wanted to tell Grace Carter I wouldn't help you, because it went against every instinct I had, but I did it anyway, didn't I? And I helped you crack your biggest case. A career maker, I believe they called it around the station?'

'That was completely different,' Leigh said with a sigh.

'And how is that?' Jasmine frowned. 'We were looking for a violent psychopath who liked to beat and rape women then too, weren't we?'

Leigh opened the door a little more. 'This isn't my investigation, Jazz. The police have their man.'

'Danny didn't do it.'

'Then I'm sure his shit-hot lawyer will prove that at his trial.'

'Leigh?' Jasmine pleaded. 'You've met Danny. You know he wouldn't do this.'

'Did you know his father is serving life for the murder of a little girl? And for dozens of other sexual offences against children?'

Jasmine frowned at her. 'So what? Weren't your parents

raging alcoholics and crackheads who used to nick whatever they could get their hands on?'

Leigh blinked at her.

'I do my homework, Leigh. Don't forget we grew up on the same streets of Manchester, and your family are very well known,' Jasmine replied coolly.

Leigh shook her head in defeat and opened the door wider to allow her visitor to step inside. 'I don't know what it is you expect me to do. I'm not even involved in the investigation,' she said as Jasmine followed her along the hallway and into the living room. There were two empty wine bottles on the coffee table and Leigh quickly tidied them away before she offered Jasmine a drink.

'I'd love a coffee, thanks,' Jasmine smiled, thinking that Leigh looked like she could use one herself.

Leigh nodded and left the room and as she sat alone, Jasmine looked around. There were very few personal effects. No photographs. No ornaments or trinkets. A faded copy of *Pride and Prejudice* sat alone in the magazine rack. There was one piece of artwork on the wall – a painting of the Liverpool waterfront, painted in hues of blue and purple. As Jasmine looked at it, she felt a wave of sadness washing over her. She was good at picking up on energy, and the one in this house was melancholy.

Leigh was a good woman. She had made mistakes, like everyone else, but Jasmine couldn't help wondering why she was so intent on denying herself happiness.

A few moments later, Leigh walked back into the room with two mugs of coffee. She handed one to Jasmine and sat down on the armchair opposite her.

'Exactly what is it you think I can help you with?' Leigh asked as she blew on the hot liquid to cool it.

'The evidence against Danny is so overwhelming that the only explanation is, someone went to great lengths to set him up.'

'Or he did it,' Leigh offered.

'Except that he didn't,' Jasmine replied.

'How can you be so sure?' Leigh frowned at her.

'Because I know Danny. I have known cruel, vicious men, Leigh, the kind that could do that to a woman, and Danny Alexander is not one of them. He is a short-tempered sod, but he is also one of the kindest men I have ever met. He would do anything for the people he loves. And despite what a rotten mother Glenda was, he still loved her. Even when he cut off contact with her, he set up a direct debit to pay all her bills every month.'

'I still don't understand where I fit in?' Leigh said.

Jasmine smiled at her. 'Yes you do, but you want me to ask you. You want me to tell you how much we need you, and that's okay.'

Leigh frowned at her.

'As you can imagine, Connor and Jake are doing all they can to find out who might have set Danny up, but their methods aren't always the most appropriate,' Jasmine said before taking a sip of her coffee.

'Yes. I'm sure A&E admissions are going up across the city,' Leigh replied.

'Exactly. And I think we both know that whoever was involved must be a little smarter than that. And I also know what a good detective you are, and given that you single-handedly solved the Ripper case, I have no doubt that your colleagues in the Major Incidents Team have sought your opinion?'

'Flattery will get you everywhere,' Leigh replied sarcastically.

Jasmine ignored the barb and went on. 'So, I wondered if there was anything about the investigation that didn't quite add up? Anything that was unexplainable? Anything that might have been overlooked because the evidence against Danny was so overwhelming?'

'And if there was?' Leigh frowned.

Jasmine narrowed her eyes at the other woman. 'You're really making me work for this, aren't you?'

Leigh shrugged in response, the hint of a smile playing on her lips. The truth was, she liked Jasmine, and there were things in the investigation that didn't sit right with her, but she wasn't about to reveal that right now.

'If there is anything, I'd appreciate you letting me know.'

'And jeopardising a murder investigation in the process?' Leigh reminded her.

'Or solving one?' Jasmine replied with a forced smile.

Leigh leaned back in her chair and the two women stared at each other for a few moments before Jasmine placed her half-empty coffee mug onto the table. 'I'll leave you to your busy day, Detective,' she said as she stood up, straightening her dress. 'Thank you for your time, and I hope you'll be in touch soon.'

Leigh didn't reply. She didn't get up to show her guest out. Jasmine knew the way to the door. Instead, she leaned against the sofa and sighed. How was it that a woman like Jasmine Carter, the wife of one of Liverpool's biggest gangsters, got to sit in her house and have the cheek to be happier and more at ease with herself and her life choices than Leigh had ever been? It wasn't because Jasmine didn't have a conscience – Leigh knew that she did – so what was it? Leigh wished that she knew.

Chapter Thirty-Two

Jasmine glanced at her phone as it vibrated on the desk in Grace's office where she had chosen to work for the day. It was a message from Leigh Moss. It simply said that she had some information.

Picking up her phone, Jasmine typed out her reply, arranging to go to Leigh's house later that evening. Just as she put her phone down, she looked up to see Connor sauntering into the room. He was dressed in her favourite dark-grey suit, with a white shirt open at the collar revealing some of the tattoos that covered his chest and wound around the base of his neck. Her stomach fluttered at the sight of him. He was the most handsome man she had ever seen, and sometimes she felt like she needed to pinch herself to prove that she wasn't dreaming and he really was all hers. She was nine years older than him, but from the moment they met, they'd had an instant and undeniable attraction, and it hadn't lessened at all in the almost two years they'd been together.

'Good afternoon, handsome,' she said as he made his way over to her.

'Afternoon, gorgeous,' he replied, leaning down to kiss her softly on the lips before perching himself on the edge of the desk beside her chair.

'Who are the flowers from?' Connor frowned as he looked at the huge bunch of white roses on the filing cabinet. Jasmine blinked at him. She had assumed they were from him, but had forgotten to ask him about them, with all of the drama going on in the past few days. Clearly they hadn't been sent by her husband – so who had sent them?

'I'm not sure. I thought you'd sent them?'

'Me? You know I hate flowers.' He narrowed his eyes at her. 'Why did you think I'd sent them?'

Jasmine swallowed. Because the note said, *All my love*. But something stopped her from telling him that. She adored her husband and she had never felt even the slightest bit afraid of him, but he was renowned for his bad temper and she didn't want to start an argument right now. What if he thought she had deliberately kept them from him? And who the hell sent them?

'I don't know. Maybe I thought you were a reformed character?' She smiled at him and his face softened.

'If you really wanted flowers, I would buy them for you. You know that,' he said, smiling back.

'I do know that,' she said, feeling a wave of guilt,

although she didn't understand where it was coming from. She hadn't asked for the flowers.

'What did the note say?' he asked.

'I can't remember now. Nothing special. They must be from a customer or something,' she replied with a shrug as the lie tripped easily off her tongue. 'Anyway, to what do I owe this pleasure?' Jasmine purred.

'I've come to ask you out on a date.' He flashed his eyebrows at her.

'Really?' She leaned back in her chair.

'Hmm.' He brushed his fingertips over her cheek. 'With everything going on, I figured we needed some fun. We could grab something to eat and then go see that new film you were fancying? And Stacey said she's more than happy to watch Paul. I think she's feeling a bit lonely.'

'Maybe we should stay in and keep her company, then?' Jasmine offered.

'No!' He took her hand in his and lifted it to his lips. 'You spend enough time looking after other people. Besides, Luke will come and pick her up when he finishes work. I'm taking you out and if you're lucky, we might even go for a drive after. I'll take the Rangey.' He winked at her before kissing her fingertips, and she laughed. When they first got together, and she had still been married to her cruel ex-husband, Sol, they had spent many an evening in secluded car parks in Connor's Range Rover.

'Then it's a date,' he said as he stood up. 'I'll pick you up at seven.'

'You're leaving already?'

'Yep. John is waiting outside for me.'

'John Brennan?'

'Yeah.'

Jasmine smiled to herself. 'Mind if I pop out and see him for five minutes? I've got something I need him to do.'

Connor held out his hand. 'Course not. Come on,' he said and they walked out together.

John Brennan shook his head in frustration as he turned off the engine of his car. Why couldn't he say no to these women? When Jasmine had asked him to do this earlier, he had thought it was a bad idea. Now he was sitting staring at Leigh Moss's front door, and he knew it was a fucking terrible one.

Despite that, he had made Jasmine a promise that he would get whatever information Leigh had relating to Danny's case, and he never went back on a promise, especially to a Carter.

His heart was in his mouth as he rang the doorbell and waited for her to answer. The last time he had been here, she'd told him in no uncertain terms to get lost. The memory of their break-up was still raw. He had completely fallen for her, a fact which had surprised him more than anyone, given that she was a copper with a bad attitude and a sharp tongue. But he saw the softer side to her too. The side of her that never felt quite good enough. The part of her that wanted to help people. Not to mention, she had the most amazing tits he had ever had the pleasure of seeing. He must have still been thinking about her tits when she opened the door.

'What are you smiling about?' she asked, snapping him from his more pleasant memories of their time together.

'Nothing.' He shook his head and cleared his throat. 'Jasmine asked me to come and speak to you.'

'For fuck's sake,' Leigh hissed. 'Why couldn't she come herself?'

'Family emergency,' John lied.

Leigh sighed deeply but then she opened the door wider and allowed him to step into the house.

'You want a drink?' she asked as she walked to the kitchen with him following close behind her.

He noted the open bottle of Chardonnay on the counter and nodded towards it. It had been a long and tiring day and an even longer week. 'I'll have a glass of that, if you're offering.'

She rolled her eyes so hard that he wondered if they'd fallen out the back of her head, but she walked to the cupboard and took out an extra wine glass, making him smile to himself. She pretended to be a moody cow, but she wasn't really. It was one of the many walls she put up around herself to keep everyone out.

Leigh poured him a large glass of wine and topped up her own before she sat at the kitchen island. John pulled up a stool and sat opposite her. He watched as she brushed a strand of her blonde hair behind her ear, and remembered the way she used to do that when she was nervous.

'You look tired, Leigh,' he said, his voice full of concern.

'I am tired, John,' she replied with a sigh.

'You not sleeping again?' he asked, remembering how difficult she found it to sleep, especially when she was working on a big case.

'Let's not pretend you're concerned about my welfare,' she sniped as she took a mouthful of wine.

'Of course I am, Leigh,' he said with a frown. 'You ended this thing between us. Not me.'

She slammed her wine glass onto the worktop. 'I had no choice.'

'You always have a choice,' he challenged her.

'Like you had a choice when Grace Carter told you to kidnap my ex-boyfriend?'

'Yes,' he snarled. 'I chose to do that, because she was my boss and she was trying to get her son out of prison. I chose to help her because I care about her.' He placed his own wine glass down. 'But you would know nothing about caring for anyone, would you?'

She pressed her lips together, her nostrils flaring as she glared at him. 'I cared about Nick,' she said eventually.

'Then go back to him. If you care about him so much, why aren't you with him, Leigh?'

She glared at him but she didn't reply.

'Shall I tell you why? It's because you've built these massive walls around yourself and you are so determined to keep from getting hurt that you don't let anyone in.'

'I let you in,' she shouted and then she bent her head, so he wouldn't see the tears in her eyes.

John swallowed as he looked at her, the guilt at hurting this woman, whom he still loved, crushing him. 'I'm sorry, Leigh. I truly am,' he said quietly, then he downed the remainder of his wine and stood up.

———————

Leigh closed her eyes. She heard the scrape of his stool being pushed back, and then his footsteps on the tiled floor. Walking away from her. Like everyone did when things got a little bit hard. But his footsteps weren't getting further away.

When she felt the heat from John's body directly behind her, she froze. What was he doing? Then his huge arms wrapped around her and her body reacted to his on instinct, leaning back against his broad chest as he pulled her close to him. She had forgotten how good it felt to be wrapped in his arms. When he planted a kiss on the top of her head, it was her undoing. She started to cry. Huge, body-wracking sobs that shuddered through her entire body. And he just held onto her, letting her cry and wail. All of the frustration and the pain that had built up over years and years feeling like it was coming out at that precise moment. It was as though once she started to feel it, she couldn't stop.

When she finally stopped crying, Leigh wiped her eyes and put her hands over John's. 'You can let me go now,' she whispered.

He released her from his embrace and stepped back, and she turned to face him, looking up at his handsome face as he looked at her with so much concern that it made her want to cry again. Despite that, she got no sense of pity from him. She hated to be pitied, but she had never felt that from John.

Another fat tear rolled down her cheek and he wiped it away with the pad of his thumb. 'I never cry,' she sniffed. 'I think you broke me.'

He stepped towards her, his six-foot-four frame towering over her as he placed his hands on her waist and bent his face close to hers. She leaned into him, her breath catching in her throat in anticipation of what he was about to do.

'Then let me fix you,' he whispered before he sealed his lips over hers.

John lay on his side, leaning on one elbow as he looked down at Leigh, both of them with smiles on their faces.

He traced his fingers over her collarbone. 'As fun as that was, I think there was something else I was supposed to be doing here tonight?' John said as he sucked on his top lip, as though he was deep in thought.

'Oh, yes. I have some information for you,' Leigh said with a flash of her eyebrows.

'Well, can you give me it, so I can get off?' John inclined his head towards the door.

'What?' Leigh opened her mouth in shock and was about to punch him in the face when he burst out laughing.

'You are so fucking easy, Detective.' He grinned at her and she laughed, reminded of the way he used to tease her relentlessly, and how much she enjoyed it. She had missed him more than she would ever admit.

'So, it's back to "Detective" now, is it?' She grinned at him as she pushed him in the chest, but he was so huge, he didn't even move an inch.

'For now.' He winked at her. 'If you do that thing I love, I might stop.'

'I'm not sure you've earned that yet.' She arched an eyebrow at him.

'Oh.' He rolled on top of her. 'And how exactly do I earn it then, Detective?' he growled as he started to tickle her, making her squeal. The information she had could wait until morning. No one would be able to do anything with it until then anyway.

Chapter Thirty-Three

Jasmine heard the footsteps behind her as she walked down the corridor of The Blue Rooms. Turning around, she saw the unmistakeable figure of John Brennan walking towards her. He had a smile on his face that made her wonder just exactly what he'd got from Leigh the night before.

'Morning, John,' she said with a smile.

'Good morning,' he replied as he jogged to reach her.

'So, how did last night go?' She flashed her eyebrows at him.

'Oh, fucking awful.' He grinned at her.

'Really?'

'Really. But Leigh did give me some information for you. Shall we?' He indicated towards Jake's office, and she linked her arm through his as they walked down the corridor together.

'You know, you seem awfully happy for a man who had

an awful time last night, John. I wonder if Leigh Moss has a smile as big as yours this morning?'

'Well, you will never know.' He winked at her and she laughed.

'Ah, a gentleman never kisses and tells,' she sighed.

'Exactly.'

'So, you did kiss?' She arched her eyebrows at him in amusement and he shook his head in exasperation. 'I knew it.'

Jasmine keyed in the code for Jake's office when they reached it and they walked inside, closing the door behind them.

'*If* anything did happen, and you two are in a better place, then I'm really pleased for you both, John,' Jasmine said in all seriousness. She had hated seeing him so down these past few months since they had broken up, and seeing how miserable Leigh was too had upset her. The two of them were made for each other, and she hoped they found a way to make their relationship work.

'Thanks, Jazz,' he said as he sat down on the sofa in the corner.

'So, what did Leigh give you – other than that hickey on your neck, obviously?'

John's hand flew to his neck and Jasmine burst out laughing. 'I'm sorry. No more teasing. What did she say?'

John leaned forward in his seat. 'She said she'd looked into the case and there were a few things in the investigation that stood out for her. Things she would have looked into further if it had been her case. She said there was what looked to be a partial ring imprint on Glenda's forehead. But it was only partial. But more interestingly, they also found traces of beeswax on the table leg.'

'Beeswax?'

'Yeah, like the table leg had been polished recently.'

'We know the table leg didn't come from Glenda's flat, and the killer brought it with them. So what if it was polished?'

'Yeah, but who the hell polishes coffee-table legs with beeswax, Jazz? Most people just wipe the top over, don't they?'

'Hmm.' She frowned. 'Someone who is very houseproud, then?'

'Maybe. But not just the kind of thing you pick up off the street. I mean, why bother polishing a table leg with beeswax before you chuck it in a skip?'

'Which is what the police are suggesting could have happened? That Danny picked up the leg from the skip over the road, from that shop clearance? But the rest of the table wasn't in there, was it?'

'No.' John shook his head. 'Leigh said it just didn't add up, and so it's the kind of thing that would have kept niggling at her.'

'Okay...' Jazz said, wondering what the significance of this was. Like Leigh, she was sure it must mean something.

'And the final thing – which is probably the most important, and Leigh suggested her colleagues were almost trying to bury it – is that there was blood from a third person on the table leg.'

'What?' Jasmine sat forward in her chair. 'And Leigh said they were trying to bury this?'

'Not in so many words.' John shook his head. 'You know that she bleeds blue.'

'So, how do they justify that? Isn't this their crucial piece of evidence?'

'Yes. But with Danny's DNA beneath Glenda's fingernails, and his blood and fingerprints on the murder weapon, they didn't have to bother with the third and have dismissed it from the investigation. Leigh said it's the decision of the Senior Investigating Officer in the case, and he decided not to pursue it any further, and charge on the evidence they already had. It doesn't change the evidence against Danny, but it's the kind of thing that Leigh would have followed up on.'

'Did Leigh say why the investigating officer didn't do that?'

John nodded and rubbed a hand over his jaw. 'She said it was either dodgy - which she doesn't think is the case with this DI. Or he was just so desperate for a quick charge that they went with the evidence they had because it was enough. After everything that happened with Barrow and the Liverpool Ripper last year, the Major Incident Team were under pressure to get a quick result on this one.'

'Wow! But that's huge,' Jasmine said. 'That blood could belong to the actual killer?'

'Maybe.' John shrugged. 'But Leigh was clear that it doesn't discount any of the other evidence against Danny.'

'So, whose blood are they suggesting it was?' Jasmine frowned.

'To quote Leigh's colleagues, some other poor fucker he beat to death.'

Jasmine shook her head in frustration. The police were so determined that Danny was their man, they were blatantly ignoring any evidence that didn't fit their perfect scenario.

'And there was one more thing,' John went on.

'Oh?' Jasmine leaned forward in her seat.

'There were minute traces of someone else's DNA on the body.'

'Another someone else or the same person whose blood was on the table leg?'

'Another someone,' John replied.

'So, why the hell hasn't that been looked into?'

'Well, it was. It was saliva. It was checked against the database and didn't match any known perpetrators. There were small droplets on Glenda's face and, according to Leigh, it could have been on her body from before the attack. That's what the investigating officer is suggesting, anyway.'

'So you think all of this is enough for Leigh to do a little digging on her own?'

'I think so,' John replied with a nod. 'I know your family have had their issues with her, but she is a woman who tries to do the right thing.'

'I know that.' Jasmine nodded. 'And please tell her thank you from me.'

'I will.'

Jasmine couldn't resist smirking at him. 'So, you're seeing her again then?'

'Stop it,' he said as he stood up.

'Okay, big guy. No more questions about Leigh.' She held her hands up in surrender.

'Hmm,' John mumbled as he started to walk out of the room, but before he did, he stopped by Jasmine's chair. He leaned down and gave her a soft kiss on her cheek. 'Thank you,' he whispered and her heart swelled.

'You're welcome,' she replied with a smile before she watched him walking out of Jake's office.

Chapter Thirty-Four

L eigh Moss sat at her computer and frowned at the case notes. When Jasmine had approached her about looking into Glenda Alexander's murder, Leigh already had the information Jasmine was asking for, because something about the whole thing just didn't sit right. It was all too neat and easy. Why the hell would someone leave the murder weapon behind with their own fingerprints and their blood on it? And how was Danny Alexander's fingerprint or blood even on it? He was arrested three days after the murder with no obvious injuries other than a small scratch on his neck.

'You wanted to see me, Leigh?' The voice at her door startled her and she jumped slightly to see her colleague DI Grosvenor standing in her office doorway.

'Hey, Kev. Yeah. Do you have a minute?'

'Sure,' he said with a smile as he walked in and sat down. 'Something bothering you?'

Leigh swallowed. It was never easy accusing your colleagues of not doing their job thoroughly, and while she wasn't going to be that blunt, that was essentially what she was about to do. 'I was just wondering if you ever looked into that partial ring print on Glenda Alexander's face?'

'Oh, yeah.' He shrugged his shoulders. 'It could have been a ring imprint. Or it could have been caused by something else.'

'Such as?'

He sat straighter in his chair. 'A button? A buckle? The poor woman's injuries were so bad, I doubt we'll ever know what that sick fuck really did to her.'

'You still don't think it's worth running more checks on that third set of blood from the murder weapon?'

'No.' He shook his head. 'Like I told you, it's probably some other poor bastard's who he's given a hiding to. It doesn't affect the investigation. We have no reason to believe he didn't act alone.'

'Have you considered any scenario where Danny didn't kill her? Because if there is even the slightest doubt, then that could be vital evidence.'

'There is no scenario that I'm satisfied with. I have no doubts it was him, Leigh.' He said with a frown.

'But you thought he might have got the table leg from the skip over the road? So, how does his blood get on it? He had no injuries, right?'

'That was just one theory, but nothing else in that skip matched the table leg. It's more likely he brought it with him.'

'Hmm.' Leigh frowned. 'And what about the other set of DNA on the victim's face?'

'No matches.' Kevin frowned back. 'I thought we already discussed this. It could have come from anywhere. A shopkeeper who spat when he talked. An old friend in the street who gave her a kiss. What the hell is this about, Leigh? Don't you have enough of your own cases to investigate?' he snapped, his frustration growing with each second.

'Of course,' she said, trying to maintain her cool. 'It's just…'

'Just what?'

'Why the hell would you leave the murder weapon and then go to the trouble of changing and destroying your clothes? It makes no sense.'

'Because he went fucking mental. He lost his mind. Clearly. And then when he could think straight again, he did what any experienced criminal like Danny Alexander does, and he got rid of the evidence.'

'But her body wasn't found for three days. Why not go back to her flat and get rid of the table leg too? You know who his boyfriend is, right? You also know that Connor Carter is one of the most experienced cleaners in the country. Why not get rid of all the evidence?'

Kevin stood up, his arms crossed over his chest as he stood over Leigh. 'Look, Leigh,' he hissed. 'Danny Alexander had means, motive and opportunity. DNA and CCTV evidence puts him at the scene of the crime. I'm not sure what else you want me to pull out of my arse to convince you this is a fucking open-and-shut case. After everything that happened with Barrow, the Chief wants this dealing with as quickly and as cleanly as possible. So, I am giving you a friendly warning to stay the fuck out of my case,' he snarled before turning around and storming out of her office with a thunderous look on his face.

Leigh leaned back in her chair and sighed. She'd already suspected that Danny Alexander wasn't the man responsible for his mother's murder, and now she was downright convinced he wasn't. And why was her colleague being so defensive? She knew why the Chief Constable wanted this case closing up 'as quickly and as cleanly as possible'. After the former Chief Superintendent was found to be the man behind the Liverpool Ripper murders, as well as a string of other offences, Merseyside Police had a huge PR job to undertake to win back the public trust. But this was not the way to go about it. Nothing about this investigation was clean. On the surface it was an open-and-shut case, but dig even a fraction beneath, and there were so many unanswered questions that it was scary. And while a Legal Aid solicitor with a huge caseload and not enough time on their hands might miss some of it, Faye Donovan would not.

So, why was DI Grosvenor intent on pressing ahead with a case that could bring the police under scrutiny again? Leigh leaned back in her chair and frowned. Grosvenor and Barrow weren't on friendly terms. In fact, there was a tangible animosity between the two men. Leigh had thought that Kevin simply didn't like their boss, but now she wondered if there was something more to it.

Chapter Thirty-Five

Leigh Moss glanced at her Sergeant, Mark Whitney, as they walked towards The Red Lion pub, the place where the King brothers had set up their new base of operations.

'I fucking hate this pair of rats,' Mark groaned as they reached the door.

'So do I, which is why I like to rattle their cages occasionally,' Leigh said with a grin as Mark pulled the door and held it open for her.

Jerrod and Devlin King were sitting at their usual spot in a booth near the back of the pub. Their minions were dotted around the place, as well as some young girls, most of whom looked underage. But it was four o'clock in the afternoon, and there was no law against them being in a pub at that time. Nevertheless, Leigh would have a word with her contacts on the licensing board and make sure that The Red Lion had a visit or two in the coming weeks.

'What can we do for you, Detective?' Jerrod sneered as Leigh and Mark approached.

'We're investigating a complaint of sexual assault. A teenage girl walking home from her friend's house on Thursday evening was dragged into some bushes by two teenage boys,' Leigh said. Thankfully a couple of passing runners had heard the girl scream and intervened. She had reported the crime but couldn't identify her attackers, other than the fact they wore North Face jackets with balaclavas, and they stank of weed. Which fit the Bridewell Blades crew to a T.

Leigh and her team had been looking into the firm for months. They were well known for a particular cruel brand of violence, as well as their complete disrespect for women. Three of the firm had been arrested and put away by Leigh's team in a big investigation a few months earlier involving the serious assault of a sixteen-year-old girl. She was one of many victims, and Leigh and her team knew without a shadow of a doubt that the King brothers were involved too. But the slippery little bastards ruled with fear and intimidation, and they'd never been charged with anything more than possession of cannabis.

'And what the fuck does that have to do with us?' Jerrod asked with a sneer as he stood up and walked towards them, his arms outstretched as though he was King frigging Solomon ruling his empire.

'It's right up your street, isn't it?' Mark snapped. 'Young girls who can't fight back?'

Jerrod stepped closer, close enough that Leigh or Mark

could reach out and grab him if they wanted to, which they wished they could. Leigh would have loved nothing more than to slap that arrogant grin off his face. She had never met anyone so in love with himself, when he had absolutely no reason to be. Jerrod King had no redeeming features whatsoever, and she wondered why anyone followed him anywhere.

She noticed that his younger brother, Devlin, was quiet for a change, and wondered if something had happened between the two of them.

'Fuck you, Detective,' Jerrod spat, and droplets of spittle landed on Leigh's face. She wiped them away with her hand, wrinkling her nose in disgust. 'Do you always give everyone a shower when you talk?'

That was met with a ripple of laughter from his minions, which enraged Jerrod's fragile ego, and he turned and glared at them all until they stopped laughing. When the pub was quiet, except for Mark chuckling beside her, Jerrod turned back to Leigh and gave her the finger. 'Unless you're going to arrest me, Detective, fuck off!' he hissed.

She rolled her eyes. One day she was going to put this little prick away for life. As he waved his hand in front of her face, the light above their heads caught Jerrod's ring, making it glint. Leigh stared at it. A small gold signet ring.

She felt the hair on the back of her neck start to tingle, as it always did when pieces of a puzzle that were eluding her started to fall into place. 'Come on, Mark. Let's go.' She nodded towards the door and he frowned at her. They hadn't asked nearly enough questions yet, but she needed to get out of there and think.

'You let him off lightly, Boss,' Mark said as they walked towards their car.

'I know.' She rubbed her hand over the back of her neck. 'You ever seen that ring he was wearing before?'

'Yeah, he always wears it. Little prick,' Mark said as he climbed into the driver's seat.

'You remember that case, the Christmas before last, of that woman on the Bridewell estate? Nadine, I think her name was?'

'God, yeah,' Mark nodded. 'Nadine Bailey. Don't think I'll ever forget it. Poor woman.' He shuddered.

'I know.' Leigh frowned. Nadine Bailey was a care worker who had been walking home from work and had been brutally raped by two youths. It had been before Leigh's time with the team, but it was an unsolved case that she had looked into when she had first taken over as DI. There was DNA evidence on the body, but it didn't match any in the system, or any of the suspects who were arrested at the time.

'Were the King brothers ever in the frame for that?'

'No. It was before their time. They moved to the estate shortly after.'

'Didn't Nadine say one of her attackers wore a signet ring on his little finger?'

'Yeah. But plenty of people do, Leigh. You thinking Jerrod for that?'

'It's not beyond him.' She frowned at the road ahead as

her mind whirred into overdrive.

'Oh, I know that. In fact, if he had been around, I'd have pegged him for it. But...'

'But what?'

'Are you sure you're not just so desperate to get him that you're looking for anything you can pin on him?'

'Maybe. We got any reason to bring him in and get a sample of his DNA, though?'

'Not lawfully, ma'am. No.' He shook his head.

Leigh sighed and leaned her head back against the headrest. That was the trouble with her job. Everything had to be one hundred per cent by the book, or trials fell apart and perpetrators were never brought to justice. But it was so frustrating when procedures tied her hands.

'They used a weapon too, right?' she said as her head snapped up again, and the niggling thought at the back of her mind had finally revealed itself.

'Yeah. Part of an old railway sleeper, if I recall,' Mark replied with a shake of his head. 'She had to have a hysterectomy.'

'You remember who your main suspects were?'

'Yeah. A couple of teenagers who had been hanging around the station all night, harassing the station staff. Police had already been called twice. They both had form too, but their DNA didn't match.'

'They're not part of the Bridewell crew now, are they?'

'No.' Mark shook his head. 'Both inside for aggravated burglary.'

'Oh.' Leigh frowned as she chewed on the inside of her cheek.

'What you thinking, Boss?' Mark frowned at her.

'Nothing yet,' Leigh said with a forced smile. She trusted Mark, and he was a good, straight copper, but she didn't want to share her theories just yet. Not until she was sure.

Chapter Thirty-Six

The smell of roast lamb wafted down the hallway as John Brennan opened the door to Leigh. 'You're late, Detective,' he said as he glanced at his watch.

'I know. I'm sorry.' She stepped inside and gave him an awkward kiss on the cheek, suddenly feeling like this was all new again.

'What the fuck was that?' he growled as he slid his arms around her waist and gave her a lingering kiss on the lips instead.

'Well, that was much better,' she said with a smile when she pulled back from him.

'Good. Now let's eat. I'm starving,' he said before walking to the kitchen.

'Me too,' she said with a deep sigh.

'Then sit your arse down and I'll dish up.' He winked at her.

Leigh sat and watched John serving the food. She had

missed his simple but delicious cooking. She had missed everything about him. On the drive over she had thought a lot about what she was about to tell him. It was wrong and she knew it was, but she was fed up of following the rules and getting nowhere.

'Something on your mind?' John asked as he sat opposite her.

'I think I've figured out who set Danny up,' she breathed and was surprised how good it felt to say that aloud.

John's mouth dropped open. 'Who?'

'The King brothers. Well, definitely one of them, at least. Jerrod.'

John narrowed his eyes at her.

'I know.' She rubbed her temples. 'They don't seem that switched on, do they? I haven't figured it all out yet, but I'm ninety per cent sure it was them.'

'I'll take ninety,' John told her. 'And I'm pretty sure Jake and Connor will too. You know I have to tell them, right?'

'Yes. But not tonight. Let me try and process it all. There are still so many unanswered questions.'

'So, we'll make them answer them, then,' John said with a frown.

'I'd feel better if I could try and at least figure some of it out. Can we please just sleep on it? They're not going anywhere, John.'

'No, but neither is Danny. He's stuck in Walton for something he didn't do.'

'One more day, John? Not even that long. Please?'

'What is it you need to figure out?'

'How did they get the weapon with Danny's fingerprints on, for a start? And how the hell did those two idiots come up with a plan this sophisticated? And most of all, why Danny? I assume they're intending on making a play for the top, as deluded as they are, so why not Jake or Connor?'

'Danny is easy pickings, isn't he? Been to prison before. His dad being who he is. If I didn't know the lad, I'd think he'd done it.'

'I suppose so.' Leigh frowned. 'But the King brothers don't think like that.'

'So someone else is involved, then?'

'I think they must be. But who?'

'I'm fucked if I know.' John ran a hand over his beard. 'I'll give you tonight, Detective. But I'm telling Jake and Connor tomorrow.'

'Okay,' she agreed. 'But don't forget, the King brothers are no good to Danny dead.'

'We all know that. Don't worry.'

'Perhaps telling them that we have their DNA on the body might help?' Leigh suggested, hoping that was true, because it would make the case against them so much stronger.

'I'm sure we'll figure out a way to make them talk. Don't worry.'

The following morning, John was already in the shower when Leigh woke up. He walked out of the en suite with a towel wrapped around his waist and she took a moment to appreciate all of those hours he spent at the gym.

'You had any revelations in the night?' he asked as he sat on the bed beside her. 'You were talking in your sleep a lot.'

'Was I? Sorry.' She stifled a yawn. 'And no. No revelations, unfortunately.'

'I'm okay to go speak to Jake and Connor, then.'

'Yes. But can I come with you?'

'Sure. If that's what you want. I'll get everyone to The Blue Rooms in an hour.'

'Good,' Leigh said with a nod. She couldn't help feeling she was about to sell her soul to the devil, but as she looked up at John Brennan drying his hair, she realised she already had.

Chapter Thirty-Seven

It was only an hour later and Jake, Connor, Jasmine, Luke and Stacey were waiting in The Blue Rooms for John and Leigh. Jake paced the floor, unable to settle. Obviously John and Leigh had some information for them, and he was praying that it was going to lead to Glenda's real killer, so they could get Danny out of prison.

Connor checked his watch and frowned. 'They should be here by now, right?'

'I'm sure they're on their way,' Jasmine said, placing her hand on Connor's arm, just as they heard footsteps coming down the corridor towards them. A few seconds later, John and Leigh appeared in the doorway. Jake noticed they were holding hands, but at that exact moment he had no interest in their relationship status; he just wanted to know what they knew.

'Morning, lads and ladies,' John greeted them.

'Morning. Come in. Sit down and tell us what you

know,' Jake ordered, desperate to find out if they had discovered who Glenda's killer was.

John and Leigh sat on the small sofa in the corner of the room while all eyes were trained on them. 'What have you found out, Leigh?' Jasmine asked.

To Jake's relief, Leigh got straight to the point. 'I think it's the King brothers who are responsible for Glenda Alexander's murder.'

'What?' Jake snapped. 'Those two thick fuckers? How?'

'I'm not sure, but I think they must have someone backing them. Someone with a lot more brains than they have,' Leigh suggested. 'But mostly because this is not their style at all. They brag about the stuff they do. They are indiscreet and loud, and this has all been too quiet, which makes me think they're working with, or for, somebody else.'

'But why?' Jake frowned. 'Why set Danny up? Just to fuck with us?'

'Maybe to cause a rift between us all?' Jasmine suggested. 'Everyone knows you and Danny are a couple. Maybe they thought you'd fall apart with him inside? Maybe they thought we'd think he actually did it?'

Jake shook his head. 'Still doesn't make sense to me. If this was about a takeover, why haven't they done anything about it? Why are they still fucking about in their little estate?'

'I don't know. There are far too many unanswered questions for my liking,' Leigh replied.

'What makes you think it was them, then?' Connor asked.

'Because Glenda had a small mark on her temple that looked like the imprint of a ring, and Jerrod King wears a signet ring. There were traces of saliva on Glenda's face, but no DNA match was found. I don't know if you've ever been unfortunate enough to be up close and personal with Jerrod King, but he spits when he talks.'

'That's all?' Luke frowned.

Jake turned to Luke and glared. If Leigh said it was the King brothers, then that was good enough for him.

'I know it doesn't seem like much, but I've been a detective for a long time. It's often the little clues that lead us to the perpetrators and not the huge, obvious ones like murder weapons with fingerprints on. Which we rarely find.'

'About that?' Jasmine interrupted. 'How did they get that table leg with Danny's blood and fingerprint on?'

'Another unanswered question. As well as there being a third set of DNA on the murder weapon. But they never ran it through the system to see if it was a match. Not that they would get a match for the King brothers because they've never been arrested for anything serious enough to warrant taking a sample.'

'So, you think it was theirs? If they get arrested for murder then the police would have to take samples, right?' Jake frowned.

'Yes, but I'm not sure it's theirs either.'

'I'm lost here.' Connor shook his head.

Leigh took a deep breath and tried to explain as clearly as she could. 'Danny touched that wooden table leg at some point, somewhere. When he did, it must have had fresh blood on it from this unknown third person, because Danny's thumb left a print. There were only a few traces of his own blood on it. Somehow, Jerrod and Devlin got hold of it and used it to kill Glenda, making sure they left it at the scene to incriminate Danny.'

'But where did Danny come into contact with this fucking table leg?' Jake frowned.

'That's the million-dollar question,' Leigh said.

'I know you might not want to consider this, Leigh, but is there any possibility of police corruption going on here?' Jasmine asked.

Leigh sighed and rubbed her temples. 'Ordinarily, I would have said no. I've known DI Grosvenor for a long time. He always seemed like he played by the book. But he is definitely rushing this one through, for some reason.'

'Any idea what that could be?' Connor asked.

'To be honest, it could be as simple as: he wants to take one of you off the streets. You lot are generally massive pains in our arses, in case you didn't know.'

'I don't buy that.' Jake shook his head. 'I know you lot hate us, but fucking with a murder investigation is kind of a massive no-no, right?'

'Yes.' Leigh nodded. 'Despite what's happened recently, we are the good guys.'

'Did you find out any more about the beeswax?' Jasmine asked.

'Beeswax?' Jake frowned.

'Shit! I forgot to mention that, mate.' Connor ran a hand through his hair. 'But it didn't seem important.'

'There were traces of beeswax on the wood too,' Leigh told Jake. 'The wood had recently been polished.'

'And who polishes a table leg?' Jasmine asked.

'Carole from our office does.' Luke frowned.

'Who is Carole?' Leigh asked, her interest significantly piqued.

'The cleaner at Cartel Securities. She's been there for years. She polishes the legs of everything. Desks. Chairs. Tables.'

'But Danny said that he didn't recognise the table leg?'

'Well, I'm not sure he pays that much attention to the furniture in our offices, Leigh,' said Luke. 'It's a big building. It's got dozens of tables in, I imagine, and apart from the one in our office, I couldn't tell you what any of them looked like either.'

Connor had been quiet during the beeswax discussion, but he suddenly spoke up. 'It's mine,' he said, loudly enough to cut through the chatter.

Everyone in the room turned to look at him.

'What's yours, Con?' Jake asked.

'The other blood on that coffee-table leg. It's mine.'

'What?'

'How did it get there?' Jasmine asked.

'I completely forgot until you mentioned the Cartel offices. It was the night of my stag do. Remember, me and Danny drank all those shots and went looking for some weed, but it was about seven o'clock in the morning, and we couldn't get hold of anyone. You two were asleep in the club, so we went to the Cartel offices because Danny said they had some pot brownies. Anyway, we were in the kitchen and I could hardly fucking stand up. Some of the lads were in because they'd finished their shift, and I fell over one of their chairs, straight onto one of those little tables. Smashed a glass and cut my hand as the table collapsed under me. It completely broke and Danny picked me up. Well, he tried, but he was as pissed as I was. I was bleeding all over the place.'

'Danny never mentioned it,' Jake said with a frown.

'I doubt he remembered, mate. We were both completely wasted and you know how he gets when he has weed. He has complete blackouts. But he picked up the glass and cut his finger. It was just a scratch though. Then he cleaned up the table parts while one of the lads took care of my hand. One of the other lads helped him take it out to the bins.'

'I remember that gash on your hand when you came home,' Jasmine said. 'You told me you'd cut yourself on a broken glass at the office.'

'That was two months ago, though?' John piped up. 'You think it's from then?'

'If the table leg had been kept in a plastic bag or something, then the blood and prints would have been undisturbed,' Leigh replied.

'So the King brothers have been planning this for a while, then?' Jake said with a frown. 'We should have dropped them off that block of flats when we had the chance,' he snarled.

Leigh shook her head and pretended she hadn't heard that particular snippet of information.

'Who helped Danny clean up, and who else was there, Con? Do you remember?' Jake asked.

'No. I was pissed. Some of the new lads, maybe? I didn't recognise them.'

'Aaron Williams, by any chance?' Luke added.

Connor frowned. 'Who's he?'

'One of the lads we took on a while ago. He hasn't been to work for a few nights. Me and John have been looking for him over the Scotland job, and the slippery fucker has been avoiding us.'

'With everything else going on, the Scottish job kind of fell down our to-do list,' John said with an apologetic shrug.

'So, someone, possibly Aaron, kept the bloodstained table leg and used it to frame Danny?' Jasmine asked with a frown. There were still so many parts of this story which just didn't make sense.

'If you think that it was your blood on there, maybe they were trying to frame you?' Leigh suggested to Connor.

Jake shook his head. 'All I know is, we're getting nowhere sitting here talking about it. We need to move and find these little cunts.' He looked between Luke and John. 'Find Aaron Williams. Today.'

Luke and John nodded their agreement.

'I'll look into the HR files and see what information I can dig up that might be useful,' Jasmine suggested.

Jake nodded at her before turning to Connor. 'That means me and you are going to find the King brothers.'

Connor cracked his knuckles. 'Yep.'

'Remember, you need them to be willing to hand themselves in,' Leigh reminded them. 'If you want Danny out, then the quickest way of proving his innocence is by proving their guilt.'

'I know,' Jake said with a sigh. 'Fucking pity, though.'

'We'll get to them one day, mate. But we got to get Danny out first,' Connor said.

Jake sucked in a breath and looked around the room. 'We all know what we're doing, then?'

'Yeah,' came the replies.

'I'm going to go back to work and if you send me his date of birth, Jazz, I can take a look into Aaron too. In case you have any problems finding him?' Leigh suggested.

John squeezed her hand in his. 'Thanks.'

'Yeah, thanks, Leigh,' Jake said. 'For everything.'

'I would do anything to take the King brothers and their crew off the streets,' she replied.

Chapter Thirty-Eight

Luke and John stood outside the small terraced house in Kirkdale. It hadn't been difficult to find Aaron Williams at all once they'd put some effort in. A quick, not-so-friendly chat with his and Chanel's upstairs neighbour had revealed that he'd decamped to his mum's a few days earlier.

John knocked on the door again and there was no answer, but a few seconds later, the rustling of binbags to the left of them made them look down the end of the street to see Aaron Williams scrambling over the huge black alley gate in nothing but a pair of shorts and trainers.

'He really is a stupid prick, isn't he?' Luke said with a roll of his eyes. 'I mean, we're six fucking doors away here.'

John chuckled softly before Luke sprinted after him, while John jumped back into his car. Luke had to give it to him, Aaron was quick on his feet and he chased him down two streets before he finally caught up with the slippery fucker. When he did, he had to rugby tackle him to stop him from running any further, and he heard the sickening snap of a bone as he did so. Fortunately, it was Aaron's wrist and he howled in pain.

'Oh, that's just the start,' Luke snarled in his ear. 'You shouldn't have run, lad.'

John's BMW X5 pulled up beside them and Luke pulled Aaron onto his feet and pushed him into the back of the car before climbing into the back seat beside him.

'I haven't done anything,' Aaron sniffed as he held onto his arm.

'So, why the fuck did you run then, you little prick?' Luke frowned at him. 'We were only calling round for a cup of tea, weren't we, John?'

'Yeah,' John replied with a nod and an exaggerated sigh. 'But now we're just a little suspicious.'

'So, you know we're wondering what that's about, Aaron?' Luke added.

Aaron turned and tried to open the car door, but it was locked.

'And now you're trying to throw yourself into moving traffic?' Luke shook his head. 'What is it you're so afraid of, lad? We only want to ask you a few questions, don't we, John?'

'Yep.'

'Answer them, and we might not cut off your balls and post them to your mum. We might even let you go,' Luke whispered.

Aaron started crying. 'It wasn't me,' he shook his head as snot ran from his nose. 'It was Jerrod and Devlin.' Luke blinked at him in astonishment, while John started to chuckle in the front seat.

'Fucking hell, lad.' Luke started to laugh too. 'You ever seen anyone cave that fast before, John?'

'No.' John shook his head.

'Jerrod and Devlin King? How do you know those little turds, then?' Luke asked.

'My girlfriend is their cousin,' Aaron nodded, wiping his nose with his uninjured hand.

'And here was me, thinking we were gonna send your balls to your ma. But you haven't got any, have you?' Luke grinned at Aaron, who continued to cry. 'I can't believe I fucking employed you.'

Aaron continued to cry as he sank back against the seat.

Luke sighed and leaned back. 'Shut the fuck up, lad, and think about what's about to happen to you if we don't get the information we need.'

Luke and John looked at the pathetic figure of Aaron Williams as he sat on a chair in the middle of the container at Nudge Richards scrapyard. They had strapped him to the chair with gaffer tape but Luke knew they weren't going to need to resort to extreme measures to get information from him. He was desperate to talk and throw his girlfriend's cousins under the bus, thinking it might save his own skin.

It wouldn't.

'So, tell us what exactly your girlfriend's idiot cousins have been up to then, Aaron?' Luke said as he pulled up a chair.

Aaron blinked at him, quiet all of a sudden, even though he had been ready to spill his guts in the car. Perhaps he thought he might have played his hand too soon?

John slapped him across the side of the head with one his giant shovel hands to remind him they were waiting for his answer.

Aaron winced in pain and shrank back when John raised his hand again. 'The raid on Cartel Securities a few months back,' Aaron sniffed.

'Oh, that?' Luke rubbed a hand over his jaw and nodded. 'I'd almost forgotten about that. Hadn't you, John? What with everything else going on?'

'Yep,' John said, nodding.

'But how the hell did your girlfriend's idiot cousins know that Danny would be going there with that money that night?'

Aaron sniffed, blinking up at him, and Luke shook his head. 'I thought this was going to go much easier than this, to be honest, Aaron, the way you were blabbing in the car. But we can make it much harder if you like.' Luke nodded to John, who picked up a pair of long-nosed pliers from the work bench beside him.

'What you going to do with them?' Aaron stammered as he stared up at John.

'Oh, come on, Aaron. You're not that naïve, are you?' Luke laughed.

'Well, to be fair, these have a lot of uses,' John grinned as he snapped them shut in his large hands.

'I suppose,' Luke conceded. 'They can pull out teeth, fingernails, even cut off fingers and toes if you apply enough pressure.'

'And pull out a tongue. Remember that fella who we did that to?' John added.

'Yeah, but it's hard to talk with no tongue, mate. Maybe we'll start with something else, eh?'

Aaron started to balk, and then he vomited all over himself and the floor in front of him.

'Fucking hell,' Luke snapped.

Aaron started to shake his head from side to side.

'You want to talk now, Aaron?' Luke asked him as he shoved his hands into his coat pockets. He wanted this over with.

Aaron nodded as his eyes flickered between Luke and John.

'I'm going to ask you some questions, and you're going to answer me straightaway. And if you don't, or I think you're lying to me, then John will remove a body part. Okay?'

Aaron nodded again, keeping his lips clamped shut in case John ripped out his tongue.

'Who told the King brothers about the money Danny had that night at Cartel Securities?'

'I did,' he sniffed.

'Why?' Luke frowned.

'It seemed like a quick way to make some money. They were supposed to grab it and go, not start a riot.'

'And the job in Scotland? Who was responsible for that?'

'Jerrod and Devlin. They took your gear.'

'And who gave them the information so they could take our gear?' Luke snarled.

'I did,' Aaron sniffed.

'For a pay-out?'

'Yes, and because they threatened to tell you if I didn't keep supplying them with information.'

Luke nodded. Aaron really was a stupid fucker, getting involved with the King brothers. He was a greedy fucker too.

'Now, tell me about the morning after Connor's stag do, when he cut his hand in Cartel Securities and you helped Danny clean up.'

Aaron's face turned from pale to translucent, and Luke knew at that moment that Leigh had been right. Aaron opened his mouth but he didn't speak.

'John,' Luke said with a sigh, and within sixty seconds, John had Aaron in a headlock and had pulled out one of his back teeth. He dropped it onto the floor while Aaron howled in pain as blood poured from his mouth.

'Don't make me ask you again,' Luke snarled.

Aaron spluttered, spitting out a large globule of blood and saliva before he spoke. 'Yeah, I helped Danny clean up, but he left most of it to me. Barking at me to sort it out, while it was him and Connor who'd made the mess.'

'And?' Luke snapped when Aaron stopped talking.

'While I was out in the back throwing everything into the big bins, Jerrod phoned me. I had a grumble about what I was doing and he told me to keep it. I had no idea they were going to use it the way they did. I swear,' he wailed.

'Keep something with Connor Carter's blood and Danny Alexander's prints on it?' Luke asked with a frown. 'And that didn't seem weird or a bit fucking off to you? What the fuck else would they want it for, Aaron?' Luke stood up and kicked Aaron in the balls in frustration, and Aaron doubled over in agony.

Luke paced up and down the small container while John stood patiently waiting for his next order. 'What was their game-plan, Aaron?' Luke asked.

'I don't know,' Aaron sniffed.

Luke walked over to him, lifting Aaron's head by his hair and bending his face close to his. 'My best mate is in fucking Walton Prison right now because of you and those fuckwit King brothers. Now, tell me what they were doing, framing Danny for murder?'

'It was Connor they wanted. Not him!' Aaron cried.

'Why?'

'They want to be the top dogs.'

'But why Connor? And why like this? And why now?'

'Some fella contacted them. He's been backing them. Apparently he knows people, and he wanted Connor out of the picture too.'

'Who is he?' Luke snarled.

'I don't know. I swear I don't know. I don't know anything else. As soon as I realised what they were going to do, I tried to get that stuff back, but they wouldn't hand it over. I'm sorry,' he sniffed as the tears ran down his face, dripping onto his bare chest.

'Who killed Glenda?' Luke finally asked.

'Jerrod and Devlin,' he sniffed.

Luke sighed and let go of Aaron's head, pushing it roughly before he walked away. Taking his phone out of his pocket, he dialled Connor's number.

'Yeah?' Connor answered.

'We found Aaron. It was the King brothers who set Danny up, only it seems like it was you they wanted.'

Connor was silent for a moment. 'Anything else we need to know about?'

'Yeah. Apparently, they're working for someone else. Someone with connections in Liverpool, but Aaron says he doesn't know who.'

'You think he's telling the truth?'

'I don't see why not. He's spilled his guts about everything else. He admitted being the one who gave that table leg to Jerrod and Devlin.'

Connor sucked in a breath. 'We might need him, then. Where are you?'

'Nudge's scrapyard. In one of the containers. You want me to keep him here and ask Nudge to keep an eye on him?'

'Yeah. Lock him in and tell him to keep his gob shut if he wants us to come back and let him out.'

'Will do. You found those two pricks yet?'

'They're at some bird's house in Bootle. We're about to pull them out of bed in about two minutes.'

'Good. Give us a shout if you need anything.'

'Will do, mate.'

Chapter Thirty-Nine

Devlin King sat on the edge of the bed and rubbed his eyes. Glancing behind him, he wrinkled his nose in disgust at the bird he'd ended up with. She was the cousin of Jerrod's new bird, Sammi, and if he hadn't been stoned off his face, he wouldn't have gone anywhere near her. She rolled over in her sleep, pulling the covers and exposing her fat, pale arse, and he shook his head. He should have gone home.

Walking to the window, he pulled the net curtains and saw the brand-new Range Rover Overfinch pulling up outside. The hairs on his forearm stood on end. Something told him this wasn't good. Cars like that didn't pull up into this street. He dropped the net curtain and kept watching. When Jake Conlon and Connor Carter stepped out of the car dressed in black tracksuits, he felt his heart start to hammer in his chest. He wasn't stupid enough not to realise that there was no way he and Jerrod could take on these two alone. They didn't even have any shooters around because coming to Sammi's house had been a last-minute thing.

He scrambled around the floor looking for his clothes, but all he could find was a pair of the fat bird's leggings.

'Fuck!' he hissed as he pulled them on. 'Jerrod!' he shouted as he stumbled around the room. 'Get the fuck up, now!'

'Oi!' The girl sat up and glared at him for waking her up.

'Shut the fuck up!' he hissed to her as he bolted from the room. He stuck his head into Sammi's room, where she and Jerrod were fast asleep, sprawled naked on top of the covers.

'Jerrod!' he shouted. 'Move your fucking arse now! They've fucking come for us,' he snarled as he pulled on his trainers, which for some reason were on Sammi's bedroom floor.

'What the fuck you on about, Dev?' Jerrod groaned just as the banging started on the front door below. It wasn't a knock, though. They were fucking coming through it.

'That's Jake Conlon and Connor Carter you can hear. Get the fuck up now!' Devlin shouted, but Jerrod was still half wasted.

'Hang on,' he slurred.

Devlin looked at his older brother. There was no way he was getting him out of this room before the two psychopaths downstairs got through the front door. He turned on his heel and legged it down the stairs two at a time before making a run for the back door. He pulled it closed behind him as he heard the splintering of wood in the hallway. He breathed in a lungful of air before he scrambled over the wall and started to run.

Once he had run as far as he could, he stopped, doubled over and wheezing as his lungs burned with the effort. A group of schoolkids walked past him and started giggling, and he looked down at himself, dressed in purple leggings and his trainers and nothing else.

When he could breathe again, he dialled Mr Savage's number.

'Yeah?' he answered after a few rings.

'They've got Jerrod,' he panted.

'Who have?' Savage snarled.

'Conlon and Carter.'

'Fuck!' Savage hissed.

'You need to help him. Get some people down here. Now!'

'Help him? If you two hadn't fucked up the plan, we'd be all plain sailing by now, kid. You're on your own.'

The line went dead and Devlin stared at the phone in his hand. 'Fucking cunt!' he spat. He was about to dial one of the crew but then he wondered what he was going to tell them. That he had abandoned their beloved leader? Left him for the two most powerful men in the North-West to do whatever the hell they were going to do? Devlin swallowed. He was probably never going to see Jerrod again. And now that Conlon and Carter obviously knew what they'd done, he was probably the most wanted man in Liverpool.

Fuck! This was all Jerrod's fault anyway. Trusting

Savage. And then he'd had to go over the top on that old bird. They were only supposed to kill her. Make it look like someone had lost their temper and clobbered her to death. It had been Jerrod's idea to have some fun with her first. Stealing some of Devlin's own tricks. Using pieces of wood to make sure those filthy sluts never enjoyed sex again was his thing. He could have killed Jerrod at the time. The last thing Devlin needed was for the bizzies to start seeing any similarities between that old bird and that fit nurse they'd followed home from the train station just before they'd moved to the Bridewell. Devlin had no idea why Jerrod had decided to do the same to the old bird. It wasn't like she was good-looking or anything, and he could enjoy watching.

Devlin King started to walk towards home, ignoring the amused glances he was attracting in his distinctive outfit. He was going to have to lie low for a while and decide what his next move was.

Chapter Forty

Jake gave a final kick against the door of the house in Bootle and, to his relief, it crashed open, sending splinters of wood flying into the hallway. As he and Connor ran inside, they heard shouting and screams upstairs and ran up them two at a time. A half-naked girl came at them as they reached the landing, demanding to know who they were, but Connor pushed her back into the room she'd come out of. 'Shut the fuck up and you won't get hurt,' he hissed as he looked around the sparsely furnished room, confirming neither of the King brothers were inside.

Jake ran into the other room, finding Jerrod King pulling on a pair of tracksuit bottoms as another girl pulled the covers over herself and began to scream.

'What the fuck?' Jerrod shouted, but Jake was in no mood for his claims of innocence. Aaron Williams had already thrown him and his brother under the bus. Now he and Connor just needed to persuade them to confess to setting Danny up. Jake walked towards him and punched Jerrod in the jaw, sending him sprawling backwards.

'There's only one of them in here, Con. You want to check downstairs?' he shouted behind him as he pulled the zip ties from his pocket. He pulled Jerrod up off the bed, twisting his arms behind his back and securing his wrists with the plastic. He pulled it as tight as he could, ensuring it pinched the little fucker's skin.

'Oi! Gerroff!' Jerrod shouted as he struggled in Jake's arms, but Jake had half a foot and about four stone on him and he overpowered him easily.

'Help me, Sammi!' Jerrod screamed like a toddler.

Jake looked up and glared at her. 'Do not fucking move!' he hissed and she nodded in compliance.

When Jerrod's hands were secure, Jake tied his ankles and lifted him, throwing him over his shoulder as the younger man struggled and shouted. 'Pass me that,' Jake said to Sammi, as he panted with the effort of restraining Jerrod, pointing to a small scrap of black fabric. Sammi handed it to him and to his disgust, he realised it was a worn thong. Rolling his eyes, he stuffed it into Jerrod's mouth, muffling his deafening shrieks.

As Jake was walking down the stairs, Connor was standing at the bottom. 'That other little prick isn't here. I checked everywhere.'

'That's all right,' Jake snarled as he shuffled Jerrod's weight on his shoulder. 'One of them will do just fine.'

Within a few minutes, Jerrod was bundled into the back

of Connor's Range Rover and they were driving to one of Jake and Connor's lock-ups near the docks.

Jerrod kicked at the passenger seat and continued screaming through the soiled underwear in his mouth. Jake punched him in the side of his head for his trouble. 'Shut the fuck up and stay still, or I will carve my name into your fucking nuts!' he snarled and Jerrod glared at him, but he did as he was told and Jake breathed a sigh of relief. He was going to have Danny out of prison soon. He could feel it.

———

Connor pulled a struggling Jerrod from the back of his car and into the lock-up, where one of their colleagues was waiting. He threw him onto the floor and then crouched to cut the ties from his legs. Jerrod kicked out instinctively, and Connor slapped him around the back of the head. Then he reached over and pulled the now soaking underwear from Jerrod's mouth and tossed it onto the pile of rubbish that would be disposed of later.

'You okay, Mal?' Connor nodded to the tall, lean man who was standing in the corner.

'Yes, Boss. Looking forward to some fun today. It's not often you let me out of my cage.' He raised his eyebrows.

'That's because you're a fucking animal, Mal,' Jake said as he slapped him on the back. Mal Freeman had worked for them for years, but he was a loose cannon and a maniac. They usually kept him busy with the kind of jobs that he couldn't get them into too much trouble with. But the unique thing about Mal was that he was also a sado-masochist, and an experienced one at that. Apparently, his services were well sought after in BDSM clubs around the country.

'Pick him up for us, would you?' Jake asked Connor as he nodded to Jerrod on the floor, before he spoke to Mal. 'Not more than a scratch on him. Okay?'

'Okay.' Mal nodded.

When Jerrod was sitting on the chair, Jake walked over to him. 'This is what is going to happen today, Jerrod. You are going to go to our friend at St Anne's Street police station, and you are going to confess to the murder of Glenda Alexander, and you are going to tell them all about how you and your fuckwit brother, with the help of Aaron Williams, set up Danny. Okay?'

Jerrod frowned when Aaron's name was mentioned and Connor laughed loudly. 'Yeah. Your cousin's fella, isn't he? He told us everything. How he gave you that coffee-table leg and you used it to frame Danny. He couldn't wait to pin the blame on you to save his own skin. Which he didn't, by the way. I reckon his heart probably packed in about half an hour ago, given what our colleagues are doing to him.'

Jerrod glared at Connor as he went on talking. 'And Danny is only their mate. Can you imagine what he's going to do to you?' He nodded towards Jake. 'He's a fucking sadistic cunt, and you fucked over his favourite person in the world.'

'Fag!' Jerrod hissed and Connor raised his hand to punch Jerrod in the face, but Jake stopped him. 'We can't, remember? We can't have him walking into the police station all battered and bruised now, can we?' Jake tutted. 'It will look like we've beaten a confession from him then.'

'Yeah,' Jerrod sneered. 'You need me. You can't hurt me.'

'Oh, I never said that.' Jake grinned at him. 'We are going to hurt you. A lot! We just can't use our usual methods – can we, Mal?'

'Nope.' Mal shook his head.

'Mal here is an expert at causing pain, Jerrod. I mean, like real, gut-wrenching pain that lasts for hours, but isn't enough to kill you – you know? You should see the things he can do with a cocktail stick.'

'Ow.' Connor winced and cupped his dick over his pants. 'Just thinking about that makes my eyes water.'

Jake chuckled. 'Oh, and Mal here is a fag like me too.' Jake winked at him. 'Only he doesn't have the same discerning tastes as me. No offence, Mal.' Jake turned to him.

'None taken, Boss,' Mal replied. 'I'll fuck anything with a heartbeat,' he said matter-of-factly. 'And I brought me some protection too. You know, so I don't leave any evidence behind.' He grinned as he pulled a huge box of condoms out of his pocket.

Jake turned back to Jerrod, who was trembling on the chair. He leaned down towards Jerrod's face and whispered in his ear: 'And his cock is fucking huge, mate. You will never take a comfortable shit ever again.'

Connor and Mal laughed but Jerrod spat in Jake's face. 'Filthy fuckers,' he snarled.

Jake wiped the saliva from his face with his sleeve. 'Well, yeah, Mal is.' He winked at Jerrod before stepping back.

'So, I'm sure you know the script. We can do this two ways. You tell us who you were working for. You agree to confess to the police, and we take you there. Or we leave you with Mal until you agree to do it anyway.'

'Fuck off! I didn't do anything!' Jerrod snarled.

Jake sucked in a breath. 'But we know you did. The police even know you did. That ring you always wear left an imprint on Glenda's face. Your DNA is on the body too.'

'The fuck it is!' Jerrod snarled. 'I wore gloves. I did everything fucking right. You will never fucking pin it on me.'

'You know how you spit when you talk, Jerrod?' Jake shrugged. 'I bet you just couldn't resist taunting poor old Glenda, could you? Telling her how clever you were. All the disgusting things you were going to do to her. She had droplets of saliva all over her face.' Jake shrugged.

Jerrod's face paled, but he continued glaring at them. 'Fuck off. If that were true, why do you need me to confess, then?'

'Oh, we don't need you to. But we'd prefer you to. You know how long those idiots in blue take to do anything. I want Danny out of Walton as soon as possible, and this is the quickest way to do it.'

'And why the fuck would I help you? If the filth are going to get me anyway,' Jerrod snapped.

Jake turned to Connor. 'Has he been listening to a word we've fucking said?' He shook his head in exasperation.

'He's fucking thick, mate. I told you that.' Connor shrugged.

'Mal.' Jake called their associate over. 'How about we give you a few hours? See how he holds up, and then we'll see if he's going to change his mind, eh?'

'Perfect!' Mal grinned at Jerrod. 'We're going to have so much fun.'

Jerrod stood up to run, but Jake pushed him back down. 'Milo Savage,' Jerrod shouted. 'It was Milo Savage. It was all his idea. He came up with the plan. But it was supposed to be you who got arrested, not Danny,' he said to Connor.

'Who the fuck is Milo Savage?' Connor frowned at Jake.

'Never heard of him.' Jake shook his head. 'Probably some name he's just plucked out of the fucking air.'

'It's not. He's not from round here, but he hates you.'

'Why?' Connor frowned.

'Something about your missus. He said she belongs to him, or something.'

'Jazz?' Connor frowned as he stepped closer to Jerrod.

'Yeah. He's fucking obsessed with her.'

Connor turned to Jake with a look of worry on his face. 'Go,' Jake said. 'Me and Mal can sort things here.'

'Yeah. I'll just go check on her,' Connor said, swallowing the lump in his throat.

When Connor had left, Jake turned his attention back to Jerrod. 'So, where were we? You ready to confess the rest of your sins now, lad?'

Jerrod looked up and stared at Mal's grinning face. 'Yeah. I'll tell them.'

'Glad to hear it, kid,' Jake said and then he slapped Mal on the shoulder. 'Sorry, fella. That means you only get half an hour.'

'What?' Jerrod spluttered. 'I said I'll tell the police I did it.'

'I know,' Jake replied with a shrug. 'Which is why Mal is going to play nice, aren't you, big fella?'

'Hmm.' Mal shrugged. 'Nice-ish.'

'Wait. No. You said!' Jerrod shouted as Mal walked towards him and strapped a ball gag onto his mouth.

'I said there were two ways this could go. And believe me, this is the easier way. But I need Mal here to show you just a fraction of what will happen to you if you go back on your word to me. I'll be back in thirty minutes. Have fun, now, won't you?' Jake winked and then he walked out of the lock-up and went to sit in his car. Once inside, he called Leigh Moss.

'Someone will be dropping the lovely Jerrod off in about forty-five minutes. Will you be waiting for him?'

'Yes. I'll make sure I'm around, and I'll get my DS to take his statement.'

'Can't you do it?' Jake asked with a frown.

'No. It has to be a sergeant or below. Don't worry. Mark is a good copper and he hates the King brothers as much as I do. What about the other one? Devlin?'

'He'd scarpered by the time we got there. But we'll find him. Jerrod's confession and his DNA will be enough to get Danny out, though, right?'

'Yes. Providing he admits he set Danny up too.'

One hour later, Jerrod King was sitting in an interview room at St Anne's Street police station giving his sworn statement that he murdered Glenda Alexander and set Danny up for the crime. Faye Donovan was already waiting in the wings, ready to demand that her client be released from custody immediately.

Chapter Forty-One

Jasmine clicked the fob on her car key and her Mercedes beeped to life. Her hand was on the door handle when she felt the arm taking hold of her elbow and squeezing hard. She gasped out loud and turned, looking into those cold blue eyes that she'd thought she'd never see again.

'Milo?' she gasped, her mouth hanging open in shock.

'Hello, Jasmine.' He smiled, showing his perfect white teeth. 'It's been a long time, sweetheart. I've missed you.'

The flowers. The note. He had called her 'sweetheart'. He used to tell her that she was the sweetest flower. Suddenly, she felt the urge to be sick. 'Milo?' she said again as her heart began to race. 'What are you doing here?'

'To take you home, where you belong. With me.' He bent his head and pressed a soft kiss on her cheek, and she froze on the spot.

'I am home. I live here now. I'm married,' she stammered.

'I can take care of that, don't worry,' he chuckled. 'I left you at the mercy of one madman. I won't make the same mistake again.'

She tried to wrench her elbow from his grip. 'Connor isn't a madman and I'm not at his mercy.'

He held on tighter to her arm. 'Jasmine!' He frowned at her. 'This was always the plan. That you and me would be together once Sol was out of the way?'

Jasmine blinked at him, conscious that she was alone in a quiet side street and Milo's grip on her arm kept growing tighter. Milo Savage had been her ex-husband's right-hand man and about a year into her marriage to Sol, the two of them had a brief but passionate affair. Jasmine had ended it when Sol started to become overly suspicious. He was a cruel and unforgiving man, and when Milo had shown her some kindness, she had latched onto it. Her life had been so empty and lonely that she had taken any warmth and compassion she could find. 'Milo. That was eight years ago,' she said with a shake of her head. 'You worked for Sol for years and we never spoke of this. Why are you talking about it now?'

'Because Sol is dead and I'm out of prison.' He frowned at her again.

'But I love Connor,' she said, and she saw the realisation dawn on his face that she was telling him the truth. She'd had no idea he'd been harbouring such thoughts for all these years.

'No.' He narrowed his eyes at her. 'You love me.'

'I don't.' She shook her head. It was kinder to be honest with him. 'I never did.' She reached out her free hand and touched his cheek. 'I'm sorry.'

The change in his face was instant as it filled with anger and hatred. He wrapped one of his huge hands around her throat and squeezed. 'Sorry? You lead me on for eight fucking years, and you're sorry?' he hissed.

'I didn't lead you on.' She choked out the words as his face grew darker with rage.

'Fucking slut!' he snarled. 'I told him that's what you were. Taking your clothes off for all of those men. Letting them feel you up for a few quid.'

'Milo! Please?' Jasmine pleaded as he gripped her throat tighter. Images of her beautiful baby boy and husband flashed through her head, and all she could think of was that she wasn't going to die in this filthy street and never see her family again.

She closed her eyes and focused on the things Connor had taught her. How to drop a man, no matter what his size. Always go for the balls. With all her strength she raised her right knee and hit Milo straight between his thighs. His eyes watered and he doubled over in pain, long enough for her to wrench herself free and open the car door.

As she climbed inside, he straightened up and made another grab for her, but she was too quick and she slammed the car door on his hand and he cursed her name, pulling his hand out of harm's way. Jazz locked the doors and started the engine. Gripping the steering wheel with shaking hands, she floored the accelerator and drove towards home as fast as she could.

Jasmine had been driving for a little over a minute when her phone started ringing. She burst out crying when she saw Connor's name and his handsome face appearing on the screen on the dash of her car.

Pressing a button on the steering wheel, she answered the call. 'Connor,' she said, her voice trembling.

'Jazz? Are you okay, babe?' he asked, the concern in his voice audible.

'Yes,' she sniffed. 'Can you come home?'

'I'm on my way there now. Where are you? Has something happened?'

'Yes, but I'm okay. I'm in the car. I'm on my way home too. I'm okay,' she repeated as she wiped her cheeks with the back of her hand.

'I'll be there as soon as I can,' he replied. 'Go straight inside the house, Jazz. Don't speak to anyone.'

'Okay. I won't,' she sniffed, wondering if Connor knew something about Milo, or whether it was just the fact that she'd clearly been crying that had him so worried.

Chapter Forty-Two

Connor's car was already at the house when Jasmine pulled into the driveway and he was standing on the step waiting for her. He jogged over to her car and pulled open the door as she turned off her engine.

'Jazz, are you okay, babe?' he asked as he pulled her out and wrapped his arms around her.

She leaned against him, inhaling the smell of him as he held onto her. 'I'm fine. Can we go inside?'

'Yeah, come on,' he agreed and with his arm around her shoulders, he guided her back inside the house.

Once they were inside, Connor took a closer look at his wife. Taking her chin in his hand, he tilted her head up to look at him and noticed the red and purple marks on her neck. 'What the hell, Jazz? Who the fuck did that to you?'

Jasmine swallowed. 'A guy called Milo,' she whispered, afraid of what she was about to have to tell him.

'Milo Savage?' He narrowed his eyes at her.

'Yes. Wait. Do you know him?'

'He's the one behind the Bridewell crew. Jerrod told us he's obsessed with you. Who the fuck is he, Jazz?'

'He used to be Sol's right-hand man. The one who was involved with the brothels and the girls he used to run. He's been in prison for a few years and I haven't seen him since he went inside.'

Connor traced his fingertips over his wife's cheek. 'Are you okay? What the fuck happened, babe?'

'I was getting into my car and he grabbed me. He…' She shook her head as the tears pricked at her eyes.

'He what?' Connor growled.

'He said that he'd come to take me home, and that we could finally be together, now that Sol was dead.'

'What?' Connor's scowl deepened as he listened to her.

'I told him he was crazy, and that I was married to you, but he wouldn't accept it. I think he really believed I was going to run off with him. When I told him that I didn't love him, he grabbed me by the throat. I swear I thought he was going to kill me, Connor. But I managed to get away.'

Connor brushed the marks on her neck with the tips of his fingers. 'Did he hurt you?'

'It's just a little tender,' she lied. Her throat felt bruised and raw, but he was already looking at her with such concern and worry that she could barely stand it.

'But why the fuck would he think that you were going to run off with him like that?' Connor frowned. 'Why would he think that you loved him?'

Jasmine swallowed. She had a feeling that Connor

wasn't going to like what she had to say next. 'Because he and I once had a thing,' she whispered.

'A thing? Like before you married Sol?'

'No. While I was married to Sol,' she admitted, feeling more ashamed of that than she ever had before.

'You had an affair with him?' Connor blinked at her.

'Yes.'

'How long for?'

'Only for a couple of months.'

'A couple of months?' Connor snapped.

'It meant nothing.'

'Well, clearly not to him. Because he's fucking obsessed with you, by all accounts.'

'He's deluded.' She shook her head.

Connor stared at his wife. 'You had *another* affair? How many others were there before me, Jazz?' He took a small, almost imperceptible step back from her, but this hurt Jasmine much more than the bruises on her neck.

'There was just him, Connor. It was eight years ago. I didn't even know you back then.'

'But you and me… What if you'd got pregnant with his baby? Would you have left Sol and married him instead?' He narrowed his eyes as he glared at her.

Jasmine blinked at him, the tears forming in her eyes as he looked at her like she was no longer the woman he knew. But what he'd just said was completely uncalled for. 'No, of course not,' she snapped.

'How do I know that?' He ran a hand through his hair. 'I

thought I was the only one, Jazz? I thought you and me were something different.'

'We are different. You are the only man I have ever loved, Connor. From the moment I met you, I knew that you were the one for me. What Milo and I had was nothing like this. I was just looking for some comfort and some compassion. You know the kind of man Sol was. Can't you understand that?'

He shook his head. 'Isn't that all I was too? Any warm body might have done?'

'How dare you say that! You know that's not true!' she hissed.

'Do I?' Connor shook his head in disgust and Jasmine felt like her heart was about to break in two.

'Yes, you do.'

'I can't…' Connor shook his head. 'I can't even look at you right now.'

'Really? Because of something I did six years before I even knew you?'

'It's not what you did, Jazz. It's the person it makes you.'

Jasmine took a step back from him. He might as well have slapped her across the face, she felt so much anger and hurt. 'And who is that?'

'A cheat. Someone I'm not sure I know,' he said with a shake of his head.

'Connor? You're being ridiculous,' she pleaded with him.

He turned on his heel and pulled his mobile phone from his pocket.

'Where are you going?' she called after him.

'I need to go and check in with Jake and make sure everything went as planned.'

'But, Connor,' she sniffed as tears threatened to spill out. She was still reeling from her encounter with Milo, and the one person she wanted to seek comfort from was about to walk out on her. But Jasmine rarely cried and she wasn't about to now, just because her husband was behaving like a jealous toddler.

'I'll post a couple of men outside,' he said as he headed for the door. 'Do not leave this fucking house, Jazz!' Then he walked out without a backward glance.

Chapter Forty-Three

Connor dialled Jake's number as soon as he was in the car, and Jake picked up after a few rings.

'Everything okay your end?' Jake asked.

'I found out who Milo Savage is,' Connor growled.

'Who?'

'I'll tell you when I get there. Did Jerrod talk? Are you still at the lock-up?'

'He did. And no, I'm on my way to the club. Mal has just dropped that little scrote off at St Anne's Street and I've let Faye know too. She said if they charge Jerrod today, Danny should be released in the morning.'

'Good,' Connor sighed. At least that was dealt with and now they could focus on finding Milo Savage before he made any more moves. 'I'll meet you at the club.'

'Okay, mate. See you there.'

Connor ended the call and put his foot down on the accelerator, desperate to get to the club as soon as possible.

He needed to tell Jake what had happened, and for his best mate to talk some sense into him, because right now all he could think about was the fact that Jasmine had had more than one affair while she was married to Sol. He knew that made him a hypocrite, but he couldn't think straight. He had thought he was the only one, and the fact that he hadn't been somehow cheapened their whole relationship. It certainly made more sense as to why he, rather than Danny, had been the intended target to take the fall for Glenda's murder.

Connor sat in Jake's office with his head in his hands and sighed loudly. After Jake had filled him in on what had happened with Jerrod, he had told Jake about the events of the past hour and his surprise at learning who Milo Savage was, and why he wanted Connor out of the picture. 'I just don't feel like I know who she is anymore, Jake,' he said as he looked up at his stepbrother with tears in his eyes.

'Course you do, Con. This is Jazz we're talking about. The woman who looks at you like you just shat the sun out of your arse.'

Jake's attempt at humour did little to lighten Connor's mood, and he shook his head and picked up the bottle of Johnny Walker before pouring himself a large measure.

'What if there were more than just him?' he said with a groan before taking a gulp of the Scotch, wincing as it burned his throat.

'So what if there were, mate? Sol Shepherd was a cunt. So what if she had a dozen affairs? That doesn't make what you two have any less real.'

'But I thought I was the only one, Jake. I thought I was different. If she could cheat on him, then she can cheat on me,' he said, swallowing the lump in his throat. He'd finally admitted it out loud. His biggest fear. That he would lose the woman he loved more than anyone else in the world.

'Fuck, mate,' Jake said as he walked around the desk and placed his hand on Connor's shoulder. 'You are *not* Sol Shepherd. Jazz hated him. She fucking adores you. You are breaking my fucking heart sitting here like this. Tearing yourself apart for something she did eight years ago.'

'I know.' He shook his head. 'But I can't get the thoughts of them out of my fucking head, Jake. The way he's been obsessed with her all these years. The fact that he had his hands on her like that, even if it was eight years ago. What if she loved him?'

'He was Sol's right-hand man. If she had wanted him, then he would have been the perfect person to take Sol out, wouldn't he? So, clearly she is telling the truth and it meant nothing to her.'

Connor swallowed another mouthful of whisky, and Jake understood that it was his ego that was hurting as much as anything else.

'Do you remember how fucking stupid we were eight years ago, Con?' he asked with a laugh. 'You and Paul tried to take out my fucking dad on the back of a scrambler bike.'

'Yeah.' Connor laughed softly. 'My dad thought your mum was going to kill us, but she saved our arses instead.'

'Yeah. You were a pair of idiots.'

'And you were an arrogant fucker who didn't have a fucking clue what he was doing,' Connor reminded him, and Jake winced at the memory of how naïve and stupid he'd once been. His mum and Michael had saved his arse too.

'And I cheated on Siobhan,' Jake said with a sigh, remembering his ill-fated marriage to his childhood sweetheart.

'Yeah, with my brother.' Connor arched an eyebrow at him.

'And you fucked her behind my back,' Jake reminded him with a grin.

'Fuck. Yeah. Sorry about that, mate,' Connor said with a shudder.

'See. We all did stupid fucked-up shit that we would never do now.'

'Hmm,' Connor said as he looked up at Jake with the hint of a smile on his face. 'I would never fuck Danny behind your back.'

Jake burst out laughing. 'Danny wouldn't touch you anyway, mate. He has standards.'

'He so fucking would.' Connor laughed too. 'I mean, you must have thought about it?'

Jake almost choked on air. 'What, me and you?'

'Yeah,' Connor replied with a nod, as he tried to keep his face as serious as possible. 'You were in love with a dude who looked exactly like me. Don't tell me you haven't thought about me and you... you know?'

Jake frowned at him. 'Are you fucking serious? You do know that's not how this works, right?'

'So you've never seen me like that?' Connor stared at him, pretending to look hurt, but he couldn't keep a straight face for long and burst out laughing, much to Jake's relief.

'You're a fucking idiot.' Jake shook his head and went to sit back down on his chair.

'I had you going for a minute, though, didn't I?' Connor laughed harder and Jake smiled at him.

'Yes, you prick!' He rolled his eyes, pleased that Connor was in a brighter mood. He waited for Connor to stop laughing before he spoke again. 'So? Milo Savage?' he asked, shifting the focus back to the reason for them being in his office.

Connor's face darkened and a vein throbbed in the thick column of his neck. 'Oh, he is going to die a very fucking slow and painful death, and I am going to enjoy every fucking second of it.'

'Good. Now we just need to find the fucker.' Jake sat back in his chair and Connor stared at him, sucking on his top lip as he considered their next move.

Chapter Forty-Four

Connor's finger hovered over the telephone icon on his iPhone as he considered whether to make the call. With a deep sigh, he pressed the button and held the phone to his ear as it rang out. He was overwhelmed by a wave of emotion when he heard the voice on the other end of the line.

'Hey, son,' his dad answered and Connor felt the tears stinging his eyes. He hadn't realised how much he'd missed him until he'd heard his voice.

'Hi, Dad.' He swallowed hard.

'Everything okay?'

'Yeah,' Connor lied. 'Just wanted to hear your voice.'

'Okay,' Michael Carter said softly. 'Jazz phoned Grace earlier too.'

Connor sucked in a deep breath. 'So you know, then?'

'Ah, Grace was vague. You know how women can be.

She didn't want to get involved, but Jazz just needed an ear, you know?'

'Yeah.' Connor wiped his eyes as a tear ran down his cheek.

'Why is it eating you up so much, son? I get that you want to kill this guy for hurting her. What else is going on?'

Connor sniffed. 'I dunno.'

'I think you do,' Michael replied.

'Paul died because of me and her. Because of what we did.'

'No!' Michael interrupted him.

'Yes, Dad. I know you tried to hide it from me, but I'm not stupid. Sol killed Paul because I was having an affair with Jazz. And now I find out I wasn't the only one,' he sniffed.

'Sol killed Paul,' Michael sucked in a breath, 'because he was a jealous egomaniac. That is not on you. It is not on Jazz. It is all on him.'

Connor shook his head. 'You won't ever convince me of that.'

'Do I need to get on a fucking plane and come smack some sense into you, kid?' his father said with a sigh.

'No.' Connor wiped his eyes, sorry for bothering his dad with something so trivial when he was thousands of miles away.

'Seriously, I can be there in six hours if you need me, son?'

'No, Dad. I'm fine. I've drunk too much whisky, that's all.'

'Okay. You know I leave you boys to do your thing as much as I can, but Jasmine loves you. You love her. Stop punishing her for something she did years before you even knew her.'

'I know you're right.'

'I'm always fucking right,' Michael said with a laugh. 'Now get your arse home and do whatever it is you need to do to make this right, so you can stop feeling like shit, and deal with this Milo cunt.'

'I will.'

'Good. I'll call you tomorrow. Night, son.'

'Night, Dad.'

———————————

Jasmine was pacing the hallway when Connor finally walked through the door. He threw his keys onto the sideboard and stared at her.

'Where have you been? I called you twice,' she said, aware of the tremor in her voice, and annoyed at herself for it. But the truth was, along with their son, this man before her was her whole world, and she hated it when they argued. They always worked as a team – a solid, unbreakable unit – but he had been so angry at her earlier, and she had never seen that side to him before.

'Out,' he growled as he walked towards her. She studied him as he approached. He wore one of his expensive tailored suits and a white shirt open at the collar. One of his many tattoos was peeking out, snaking around the base of his neck. It was the one he'd got when their son was born. As he edged closer, she caught the smell of whisky on him, and she instinctively took a step back as a flashback of an incident with Sol almost knocked the breath from her lungs. He had come home drunk and accused her of an affair with some man whom she hadn't even recalled meeting. He accused her and punished her for the alleged misdemeanours so often, she wondered if that was why she finally gave in to Milo's advances. If Sol was going to beat her for it anyway, why not at least do something to deserve it?

Connor's face settled into a scowl. 'Jazz?' he said as he edged closer, while she took another step back.

'Jazz?' he said again as he reached out his hand, and she flinched. She had never been even the tiniest bit scared of him before today, even though he was one of the most feared and ruthless men in the North-West. But the smell of the whisky, and the look on his face, took her to a place she thought she'd left behind a long time ago.

Connor's heart almost broke in two as he looked at his strong, beautiful wife, practically cowering as approached her. She took another step backwards until she was flat against the wall and had nowhere left to go, and he realised with sudden clarity what a complete idiot he'd been.

'Babe,' he said as he slid one arm around her waist, while he brushed the fingertips of his other hand over the soft skin of her cheek. 'I'm sorry I've been acting like a jealous prick.'

'I'm sorry I didn't tell you about Milo,' she whispered as she looked up at him through her long dark lashes.

'I would never, ever hurt you. You know that, right?'

'I know,' she whispered.

'But I am going to hurt him,' he said, his eyes darkening. 'He's going to pay for everything he has done to you, and to our family.'

She nodded at him. 'I know,' she said again.

'I love you so fucking much, Jazz,' he breathed as he bent his head closer to hers. 'If anything ever happened to you…'

'I love you too,' she replied as she slipped her arms around his neck and pulled him closer to her until her lips were brushing his. Connor pressed closer against her and she felt the groan rumble through his chest. As he sealed his mouth over hers, all thoughts of Sol and Milo were forgotten.

Chapter Forty-Five

Danny Alexander stepped out of the gates of Walton Prison and blinked in the bright morning sun. He'd been told a little before midnight that he'd be out the following morning and had thought he must be dreaming, but here he was. All charges had been dropped and he was a free man. He could hardly believe it, but then Jake Conlon was a miracle worker.

As Danny looked across the road, he saw Jake standing there, leaning against his silver Aston Martin, in his designer suit and sunglasses, looking like he'd just walked off a photoshoot for *Esquire*. Slinging his holdall over his shoulder, Danny waited for a break in the traffic and then jogged over the busy road. He wasn't usually one for public displays of affection, but he had never been as happy to see anyone before in his entire life. So, when Jake pulled him into a massive hug and kissed him, he responded in kind, not giving a fuck about who might walk past and see.

'Is this my welcoming party, then?' Danny grinned when he pulled back from him.

'I convinced them all to let me pick you up on my own. I thought you'd want to go home for a shower first.'

'Yep.' Danny grinned, looking down at his clothes. He felt like he needed about two hundred showers to get rid of the prison grime.

'And,' Jake smiled as he slipped his hand beneath Danny's coat, 'I wanted you to myself for a bit too.'

Danny flashed his eyebrows at him. 'You missed me, then?'

'Too fucking much. Now get in the car and let's get you home.'

Danny didn't require telling for a second time and he walked around to the passenger seat and climbed inside, inhaling the new-car smell. Jake went through new cars like other people did shoes. 'This is a nice motor.'

'Glad you like it, because it's yours,' Jake said with a smile as he started the engine.

'What? Fuck off. You're not buying me a car,' Danny said with a laugh.

'I'm buying you whatever the fuck I want to buy you.' Jake laughed too. 'So, you'd better get used to it.'

Danny leaned back against the headrest, wondering what the hell he had ever done to deserve someone like Jake. 'I might just do that,' he said quietly.

A few hours later, Danny was sitting with a pint in his hand in the back room of Grazia's restaurant, another of the Carter family's establishments. He looked around at the familiar faces and couldn't help but smile to himself. Luke and Stacey were certainly much friendlier than they had been before he'd gone inside, and he knew they were still working through things but he hoped they sorted themselves out. They were standing close together and Luke had his hand on Stacey's back as she laughed about something. The sight made Danny smile. The two of them deserved to be happy. He and Luke were good now, too. Being sent down for murder and spending two weeks in Walton Prison certainly put things into perspective, and he had realised that Luke had only done what he did because he cared about him and Stacey so much. Throughout his life, Luke had always been there for him, just like a brother, and there was no way he was going to let something that happened years earlier come between them.

The room held a small, select gathering of people. Mostly Connor's family. His uncle Sean and his wife and daughters. Connor's grandfather Pat and his wife, Sue. As well as some of their most trusted employees, including John Brennan, who was standing in a corner, with an arm wrapped around none other than DI Leigh Moss. Jake had told him how instrumental Leigh had been in helping to find out who had really killed his mother. Devlin King had disappeared and was still on the run, but there was plenty of time to catch up with him and make him pay. And Danny would make sure that he did, along with his sick older brother too. If he thought that prison was going to protect him, he was sadly mistaken.

Jake walked over to him and slipped an arm around his waist. 'You okay?' he asked.

Danny looked at him and smiled. 'Better than okay,' he replied, giving him a brief kiss on the lips.

'That's the second time you've kissed me in public today, Dan.' Jake arched an eyebrow at him. 'Two weeks of jail time, and you're a changed man?'

'Fuck off,' Danny said, giving him a nudge in the ribs as his cheeks flushed pink.

'Ah, there's my Danny,' Jake laughed.

Danny laughed too. They had plenty to do in the coming weeks. Finding Devlin, along with Milo Savage, was their top priority. But, it could wait for one day. For today, all Danny wanted to do was spend time with the people he loved most in the world. The people he was starting to realise loved him too.

Chapter Forty-Six

Jasmine placed Paul in his pram and sat back down in her new expensive leather chair with a smile. After everything that had happened, she was happy to make The Blue Rooms her new base. It made her feel safe and reassured to be around Connor and Jake, especially as Milo was still out there somewhere. Connor and Jake had made finding him their priority, but it seemed all they were finding were dead-end leads, as though Milo was always one step ahead of them. So, Connor had insisted that she always have one of his bouncers with her wherever she went. It was annoying and claustrophobic, but she could understand her husband's concerns. Her current security detail for the day was sitting in the bar in The Blue Rooms watching the football. She had sent him in there when he'd been getting under her feet.

Besides the added security at Jake's club, it was also the place where Stacey worked, and Jasmine and she had become great friends in the past few months. It had been Jake's suggestion to turn a part of the old store-room into an office for Jasmine, and she had an idea it was going to turn out to be the perfect solution.

As she looked at her sleeping son, she felt a rush of happiness. She had a husband she adored, a beautiful son who had made both of their lives complete. She was part of a family who loved and cared for her. And the icing on the cake was that she felt like she had finally found her place in the new order of things. Grace Carter's shoes had been huge ones to fill, but Grace had been right – people weren't looking for a new Grace, they just needed someone who could run things as well as she had. And while Jasmine wasn't arrogant enough to think she was quite there yet, she knew she was on the right track.

The sound of footsteps and giggling from just outside the door made Jasmine look up. She smiled as she saw Stacey walking into the room with Jake's daughter, Isla. Now that Jake and Danny were serious, and little Isla was aware of their relationship, Stacey had revelled in her new status as Isla's aunt. It was lovely to watch their relationship developing.

'Here they are,' Stacey said as they walked into the office. 'Isla has been pestering me to come and see you both all day. She is obsessed with babies,' she said with a smile as she held onto Isla's hand.

'Oh, he's just fallen asleep,' Jasmine replied. 'But he'll be awake again soon. And your dad and Uncle Connor will be here shortly, if you want to hang around?' She said the last part to Stacey, who nodded her agreement.

'Your dad and Danny are taking you out for pizza later, aren't they?' Stacey said as she checked her watch. 'I thought they would have been back by now.'

'Connor called me half an hour ago to say they got stuck in some traffic on the M6,' Jasmine replied. 'They shouldn't be too much longer, though.'

'Can I spin in your new chair, Aunty Jazz?' Isla asked, showing off her missing front tooth which had fallen out a few days earlier.

'Of course you can, princess,' Jasmine replied as she stood up and allowed her niece to sit down.

'How are things with you and Luke?' Jasmine asked as she perched on the edge of the desk opposite Stacey while Isla spun around in her chair.

Stacey's cheeks flushed pink. 'We're getting there,' she replied. 'I still haven't completely forgiven him, Jazz. We had a huge argument about it again last night. But I guess I can't live without him either.'

'Well, there's a lot to be said for passion in a relationship,' Jasmine said with a grin.

'Hmm, and the make-up sex is hot!' Stacey whispered before she started to laugh.

Jasmine laughed too and was about to ask for further detail when they heard more footsteps outside. She looked up, expecting to see Connor and Jake, but it was neither of them. Instead, a scrawny kid with a goatee, who looked like he hadn't washed in a week, walked into her office.

'How the hell did you get in here?' Jasmine asked as she stood tall. It was mid-afternoon and there was no additional security on at the club, so the doors should have been locked.

'Shit! I must have left the door open,' Stacey said.

The kid bared his yellowed teeth like a rabid dog as he scowled at the two of them. 'Women like you should be more careful,' he snarled.

Stacey ran around the desk to Isla while Jasmine squared up to their intruder. 'I don't know who the hell you are, but you need to leave. Right now!'

He stepped towards her, pressing his face close to hers so she could smell his rancid breath. 'Or what?' he hissed.

Jasmine was about to give him a right hook when she saw his hand raised, and the unmistakeable glint of the metal barrel of a gun as he lifted it to her forehead. The steel was cold against her temple and she shuddered as the unknown youth stepped even closer, invading every inch of her personal space.

Stacey gasped behind her, indicating that she had now seen the gun too. Jasmine swallowed hard. 'What do you want?' she asked, the tremor in her voice audible.

'I want what your cunt of a husband took from me. My brother is rotting in a cell because of that prick. All of my soldiers have been fucking killed or maimed.'

That was when she realised she was dealing with the missing King brother.

'Devlin,' she said softly. 'I can give you what you want.

But please let my friend and the kids go. They are nothing to do with this.'

'That's his kid, isn't it?' he snarled, nodding his head towards Paul sleeping in the pram. The bile in Jasmine's throat burned raw and she fought the urge to throw up all over Devlin.

'Connor and Jake will be back here soon with half a dozen of their men. I can stall them. I will do anything you want if you let them go,' she pleaded, her voice trembling with every word. 'Please, Devlin?'

'Anything?' His tongue darted out of his mouth and he licked his lips before his eyes dropped to Jasmine's cleavage.

'Y-yes. Anything,' she stammered. 'Just let them go.'

'Get the fuck out!' Devlin snarled to Stacey.

'But Jazz!' Stacey said as Isla began to cry.

'Just get the kids out of here, Stacey. Now!' Jasmine barked.

'I can't just leave you…'

'Just go!'

'Yeah, go before I change my mind,' Devlin sneered.

Stacey didn't need telling again. Scooping Isla up into her arms, she took hold of the pram before stealing a final glance at Jasmine, who simply nodded. The most important thing was that the kids were safe.

Jasmine watched as Stacey rushed out of the office. Devlin kept the gun pressed against her temple as her heart raced in her chest. As soon as Stacey was gone, Devlin grabbed

Jasmine's breast and squeezed hard. 'Let's me and you go somewhere for some fun, then, baby,' he sneered. 'As long as you can keep me satisfied, I might just keep you alive.'

Jasmine shrank back from his touch. He was shorter than she was in her heels, but she cowered before him, stooping her shoulders slightly to make sure she wasn't looking down at him. 'Okay.' She licked her lips as her breathing came faster and heavier. 'Let me grab my car key and I'll drive us.'

He narrowed his eyes at her. 'Where is it?'

'In my handbag.' She nodded to her Celine bag on the floor beside her chair.

'Get it.' He indicated the bag and Jasmine moved around the desk.

Her blood thundered in her ears as she crouched down to reach for her bag before removing the car key. At least it looked like a car key. Connor had got it specially made for her after the incident with Milo. He was so protective of her.

Devlin narrowed his eyes at her and she held out her hand, showing him the innocent-looking fob with the Mercedes logo on it.

'Let's go,' he snarled, lowering his gun and grabbing her by the elbow.

'Yes, let's,' Jasmine replied, with no hint of a tremor in her voice now that she no longer had to pretend to be a terrified, helpless woman. Men like him always underestimated women like her. As she pressed the small button on the fob, the sharp blade popped out. Using all of her strength, Jasmine swung her free arm to Devlin's throat, forcing the blade deep inside. The look in his eyes as he staggered backwards, clutching his throat, was one of pure shock and terror.

Jasmine held the blade aloft as Devlin crumpled to the floor with blood spurting between his fingers. She'd made sure to hit a main artery so she didn't have to watch him dying for too long. As he lay on the floor of her office, bleeding a bright-crimson stain into her beautiful new cream rug, she stood over him.

'I'm glad that the last thing you'll see before you leave this earth is my face, you filthy creep,' she spat. 'I have taken down men who would use you as a toothpick, you disgusting little scrote.'

He opened his mouth to speak, but all that could be heard was the sound of him spluttering and choking on his own blood.

Jasmine watched as the blood pooled around his body and the last of his life ebbed away from him. When she heard footsteps running down the corridor a few moments later, she knew that it was the cavalry coming. But she was perfectly capable of looking after herself. Nobody threatened her or her family and got away with it.

She was Jasmine Carter.

Connor pulled his car into his driveway and turned off the engine.

'You okay, mate?' Jake asked.

Connor turned to him and shook his head. 'I can't stop thinking about what could have happened, Jake.'

'I know. Me too,' he admitted. His own daughter had been in his club when that cunt Devlin had bounced in, threatening people with a gun. He was more than impressed with the way Jasmine had handled him, but the 'what if?'s were running around his mind too. Luke and Danny were currently ensuring that Devlin's body would never be found, while Jake and Connor were about to go into a family dinner and pretend that everything was fine. It was what they did, after all.

'And that cunt Savage is still out there,' Connor said as he ran a hand over his jaw. 'How the fuck do I ever leave either of them alone again, Jake?' he asked, referring to his wife and son.

'We'll step up security. We'll find Milo Savage and we'll deal with him. I promise you.'

'What if this isn't the end of it, though? There were strings being pulled in that investigation into Danny that Milo did not have the clout to pull. So who did? Who else was behind all this? What if this is something much bigger than we realise? I feel like we don't know who our enemies are anymore. We let that Aaron kid get hold of mine and Danny's blood, just like that. If the King brothers weren't such fucking incompetent pricks, one of us could have gone down for murder.'

'I know. We'll be more careful in future,' Jake insisted.

'But we are careful. How can we be any more careful when we don't know who the fuck is out to get us, Jake? It feels like everyone wants to take us down.'

Connor stared at him and Jake searched for the right answer, but he couldn't find it. He wished his mum and Michael were there.

Jasmine was staring out of the window watching her niece play in the garden. Isla didn't seem to have been too affected by what had happened in the club earlier, thanks to Stacey shielding her from most of what had happened. Paul was safely nestled in the arms of his Great Auntie Sophia, and Stacey was sitting on the patio talking to Sean and

Patrick. Jasmine smiled when she felt two strong arms around her waist. The tension she'd been feeling all evening suddenly slipped from her shoulders as Connor brushed her hair back from her face and nuzzled her neck.

'Is everything taken care of?' she asked.

'Yes. All sorted. Jake is here and Danny and Luke are on their way too.'

'Good,' she said with a soft sigh.

'We could have cancelled, you know?'

'We can't cancel family dinner night,' she said with a shake of her head. 'Family is the most important thing in the world.'

The whole family got together one night a week for dinner, and they took turns to host. There was no way Jasmine was going to let what happened with Devlin earlier put a stop to it. She only wished that Grace and Michael and their two youngest children could be there too. But they would Facetime later, and they would be home for a visit in a few weeks.

'Are you okay?' Connor asked, his lips brushing over her ear and making her stomach flutter.

'Yes, I'm fine. Promise.'

'I swear I felt like my heart was going to pack in when Stacey told me he was in there with you today, Jazz. I have never moved so fast in my entire life.'

She placed her hands over his and leaned back against his hard chest. 'I told you I can take care of myself, didn't I?' she said with a laugh.

'I know. You are a fucking warrior, babe. But I will

always worry about you anyway. There is no way he should have even been able to get to you. I'll make sure there is always security on that club when you're there from now on.'

'You don't have to do that, Connor.'

He pulled back and spun her around in his arms. 'Yes I do. You and Paul are the most important things in the world to me, Jazz. I never want either of you in that situation again. I know you handled it, babe, but you shouldn't have had to. And Milo Savage is still out there somewhere.'

'Okay,' she said, relenting, because she knew there was no way he would back down, and his overprotectiveness was one of the many things she loved about him. 'I would never have let him hurt our baby, though.'

'I know,' he said as he pressed a soft kiss on her temple. 'You make me happier than I ever dreamed possible, you know that? I love you so fucking much.'

Jasmine smiled and rested her cheek against his chest. 'I love you too, Connor,' she breathed. This was the kind of happiness that she had only ever dreamed of before. The kind that wasn't meant for people like her. She supposed that every dog really did have its day, even ones with secrets as dark as hers.

Acknowledgments

As always, I would like to thank the wonderful team at One More Chapter for believing in me and bringing these books to life, especially Charlotte Ledger and Kim Young whose support of the Bad Blood series has helped it go from strength to strength. I'd also love to thank my amazing editor, Jennie Rothwell for championing the Carters and helping to shape the stories of the next generation. Your advice and support has been invaluable to me.

Most of all, I'd love to thank all of the readers who have supported me and who have bought or read my books. You have made my dreams come true.

I couldn't do this without the support of other authors too, and the crime writing community are a particularly lovely and supportive group of people. But, I'd like to give a special mention to Mary Torjussen and Amanda Brooke, for always being willing to lend a listening ear and for putting up with me and my Monday night ramblings. I would be lost without you both.

To all of my friends who put up with my constant writing chatter. There are too many to mention, and I love you all! A huge thank-you to my family for their constant love and support.

And finally, but most especially, to Eric – who supports every crazy decision I make, and my incredible boys – who continue to inspire and amaze me every single day.

Read on for an extract from Part of the Family...

You're either with them

The Carters have always run the streets of Liverpool, but now there's a new family in town who think it's time to challenge the system.

Or against them

And when threats are made, both loyalty and money is at stake. Of course the Carters will seek revenge, but first Grace and her boys must find out who is responsible.

The decision is yours

Being at the top of your game is tough, especially when your enemies – both old and new – want to take you down. Now it's time for the fight of their lives. The only question is, who will win?

Prologue

I put the gun on the table in front of me and stood up, ducking slightly so I didn't bang my head on the ceiling. Picking up the empty takeaway carton, I stuffed it into the overflowing rubbish bin, pushing it down with my fist so it didn't spill back out onto the floor. The smell of rotting food jumped out at me as the boxes were squashed into the small space. I should probably take it down to the huge recycling containers out at the front of the park, but I could hear the rain hammering on the roof of the caravan and it was a five-minute walk. I could cope with the smell until the morning.

Turning on the old television, I flicked through the channels to find something to watch before settling on reruns of **The Big Bang Theory.** *I'd seen every single episode countless times, but I could watch them over and over again. It was my go-to programme – the television equivalent of chicken soup. And I deserved some comfort, didn't I? After everything I'd been* *through, I deserved more than an old leaky caravan and a crappy twenty-four-inch telly.*

I had nothing.

I had no one.

I choked back the tears. The time for feeling sorry for myself was over. Because time was the only thing I had left and I would use it to carefully plan my revenge. Everyone thought I was stupid, but I was cleverer than all of them. And soon they would learn that truth.

I might not have strength or brute force on my side, but I had more brains than the lot of them put together. I eyed the Baikal handgun on the coffee table. It was a beautiful piece of kit. I loved the way it felt in my hand. I liked the way it made me feel. Powerful – as though I could take on anyone. I kept it close to me at all times – just in case someone found me. I'd even fired it a couple of times. A few practice shots to make sure I knew exactly what to do when the time came.

And my time would come soon. I just had to find out a little more information about my target and figure out the best time to strike. I needed him to be alone, for obvious reasons, but I also wanted there to be no one there to help him as he felt his lifeblood seep from his veins. I'd enjoy watching him – helpless and incapacitated, and in pain. Then they would all feel the pain of losing him too – and they would know exactly what it felt like to have someone you loved ripped away from you.

I sat back against the old sofa cushions and smiled to myself, content in the knowledge that Michael Carter's days were numbered.

Prologue

Tick, Tock, Michael.
Tick, Tock.

Chapter One

Grace Carter opened the passenger door of Luke Sullivan's car and climbed inside.

'Thanks for picking me up,' she said with a smile.

'No problem. You ready for this?' he asked her.

She nodded. She'd thought about nothing else all weekend. 'Ready as I'll ever be. You?'

'I'm looking forward to getting some answers, but I'm not especially happy about who we have to see to get them.'

'Well, I don't suppose we have much choice, do we?' Grace asked.

'Unfortunately not,' he said as he pulled out of Grace's driveway.

Grace leaned back against the soft leather headrest and closed her eyes. It had been a little over a week since she'd discovered that Luke Sullivan was her half-brother. He'd been born three months after her father died and neither she nor Luke had had any idea of their connection. That was until Glenda Alexander, the mother of Luke's best mate, Danny, had surprised them with the information eight days before. Glenda had even produced a photograph of Luke's pregnant mother and Grace's father, looking every inch the happy expectant couple, as proof.

Grace had refused to believe it at first. The photograph had knocked the wind from her, but it wasn't absolute proof. They could just have been friends. But unbeknownst to all of them, her father-in-law, Patrick, who had known Grace's father, Pete, in his younger years, had seen the resemblance between Luke and Pete immediately and had done some digging of his own. His source had found some old financial records and discovered that Grace's father had a secret will and had left Luke's mum, Maggie, a large sum of money. That seemed to prove beyond all doubt that Pete Sumner had indeed been Luke's father too.

The truth of the revelation had completely floored Grace. She had always idolised her father. There had only been the two of them when she was growing up, and they had been incredibly close – or at least that was what she'd thought. Now she knew that her father had been lying to her, she wondered what other secrets he had kept from her. Did she have any other half-siblings out there in the world? To think that all she had ever wanted was a brother or sister, and she'd had one in Luke for the past twenty-eight years.

Why hadn't her father told her that he'd met someone else? She liked to think he would have known she'd have been thrilled about the possibility of their family becoming more than just the two of them. Hadn't he known her at all? Had he been ashamed of her? Or ashamed of Luke's mother Maggie? None of it made sense to her. She had discussed the situation over and over with Michael, who had tried to assure her that her father would probably have told her when the time was right, had he not died unexpectedly. But Grace wasn't so sure. She wished she could believe him but there was no escaping the fact that for whatever reason, he had kept it from her.

The one thing Grace did believe was that Luke had been as in the dark as she was about the whole thing. It begged the question why his mother had never told him who his father really was either. Had Maggie known about Grace, and if so, why hadn't she told Luke that he had a half-sister? Or why hadn't she come to find Grace to tell her about Luke? And most puzzling of all, why did Glenda Alexander have the only photograph of Grace's father and Luke's mother together? Glenda had hardly known Luke's mother. Luke's friendship with Glenda's son Danny had been the only connection between the two women. Whatever the case, it seemed that Glenda Alexander was the only person who might have answers to their many questions. And whilst Grace believed Luke and Danny when they told her Glenda couldn't be trusted, what other choice did she have?

Grace opened her eyes and looked across at Luke. He was the one good thing to come out of the whole sorry mess. She smiled – her brother. The two of them had spent the last week trying to process this new information that had been landed on them, and they'd grown even closer as a result.

'How is your throat now?' she asked as she noted the fading bruises on his neck. When Glenda had revealed that Luke and Grace had a relationship of some sort, she had done it in a way that had made Michael think she and Luke were having an affair. His response had been to grab Luke by the throat and try to strangle the truth from him. Fortunately, Grace had arrived in time. Michael felt bad about the whole thing now and had apologised to Luke and Grace, but at the time he had believed himself to be entirely justified.

Luke rubbed at his neck. 'Not too bad,' he said with a soft chuckle. 'But remind me never to get on your husband's bad side.'

'Well, don't worry, you've got your big sister to look out for you now,' she said, starting to laugh.

Luke laughed too. 'Fucking hell. Grace Carter is my big sister. I wish I'd known that when I was in school and Fat Barry used to try and steal my dinner money.'

'Fat Barry?' she asked.

'Yeah. He was a horrible fucker. The school bully. Until me and Danny fought back one day, anyway. He never messed with us, or anyone else after that, actually.'

'Maybe you don't need a big sister to look out for you after all then?' she said with a smile.

'Still nice to have one though,' he said quietly.

'Yeah,' Grace replied softly.

Suddenly, there was too much emotion in the confines of the car to deal with.

'So,' Grace said with a wicked grin, in an attempt to change the subject. 'Who did you spend the afternoon in a hotel with then?'

He laughed again. 'What?'

'You heard me. Michael said you were acting all cagey about a mystery woman—'

'Who he assumed was you,' Luke interrupted her.

'Yes. So, who was she?'

He shook his head. 'I'd rather not say. Not yet.'

'Aw, come on, Luke. You can tell me anything.' She gave him a playful nudge on the arm.

He took a deep breath and she thought he was about to tell her when they were interrupted by Grace's phone ringing.

'Saved by the bell,' he said instead.

Grace answered the phone to Jake. 'Hiya, Son.'

'Hiya, Mum. Is Michael with you? He's not answering his phone.'

'No, I'm with Luke. We're on our way to see Glenda.'

'Oh yeah, I forgot.'

'Have you tried the house phone?' Grace replied.

'Yeah. There's no answer.'

Grace checked the time on her watch. 'Maybe he's at the gym?' she suggested.

'I'll try him again in a bit.'

'Is everything okay?' she asked.

'Yeah. Everything's fine. I just need to ask him about something, that's all,' he replied.

'Okay. I'll let you know if I speak to him.'

Grace ended the call and tried Michael's number herself but it went straight to voicemail. He was probably at the gym like she'd said, and sometimes the reception there was sketchy. She'd try him again later.

Available now in ebook and paperback

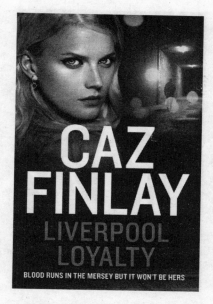

The Bad Blood Series

All titles available now in ebook and paperback